THE UNIFORM OF GLORY

NOVELS *by* P. C. WREN

BEAU GESTE
BEAU SABREUR
BEAU IDEAL
GOOD GESTES
SOLDIERS OF MISFORTUNE
THE WAGES OF VIRTUE
STEPSONS OF FRANCE
THE SNAKE AND THE SWORD
FATHER GREGORY
DEW AND MILDEW
DRIFTWOOD SPARS
THE YOUNG STAGERS
THE MAMMON OF RIGHTEOUSNESS
MYSTERIOUS WAYE
VALIANT DUST
FLAWED BLADES
ACTION AND PASSION
PORT O' MISSING MEN
BEGGARS' HORSES
SPANISH MAINE
EXPLOSION
SINBAD THE SAILOR
BUBBLE REPUTATION
FORT IN THE JUNGLE
THE MAN OF A GHOST
WORTH WHILE
ROUGH SHOOTING
CARDBOARD CASTLE
PAPER PRISON
THE DISAPPEARANCE OF GENERAL
   JASON
TWO FEET FROM HEAVEN

EDITED *by* P. C. WREN

SOWING GLORY

THE UNIFORM OF GLORY

being

The True Story of

A FREE FRENCHMAN'S
NIGHT OUT

BY

PERCIVAL CHRISTOPHER WREN

THE BOOK CLUB
121, CHARING CROSS ROAD
LONDON, W.C. 2

This Edition 1943

THIS BOOK IS PRODUCED IN COMPLETE
CONFORMITY WITH THE AUTHORIZED
ECONOMY STANDARDS

MADE AND PRINTED IN GREAT BRITAIN BY
EBENEZER BAYLIS AND SON, LTD., THE
TRINITY PRESS, WORCESTER, AND LONDON

A*

And over the seas we were bidden
A country to take and to keep;
And far with the brave I have ridden,
And now with the brave I shall sleep.

A. E. Housman.

CONTENTS

CHAPTER I

NOTORIOUSLY, it is a long worm that has no turning, and we have it on high authority that a crowded hour of glorious life is worth an age without a name.

This artless story is the veracious account of the bold turning of a down-trodden worm, and of the crowded hour of glory that he enjoyed; an hour for which he was prepared to pay in full and to grudge nothing of the payment.

Denis Ducros had seen better days, University days at the Sorbonne in Paris, and lovely long days in Provence, where, a scion of the *petite noblesse*, life had gone very well until it had gone suddenly and completely awry.

And now Denis was a servant, and a good one, who spent most of his life behind a green baize apron; much of it behind a green baize door in a little room in which he cleaned silver and his master's accoutrements; some of it behind his master's chair, where he faithfully and efficiently strove to anticipate that master's every want as he nobly enjoyed the pleasures of the table; and a little, a very little, of it in dreams.

He would have spent more time in dreaming had he not been too busy by day and too weary by night.

Nevertheless, at times, when his work was mechanical and the skilful hand polished the refulgent boot, or spur, or sword, or button, without conscious direction of the errant mind, Denis would think long thoughts that would have surprised all those who knew him, his master most of all.

For Denis, the deft valet, the accomplished house-man, the most servant-like of admirable servants, was at times strongly conscious of the fact that he had a soul above his present station, a mind above his menial tasks, and disturbing intimations of immortality.

Seated in his cubby-hole, upon an up-turned box, he would, upon occasion, see Denis not thus occupied with button-stick and brush, but mounted on a noble charger, riding at the head of victorious troops through streets lined by acclaiming crowds.

Slowly turning his cold, haughty and imperious face from side to side, he would glance up at the balconies from which bright eyes shone upon him, and white hands fluttered enchanting kisses from lovely lips.

Nice work if you can get it.

Or even in the very act of peeling potatoes, beneath the ringing scourge of the sharp tongue of the fat Natalie, the *bonne à tout faire* who loved him, he would see himself seated at a table before a tent, beneath an Army Commander's flag; and, as men galloped up, flung themselves from their panting, sweating horses, and smartly saluting, gave him written messages from his Brigadiers, he would coldly, calmly and quietly issue his orders in reply. The brain at the centre of the military web, directing the battle, riding the storm. He had once seen the great Marshal Lyautey.

Very nice work if . . .

"And is it to be supposed, my little cabbage, that the potato will peel itself if you gape at it long enough?" fat Natalie would ask, and shatter the bright brief beginnings of a dream.

From time to time, though comparatively rarely, he would, when soaping a saddle, or suppling a bridle-rein, see himself arrayed in a perfectly-fitting uniform with gold five-*galoned* sleeves, such as those his master wore, entering the boudoir, a nest of silk and satin, and a lovely and most loving woman, a famous beauty, or leader of rank and fashion; and as, advancing with outstretched arms, he gracefully sank upon one knee, she would take his face between her small white hands and . . .

"*Denis!* Where's that damned scoundrel Denis?" the Colonel would roar.

And it would not be into the presence of a lovely welcoming woman that Denis would then hasten.

For it was the Colonel's admirable way to roar loudly at Denis, it being his belief that thus, and only thus, is the best to be got from servants—menservants, that is to say

—for the Colonel, albeit a brave and much decorated warrior, had never been heard to roar at fat Natalie.

What the Colonel thought of Denis, if he thought of him at all, is not known; but what Denis thought of the Colonel was that he was a super-man, a hero of romance ornamenting a prosaic world, a model and a pattern to all men.

A truly humble creature whose soul had been too long swaddled in green baize, Denis had one secret source of pride, legitimate and sustaining pride—he was undeniably very like the Colonel in appearance.

It is to be doubted that the Colonel had ever noticed this interesting fact; and indeed the resemblance was not marked when Denis in shirt-sleeves, apron and slippers was doing a job of work in which coal, potatoes, or greasy crockery played a part, and the Colonel was arrayed in the perfectly-fitting smart uniform of his famous Corps. Nor, when his hair was rough, his moustache untrimmed and his face ill-shaven, was the servant's resemblance to his master that of a twin brother.

Nevertheless, once, in the dusk—but by no means in the dark—when Denis in his walking-out uniform came suddenly upon Natalie by the front door of the Colonel's quarters, she had exclaimed,

"*Toi! ... Mon Dieu! Salaud*, I thought it was *Monsieur le Colonel* himself."

And never, never once in the whole of his life, since the day when he had been born of a Provençal father and an Irish mother, had Denis Ducros heard sweeter words, or any sounds that had given him a tithe of the pleasure that these did.

He, Denis Ducros, *soldat première classe*, the Colonel's *ordonnance*, servant, batman, butler, horseman and valet, had been mistaken for the bravest, finest and handsomest man in the Nineteenth Army Corps of Africa, if not in the whole French army.

He had always known it himself, and now someone else had recognised it. Fat Natalie Dupont, who greatly loved, but did not fear, him; and whom he greatly feared but did not love.

And at sunset on this Day of the Great Fête of the

Republic, also the greatest day of all his life, the day on which he rose to his full stature, to the apex of his possibilities, and even to the height of his imagination, Denis stood before the mirror in the Colonel's exiguous dressing-room, and, catching sight of the reflection of his own face, was reminded of the indisputable truth. Closely his form and features resembled those of the Colonel; and, as he finished brushing the Colonel's *képi*, he did what he had never dared to do before.

He placed it on his own head.

C'est le premier pas qui coute, and this was the first step upon that path upward or downward, according to the point of view, that led to the great, the sudden, the tremendous uprising and self-assertion of the romantic soul of Denis Ducros.

The *képi* fitted beautifully; and, by stepping backward he contrived to see nothing of himself in the mirror but his *képi*-adorned head.

Most pleasing. Most satisfactory and . . . stimulating.

Why, it would only be a couple of minutes' work with the Colonel's nail-scissors to render his moustache an exact imitation of that of his handsome and debonair exemplar, a closely-trimmed, lip-exposing ornament of a bronzed and martial face.

The nail-scissors were, as he knew, in the right-hand corner of the top left-hand drawer. There and nowhere else, always and inevitably, save when the Colonel was using them for the trimming of his well-kept nails.

Deftly clipping, from the corners of his mouth toward his nose, Denis quickly reproduced an admirable facsimile of the Colonel's moustache, a thorny bristling hedge that adorned, while not concealing, the firm mouth and whitely shining teeth, occasionally displayed by the Colonel's slow sardonic smile.

Denis practised one.

First slowly, and then sardonically.

Yes, that was right. That was excellent. The very smile, combining faint amusement, slight contempt, and a sense of thoughts unuttered—and just as well left unuttered perhaps.

Usually it followed upon the observation,

"*Ah! . . . Indeed?*" with which the Colonel was wont to greet some statement which, up to that moment, had seemed sane and sound and reasonable, but forthwith was seen and heard and known for the incredible puerile piffle that it surely must be.

Again stepping back to the point from where he could see nothing but his face and the *képi*, Denis regarded himself coldly, his face unwontedly austere and hard.

"*Ah! . . . Indeed?*" said he aloud, and smiled slowly and sardonically. Marvellous.

It *was* the Colonel.

There, in the mirror, Colonel Rochefort regarded Denis Ducros so coldly, so balefully, that Denis faltered, flushed with shame, and swiftly removed the *képi* from the unworthy head that presumptuously dishonoured it. And there in the mirror was Denis Ducros again, laughing at his own folly in permitting himself to frighten himself.

He replaced the *képi* and the smile—and uneasily looked away from it.

Merciful Heaven! Suppose it *had* been the Colonel there in the mirror! But he was safe in bed, poor gentleman, or Denis would not have been in the dressing-room posturing before the mirror. Safe in bed for two or three days at least, suffering, as not infrequently he did, from an attack of malaria.

As he treated these attacks according to a prescription of his own, of which the main ingredient was neat cognac, and the remainder was of an alcoholic nature, the malaria was apt to affect his liver. And this malarial affection of his liver was apt to influence his judgment.

Sometimes Denis called it his misjudgment, at others, his temper.

But as his ancient enemy had attacked him only an hour ago, and he had swiftly riposted with a tumbler full of the mixture, he was certain to be asleep and to remain in that happy state for many hours to come . . .

Denis gazed respectfully at the face in the mirror. Marvellous.

13

Yes, it was marvellous, but it wasn't perfect. There was something missing.

Of course there was.

And Denis laughed in a manner which made his face much less like that of his master; much more happy-looking, care-free, kindly and simple.

Something missing indeed! A most important, if not essential something. And that, nothing less than the beautiful tortoise-shell-rimmed monocle which the Colonel seemed almost to throw into his eye and to hold there as firmly fixed as were the teeth in his head. As its proprietor rarely wore it in bed, it would be where it always was when not in use, in the box sacred to personal trinkets, such as links, studs, spare watch, and other jewellery, that reposed on top of the chest of drawers.

It would be rather a lark to stick it in his eye and further increase the remarkable likeness.

Most appalling impudence, but as the Colonel would never know . . .

Yes. Having gone to the trouble of trimming his moustache, he'd go the whole hog.

Well! Really! One would hardly believe it. For two pins he'd call for Natalie, bid her shut her eyes, and when he gave the word, open them and look in the mirror.

He'd wager a dozen of *pinard*[1] that she'd ejaculate with respectful amazement,

"M'sieur le Colonel!"

Yes; but there'd be no respect, and it would be he who would provide the amazement, when she turned from the mirror and looked at him. She'd be worse than the Colonel himself, in her ferocious indignation at such outrageous rascality.

No. There could be no applauding spectators of this remarkable piece of impersonation.

A pity.

Also rather a pity that he had to screw up the left-hand side of his face just a little, for the greater security of the monocle; for its rightful owner contracted not the smallest muscle of his cheek or eye. His face gave the monocle no

[1]Cheap red wine.

14

more encouragement, so to speak, than a wall gives a window. Yet the crystal disc sat as securely in its place as does a pane of glass in a window-frame.

However, practice makes perfect.

Unfortunately there was but little time for practice, for he had the uniform to brush, and the buttons, spurs, and riding-boots to polish, before he left the Colonel's quarters for his usual Thursday evening-out. And this was Fête Day too, and out he would go *coûte qui coûte*.

But it really was rather hard that Natalie should not see just his head—over a wall say—with *képi*, monocle and trimmed moustache.

Talk about mistaking him, in the dusk, for the Colonel!

She'd *know*, in broad daylight, that it was the Colonel, especially if she spoke and he said,

"*Ah! . . . Indeed?*" and smiled his slow sardonic smile.

Especially if he didn't drop the monocle in the effort of producing the smile. Something like the dog and the shadow, that would be. And what a waggish dog he was! He, Denis Ducros, wearing the Colonel's *képi*, monocle and moustache!

Slowly and sardonically he again smiled into the mirror.

"*Ah! . . . Indeed?*" he said, and dropped the monocle. "*Peste!*"

That spoiled the show completely. Sad, for it was otherwise a perfect performance, and to the man with the soul of an artist, quite a little disappointment.

Of course he had the soul of an artist, or at any rate of an *artiste*, and ought really to have been an actor. He would have been another Cocquelin or another Guitry. He would have been another anything-you-like where character-parts and perfect impersonation were required.

Replacing the monocle, Denis endeavoured to screw it tightly into his eye, and to hold it there without obvious muscular effort.

No. It wasn't absolute perfection. The face was that of the Colonel all right, but it was the Colonel suffering a spasm of pain or emotion. And Colonel Rochefort did not permit his face to register the fact, when suffering spasms of pain or emotion.

"*Sacré bleu!*" An idea! The little gum-bottle on the Colonel's office-room table!

If he carefully smeared the broad tortoise-shell gallery with some of that thick gum, waited until it was nearly dry, and then carefully placed it in his eye, it would undoubtedly stick. Then he could keep his countenance as cold, austere and expressionless as the Colonel's. He could smile as slowly and sardonically as he liked, without having to spoil the effect by an anxious contraction of his facial muscles.

Yes. As a true artist for whom nothing but perfection could be satisfactory, he had to admit that the face in the mirror was not completely and truly that of the Colonel as seen in public. That look of strain and anxiety was . . .

"*Denis!* . . . DENIS! . . . *Sacré salaud!* . . ."

. . . was instantly replaced by one of infinitely greater strain and anxiety. Yea, of consternation and alarm. *Bon Dieu de Grace!* Suppose the Old Devil jumped out of bed, strode into the dressing-room and caught him with the *képi* on his head, the monocle in his eye!

Swiftly removing *képi* and monocle, the frightened Denis flung the one on to the chest of drawers, slipped the other into his pocket, and bounded across to the door that opened into the Colonel's bedroom.

"Ah! There you are, you species of besotted imbecile," growled the Colonel as Denis entered the darkened room.

"Get me another bottle of cognac. And listen . . . Hang the DO NOT DISTURB notice on the door; and do not bring my coffee in the morning, until I call for it. Tell Madame that I shall not be present at dinner . . . that I do not wish to be awakened on *any* account."

Swiftly Denis returned with a litre bottle of the Colonel's favourite *fine.*

"Understand, you accident?" growled the Colonel as Denis deftly opened the bottle in his presence. "I am *not* to be disturbed by *anybody* for *anything.*"

"*Oui, oui, Monsieur le Colonel. Je comprends.* Not until *Monsieur le Colonel* is pleased to disturb himself and to ring."

Fading discreetly from the room, Denis softly closed the door, and, from a drawer in the Office table, took the

16

printed card which bore the legend DO NOT DISTURB and signified to all men and one woman that, whether in office or bedroom, the Colonel wished to be alone.

That was all right. The Old Devil wouldn't budge now for the next twelve hours at least, when he would suddenly appear where least expected, neat, sleek and dapper as a young tom-cat, and ferocious as an elderly leopard.

Returning to his work, Denis took his master's handsome black-and-gold tunic from the back of the chair over which he had hung it, and began most scrupulously to brush it.

For the thousandth time he admired the beautiful *galons* of gold braid that ornamented it five-deep from cuff to elbow; the buttons and badges that seemed to be of purest gold; the lovely heart-stirring array of medals and decorations. What must it feel like to have the right to wear such a tunic as that?

What would it feel like, merely to slip it on? Just to see how it fitted. How it fitted the figure of a man who was known and admitted closely to resemble the famous Colonel Rochefort, of *La Légion Etrangère*.

What a thing to do! He was certainly going it to-night. One would think that he had opened the bottle downstairs and had been tasting its contents. Whereas he had had nothing since his tumbler of *pinard* after giving the Colonel his lunch.

What a thing to do! Nevertheless a thing to be done well if done at all.

The *képi* . . . the monocle . . . the moustache . . . the tunic . . .

And then he could behold a good half of himself. His better half, so to speak; and see how far that part of him resembled the upper half of the Colonel.

But first of all to prepare the monocle.

It was the easy and delightful work of but a couple of minutes carefully to coat with gum the flat upper rim of the gallery of the monocle, that would lie just beneath his eyebrow, and the edge of the lower one that would fit into his eye socket.

And then some smart work on his hair with the Colonel's

own stiff brushes, and a beautiful polish with the help of the Colonel's own brilliantine.

It wasn't right. It went against one's conscience; but surely a man who had spent so much time and energy in polishing the Colonel's leather and bright-work, might give his own head a polish?

And then, by the Name of a Name of a Little Pink Dog, he would not only look like the Colonel, but he would smell like him.

Industriously he oiled and polished.

And now, if such an utter impossibility were in any wise possible, he looked even more like him than before—with his hair brushed straight back as the Colonel brushed his —especially when he took the *képi* off.

And now for the monocle.

Perfect. The gum neither wet nor dry, but sticky as a fly-paper. He would put it in his face and hold it pressed in tightly, until it was as firmly attached as his ear or his nose.

Seating himself in the Colonel's chair, Denis almost unconsciously assumed the exact position invariably taken by the Colonel when waiting for Denis to attach his spurs to his boots, and softly hummed a little air that was the Colonel's current favourite.

By the Father of all Good Soldiers, he was beginning not only to look and to smell, but to sound like the Colonel!

Beneath his breath he issued orders and uttered orderly-room imprecations in the Colonel's best manner.

In imagination he had Sergeant-Major Lejaune up before him, listened to that terrible man's faltering excuses, observed with cold contempt,

"*Ah! . . . Indeed?*"

And smiled a devastatingly slow, sardonic smile.

Anon, he rose to his feet, placed the *képi* on his anointed head, not only at the exact angle, but in the Colonel's exact manner, with the inevitable little tap on top, that crowned the work. And then, with swiftly beating heart, he slipped his right arm into the right sleeve of the tunic and, in the exact style and manner of his master, assumed the sombrely refulgent garment, hooked it beneath his chin, and fastened the big bright buttons.

18

A perfect fit! Comfortably tight at the waist, comfortably accommodating across the chest. No looseness anywhere. No cutting underneath the arms. Rather might he have been made for the tunic by the Divine Architect Himself, than the tunic for him by mortal military tailor.

Now for the mirror. But first to lock the door that opened on to the landing, lest fat Natalie, who had the nerve and imprudence to do anything, should open it and put her head into the Colonel's dressing-room, in search of the Colonel's batman, whom, indeed she appeared to regard as being her batman also . . .

And now . . .

"*Could* it be? Could it be that that magnificent figure was but a reflection in the mirror? And the reflection moreover of Denis Ducros? A poor servant, who was even a still poorer soldier. Could that perfect picture of a *beau sabreur*, that complete portrait of an officer and a gentleman, and an elegant but most dangerous-looking warrior, be *himself*?"

That surely was not Denis Ducros?

"*Not? Ah! . . . Indeed?*" replied the figure in the glass. And Denis all but fell away, collapsing in stricken fear before the Colonel's cold regard. Actually he shuffled back, catching sight, as he did so, of his own deplorable *pantalons* and house-slippers.

Stepping forward again, he included these reassuring incongruous nether-details in the mirror portrait.

Yes, that was Denis Ducros all right, that lower half anyway, an authentic, domestic servant. He who had first been *soldat simple*, officer's *ordonnance*, then Colonel's batman, valet, butler and houseman. Madame's servant really.

What a remarkable picture!

Officer and gentleman, from the crown of his head to the middle of his body; menial domestic from his middle to his shapeless great house-shoes.

Well, he must step back once again and admire the upper part before removing the borrowed plumes that made him look so fine a bird.

Yes, it was astounding—not only the actual likeness, but the whole bearing, deportment, aura and atmosphere.

19

Surely the personality of something fine and worthy shone through? Surely no complete clod, no mere miserable bale of cannon-fodder could have filled the Colonel's tunic and looked so really authentic a Colonel, as did the figure in the glass? Why, until one's eye reached the ill-fitting, grease-spotted over-alls, and saw the hall-mark, the livery, the stigmata of domestic service and . . .

And suddenly the stifled soul of Denis Ducros cried aloud from the depths of its abasement.

Suddenly it rose upward, with a mighty surging, from those dismal deeps, threw off its swaddling clothes of cramping discipline, stood forth, and manifested itself as worthy of its great and noble ancestors, Brian Boru on the one side and d'Artagnan, if not du Guesclin, on the other.

Would the mighty warrior-king have patiently worn the houseman's greasy trousers?

Would du Guesclin, who won the Hundred Years War —or some such prolonged argument with the English— have sat down, contented, in their ignoble baggy seat?

The blood of Brian Boru and of Bertrand du Guesclin, or of his authentically Connaught mother and Provençal father, went swiftly to Denis's head, his hands to the buttons of his trousers.

In scarcely longer than it takes to tell, the shapeless old garments had fallen—fit only to fall—and Denis, with shining eyes, compressed lips, and dilated nostrils through which he drew quick breath, seized with hands that trembled, the Colonel's beautiful red riding breeches, with their double stripe of black braid, from where they hung neatly folded over the back of a chair.

Panting with excitement, he drew them on, buttoned them about the knees, smoothed them so that they fitted there like a glove, fastened and braced them to the right height, and stood, a Colonel revealed, perfect from head to knee.

But it was not enough! His hour and his madness were upon him, and he must be fulfilled.

It was the Colonel's beautiful riding boots that were fulfilled.

As one possessed, he seized the left-hand boot, hauled

out the eighteen-inch-long centre tongue of the tree, shook out the back piece, drew out the front piece and foot, hooked his fingers through the interior loops in the top of the leg, and, just in the Colonel's own manner, with identically similar grunts, and brief, pointed orisons to Higher Powers, drew the boot on, stamped his foot once, and then adjusted the knee of the black-leather-strapped breeches within the top of the boot.

As in the case of the *képi*, the tunic, the breeches, a perfect fit.

Absolutely comfortable.

Why! Had his Mama known Colonel Rochefort's Papa, he himself might have been . . .

But that was quite enough of that line of thought! With even greater speed, Denis assumed the other boot, and having arranged boots and breeches to his fastidious liking he strapped on the silver-shining spurs that so often he had polished and fastened upon his master's feet.

Now for the mirror . . .

Now there would be something to look at. Literally *cap à pie* he would be correct.

Well! Well!

Enraptured, Denis stared.

Not at himself, Denis Ducros, so much as at Denis Ducros' reincarnation as Colonel Louis Rochefort.

Unconsciously he struck one of the Rochefort poses, left hand on hip, left foot advanced, left knee slightly bent, two middle fingers of right hand thrust between the fourth and fifth buttons of the tunic.

But there was something missing. What was it? Of course. Gloves and cane. One glove on the left hand, the cane clutched by the middle, together with the other glove.

So. That was it. Why, the greatest living portrait painter could come and paint that reflection in the glass, and not trouble Colonel Rochefort for a single sitting; and not a crapulous critic could be found to deny its perfect likeness to the man who was not its original.

Sacré Nom! If the bedroom door opened now, and the Colonel entered the room, he'd have a fit. It would be he, rather than Denis, who would collapse in fright. After one horrified glance, one agonised incredulous stare, he would cry,

"*Mon Dieu!* It has come! I am mad ... God help me and forgive me."

And a man who, like Marshal Ney, had been called the bravest of the brave would flinch and quail. He'd cringe before his servant, Denis Ducros, the worthless, idle, and good-for-nothing *scélérat*, whom he was always threatening to kick back into the ranks, and whose progress he had indeed upon occasions accelerated by the not wholly playful application of one of these very boots to the baggy seat of those very fallen *pantalons*.

Almost Denis wished that the Colonel would come into the room. But not quite. No, no. He himself might be going mad, but he had not yet *quite* gone.

Nevertheless, it would be splendid fun if fat Natalie came in. He'd unlock the door. For, sooner or later, she was bound to come in search of him, if he made no reply to her agonised caterwaulings that he should come and help her with the vegetables, or something of the sort. And to come and help the good Natalie with a job, simply meant to do the job for her.

Or should he go downstairs, and, in the *rôle* of *M'sieur le Colonel*, frighten the life out of her? But there'd be no great fun in doing that, unless later he revealed himself, and that might be dangerous.

He did not think that fat Natalie would give him away, but she'd be quite capable of sticking a knife in him if he made a complete and utter fool of her, and a badly frightened one at that.

Nevertheless, Denis unlocked the door before returning to the most delightful spot on earth—his place before the mirror, his place from which he could see Denis Ducros as he ought to be; clad, not in shining armour as his ancestors had been, but in the shining and beautiful uniform which represented it.

Yes; there before him in the magic glass, stood the true Denis Ducros, leader of men, commander of armies, lover of beautiful ladies.

Le brave Général, Denis Ducros, who rode on white

22

horses, into conquered cities, acclaimed by admiring multitudes, the recipient of welcoming kisses blown by small white hands from lovely coral lips . . .

His eye fell upon his green baize apron, and his discarded trousers and house slippers.

Not so good.

But away with the foolish thought.

Did not every emergent butterfly see lying beside its magnificent beautiful form, the miserable shell of the chrysalis from which it had burst forth. The life of the butterfly might be short, but it was glorious and free. The life of "Colonel" Denis Ducros might be short, but during those few minutes it should be glorious and free. For was he not glorious to behold, there in the mirror; was he not free, if only for a few fleeting moments, to imagine himself playing the part for which he was dressed; to imagine himself a distinguished and decorated soldier, whose high rank would undoubtedly be yet higher, if not indeed of the very highest in the military hierarchy?

Dreams are free, easy, cheap and fine . . .

"Pah!" he ejaculated, as he kicked the offending garments out of his sight, out of his life, his new butterfly life of a few glorious minutes, a glorious hour even.

Pacing, as the Colonel paced when thinking out some knotty problem of regimental economy, discipline or tactics, Denis strode to and fro across the little room, halting from time to time to admire himself in the mirror, to remember and practise some newly remembered attitude or gesture sacred to the Colonel. Each gave him more joyous satisfaction, more complete confidence; and each increased the *tempo* of his madness.

Then chance, or fate, intervened, using as so often she does, a woman for her instrument.

The door swiftly but softly opened, the head of Natalie appeared, even as she uttered in a venomous stage whisper,

"Denis Ducros, you lazy hound, I thought . . ." and as her bright and bold black eyes fell upon the resplendent figure before her, her tone changed as swiftly as the tenor of her words.

"Oh! M'sieur le Colonel!" she cooed. "A thousand pardons! Excuse and forgive me. I thought . . ."

"Ah! . . . Indeed?" smiled Denis sarcastically. "You thought? You must not attempt to think, my good woman. Nature has not equipped you with the apparatus for thinking."

And before Denis's cold stare, the overbearing virago who was his *bête noir*, cowered and shrank from the room.

"Ha!" ejaculated Denis in the Colonel's manner triumphant; and, turning to the mirror, gave the right side of his moustache a brushing-upward flick with his right hand.

So the omniscient and undeceivable know-all did not know *le légionnaire* Denis Ducros from *M'sieur le Colonel* Louis Rochefort in the still-bright light of the setting sun!

Should he now go downstairs and terrify her to death; then, revealing himself for the man he was, give her a humiliation she would remember?

It was a temptation.

But away with it. How puerile. How unworthy—to use up the precious minutes of his glorious incarnation, in so base a pursuit as the discomfiture of a fat *bonne à tout faire*. What mattered it should she never know? *He* knew.

He knew that he had been mistaken for Colonel Rochefort of the Legion and by a woman who saw him every day and all day—and hoped to see him all night.

And if a woman, why not a man? Why not all men? In that moment Denis Ducros fell from grace—and rose to the full height of his imaginative Provençal-Irish stature.

"Ha!" he said again, in the Colonel's own voice, excellent mimic that he was, *"Ordonnance! Denis!* Where the devil are my cane and gloves?"

"But in your hand, *M'sieur le Colonel*," he answered himself in his own voice. "The left glove on the left hand, the right glove wrapped about the cane."

"Ha! Then why the devil couldn't you say so," growled Denis the Colonel to Denis the batman.

Another happy thought.

"And my silk handkerchief, species of *imbécile*!" The Colonel invariably carried a large silk handkerchief in his left cuff and frequently applied it to his nose—perhaps because he preferred the odour of its perfume to that of *les légionnaires* and other disgusting smells; or because he preferred to breathe as little dust as possible.

Taking the handkerchief from the drawer, Denis shook it out and transferred it to the left cuff of his tunic. He would know exactly how and when and where to produce that valuable piece of evidence and stage-property.

For he was going *out*.

He was going to act upon a wider stage, and before a bigger, better, worthier audience than Natalie Legros.

The well-known flourish of that familiar square of silk would carry conviction even where conviction was not needed.

H'm! An unpleasant word, conviction. But never mind. Away with it. Perish the thought, pleasant or unpleasant. He was going *out*. And *coûte qui coûte*, he was going to be a Colonel for an hour, a distinguished officer and a fine gentleman, even if he became thereafter and therefore, a quite undistinguished member of a Penal Battalion.

Then, opening the outer door of the room, Denis Ducros descended the stairs from the Colonel's quarters and swaggered out into the rosy light of the beautiful spring evening.

So lovely a light, and so beautiful an evening was it, that even the hideous great yellow barracks, and the vast gravelled parade-ground, bordered by Company-offices, store-rooms, Guard-house and *cellule*-punishment prison, and bounded on the side opposite the barracks by lofty iron railings and great gates, looked a little less ugly and forbiddingly utilitarian than usual.

Beauty is, moreover, in the eye of the beholder; and that of Denis, viewing it from the lofty altitude of his new temporary rank, looked upon it for the first time with favour, obtaining for the first time as it were, a bird's-eye instead of a worm's-eye view.

To think that he should have lived to tread this un-hallowed ground with the haughty and spurning foot of a master, a proud conqueror; and to look upon this familiar and detested scene with the gaze, as it were, of a pro-prietor, of one who is monarch of all he surveys.

Literally, he saw the world in a new light, a roseate light indeed, as the beautiful butterfly of that humble little grub; no longer a domestic soldier-servant, but an uplifted *tête montée* Gallic-Irishman, on top of the world and on top of his form. . . .

What should he do first?

He would take a preliminary canter, or rather a dignified stroll, across the parade-ground, and match the virtue and value of his disguise against the eyesight and observation of such of his comrades and superiors as he might encounter.

And, in that hour of his uplifting, he felt that there could arise no emergency with which he would not be most competent to cope—and in the true Rochefort vein and manner.

Confidently he strode forward on the path of glory that would lead but . . . whither?

Three *légionnaires* approached on their way from the main gates to their *chambrée*.

Now for the second test.

Drawing a deep breath, he gazed upon them haughtily, enquiringly, indeed suspiciously, as in the manner of Colonel Rochefort—whose attitude towards *les légionnaires*, whom greatly he loved and whom mightily he chastened—was that of one who knew their wicked hearts so well as to be only too aware that they were doing wrong, had just done something wrong, or were about to do something wrong.

The swift turn of the head, the hard penetrating glance were in the authentic vein. Would the disguise work?

It worked.

It worked most satisfactorily and completely.

Whether it would have done so as perfectly and for as long, in the broad daylight of high noon is unknown; but in the rosy evening light, soon to turn towards dusk, it seemed evident that whosoever beheld him, would behold Colonel Louis Rochefort. For the salutes were swift and spontaneous.

There was no doubtful look upon any of the three well-known faces. There was no hesitation, no second glance,

26

as the respectful eyes that were turned to him resumed their stare to the front; and benignly the smartly quivering salutes were acknowledged with a finger-tip of the right hand to a gold-embroidered *képi*.

Good fellows.

Excellent fellows.

Bons camarades et bons légionnaires.

Bad men all, but bad men of the best sort. *Mauvais sujets*, but certainly not of the gaol-bird class.

Now, one of the most widely spread and completely erroneous of all misconceptions concerning the French Foreign Legion is the popular belief that, if not exactly a unique collection and assortment of crooks and criminals, it is composed very largely of this undesirable class of people. There could scarcely be a bigger mistake; and, as Denis was well aware, there are some wonderful mistakes published on this subject by those who are subsidised to slander the Legion; by journalists who have listened to the lies of the Old Soldier, more-than-willing to turn a dishonest penny and give good measure therefor; and by those equally dishonest persons who know nothing whatever about the subject.

The majority of the men of the French Foreign Legion are not criminals. But a small minority of them are, and so is a small minority of any other regiment in the world.

Anyone who thinks that this magnificent Regiment is a robbers' roost, a rogues' Alsatia, and a scoundrels' asylum, imagines a vain thing.

On the other hand, the word asylum reminds one of the indubitable fact that there is a small proportion of *légionnaires* who should be in an asylum, and these men definitely outnumber those who should be in prison.

This statement, again, must not be taken as suggesting that the French Foreign Legion consists largely of cheerful lunatics; but it is undeniably true that, while there is no greater proportion of criminals in the French Foreign Legion than there is in any other regiment, there is certainly a greater proportion of men who are what is termed "queer"; men who are slightly unbalanced, and who are, on the whole, a little more mad than the rest of us.

And of course, there are again those who, while normally sane and sober as a judge, go completely, if temporarily, insane under the influence of *le cafard*.

And as Denis knew, the three men in the act of saluting him were representative respectively of each of these three classes.

Hans Müller, the German-Swiss, was not really a criminal, though there might be narrow-minded civilians who would regard him as one; Ivan Dobroff was not really a lunatic, though few doctors would decline to certify him as one; and Michel Aubraine was a man of well-balanced and noble mind, save when suffering from an attack of *le cafard*, the influence of which was to make him behave either as a criminal or as a lunatic, when not as both—the complete criminal-lunatic in fact.

Good fellows.

Excellent fellows.

He would have liked to greet them with a kindly, *"Bon soir, mes chers enfants! Dieu vous bénisse!"* But that would not have been in character, for assuredly it was not the habit of *le bon Colonel*, Louis Rochefort, thus to greet and bless his regimental children. Curses came much more readily to the firm lips beneath that trim little hedge of a moustache, and he appeared to regard his little ones rather as *sales cochons*, *scélérats*, and *salauds*, than as *ses chers enfants*.

No, Colonel Denis Ducros must act in character, must play his part as perfectly as he looked it, and not fail to give a flawless impersonation. He must repress his benevolent and comradely instincts in the interest of his Art.

A pity though, for he highly approved these three cheerful blackguards, and would have liked to do something to add to their gaiety, to ameliorate the asperities of their path which they themselves did nothing to smooth, and to send them on their way rejoicing—to continue celebrating the Great Fête Day of *la République*.

Especially Michel Aubraine, with whom he had a tenuous tie of blood and many traits in common. He was fond of him, for they held similar views on life, and enjoyed a common sense of humour.

Michel Aubraine (whose grandfather had spelt it Michael O'Brien) had once, under the influence of *le cafard*, made Legion history by burgling the house of *Monsieur le Maire* and stealing, or, let us say, borrowing without his knowledge and consent, his complete official dress, his red, white and blue sash of office, his chain, his top-hat, his gold-mounted stick and his patent leather shoes, which were really much too small for him.

In these borrowed plumes, Michel Aubraine had called on the Commander-in-Chief in Algeria, then visiting Sidi-bel-Abbès on a tour of inspection, and had begged him, in the name of France, their common Mother, to insist that France treated her French Foreign Legion in a somewhat more motherly manner, with fewer kicks and more ha'pence.

The tale of this deed was told in *café* and canteen and *chambrée*, in *caserne* and camp, to this day, with deep chuckles, and even deeper approval.

Michel Aubraine, who, Parisian born and bred, gay insouciant *boulevardier* before his fall, was, as he said, of "Cork extraction," and probably the descendant of some Captain Michael O'Brien who had come to France to seek his fortune in the *Corps du Garde* and the French wars.

There are many people, among them canny Scots and sober Saxons, who regard the Irish as mad, and will say of the gentleman from Kilkenny or Killaloe, that he's "Irish and unaccountable."

To this type of merry madness and unaccountability, Michel Aubraine added the temperamental effervescence alleged to be partly Gallic; and when the mood descended upon him and the fit seized him, he would do things which nobody's maiden aunt could be expected to approve.

But Denis Ducros approved; admired Michel wholly, and loved him greatly.

Nevertheless, to describe Michel as any more insane or criminal than was Denis himself, would be a complete misuse of words.

And how Denis would have loved to disclose himself to Michel!

And how Michel would have loved the disclosure! A feat after his own heart. A feat rivalling, nay excelling, his own calling on the General in the *rôle* of *Monsieur le Maire*.

A wink and a word to Michel, and he would follow Denis about, from the beginning to the end of this joyous adventure, thrilled and delighted beyond all telling.

Yes, and beyond all self-restraint too, probably. It was a temptation, but it must be resisted. Michel would know soon enough, and it would give him infinite delight to remind Michel of how, together with Hans Müller and Ivan Dobroff, he had, with most punctilious respect and impeccable smartness, saluted his old *copain*, the Colonel's batman!

Yes, he would know soon enough.

But it might be many a long day before they could laugh over it together and really enjoy the joke; for there was no denying that the butterfly's brief summer evening would almost certainly be followed by a long chill winter of discontent.

It would mean cells.

Thirty days cells, at least; and almost certainly the loss of his soft job, and the return to hoe his hard row, to live in the ranks, wherein he would be especially and extra-bitterly harried by *l'Adjudant* Buehl, Sergeant-Major Schnitzel, and by Sergeant Schumacher, all of whom he knew to hate him and to deplore his escape—from their sphere of unkind activities, to the haven of the Colonel's *ménage*.

Should he go back while there was yet time, go back before any harm was done? Go back content with having *been* the Colonel, and been so recognised by his enemy, fat Natalie, and saluted by his friends *les légionnaires* Müller, Dobroff, and, above all, by Michel Aubraine, the clever, the joyous, reckless, gay and care-free creature, the amusing rascal whom, of all men, save the grim Colonel Louis Rochefort, he most admired?

Granted that, by putting on the Colonel's uniform, swaggering across the parade-ground, and being saluted by his *copains*, he had perhaps equalled Michel's feat of calling on the General in the Mayor's clothing and insignia—should he now exceed and excel it by turning out the Guard and inspecting it?

30

That would be a really memorable feat.

Who was the Sergeant of the Guard, to-night? What a holy joy if it were one of his especial enemies, and he could make a fool of him!

Not that it was a really healthy pastime, making fools of sergeants. No, apart from whatever official punishment he got, beginning probably with thirty days' solitary confinement in a dark cell, that sergeant would have a little of his own to add unofficially; something quite unpleasant.

And would not the worst punishment of all be the loss of his job?

For surely Denis Ducros was infinitely better off in such a position than he had been when in the ranks; a position in which he had long been exempt from gruelling marches, the wearisome and monotonous drills, guard duties and fatigues, and the boring routine of barrack life? If ever a rascally rogue of a *légionnaire* found himself in clover, or on velvet, surely it was Denis Ducros, with his light and easy duties, his considerable leisure, his opportunities of hearing so much interesting officers' gossip at table, and below-stairs gossip from Natalie; not to mention his access to an elegant sufficiency of food, wine and tobacco?

Yes, one would have thought that the most volatile of *garçons* or the maddest of "gossoons" would have been at some pains to retain so infinitely desirable a post.

But away with prudence; perish wisdom and discretion; all three but the coward's names for cowardice, and he had had enough of all three.

Was not his hour come?

Did he not know that, when the mood descended upon him and the fit seized him, as occasionally it did, he must break out, run wild, lose control, have his fling, and do the damnedest things?

For a thousand days he might be the humble little man whose pay was a ha'penny a day, and whose right to life, liberty and the pursuit of happiness was non-existent.

But on the thousand-and-first—when the moment came —and if *le bon Dieu* alone knows what brings the moment to the real Irishman, perhaps not He Himself, knows what brings it to the hybrid Gallic Hibernian—he must arise

31

and go to his father, the Devil; kick over the traces; cut loose; run amok; and throw his bonnet, *beret* or *képi*, over the nearest windmill.

"I must be mad," whispered Denis to himself, "even to think of such a thing . . . I *am* mad . . . Praise God from whom all blessings flow, I am as mad as a March hare. I will turn out the Guard. I will inspect it. And, Heaven and my great ancestors helping me, I will turn the Sergeant of the Guard not only out, but inside out."

Sacré véto! The Sergeant of the Guard.

Yes. He would certainly inspect the Guard and if, in doing so, he must still repress his benevolent and philanthropic instincts with regard to his comrades, the Sergeant of the Guard was another matter.

There he could do a little good of a different kind. Give himself a little real pleasure and still remain well within the scope and confines of his part.

If he could get away with it, that is.

But he could. Of course he could.

It was when an actor lived his part and actually felt himself to *be* the character he was impersonating, that he acted perfectly and carried complete conviction.

"*Ha!*" he said aloud in the very voice and manner of the Colonel, as he smartly smacked the left leg of his riding boot with his cane, and—took the second step along the path of glory that could lead but to the cells.

As he strode across the vast parade-ground, men engaged on various fatigues, or proceeding forth from barracks, in their smart array for walking-out, to enjoy the Fête Day celebrations, froze to attention if laden with bucket and broom, or, if empty-handed, saluted with the swift rigid smartness of toy automata.

As he approached the Guard-house, there was a sudden shout, swift movement; and, within one minute of the alarm, the Guard was turned out, was presenting arms with perfect precision, and standing to attention like a group of graven images.

Denis halted in his stride, meticulously returned the Guard's salute, and gravely eyed its Sergeant.

Good. His luck was in.

Of all the men he hated, and they were not very many really, he hated, yea loathed and detested, this Prussian brute, Schumacher, a bully, a brute and a ruffian if ever there were one; a base and pig-like lout whose genuine joy and pleasure it was to make trouble, bring punishment, and cause suffering.

If there were one thing he loved more than to catch the wrong-doer, and punish him as savagely as lay in his power, it was to accuse the innocent of an offence, punish him for its alleged commission, and add extra punishment for the further offence of denial and protest.

With left foot extended, left hand holding glove and cane clenched, and the fingers of the right hand stroking his moustache, Denis considered Sergeant Schumacher with disconcerting attention, or what would have been most disconcerting to anyone less sure of his unquestionable correctness than was the good Sergeant Schumacher.

"Now what would that be?" murmured Denis aloud, as he studied the motionless form of the big Prussian, and felt inwardly thankful that the latter, together with the rest of the Guard, was staring straight to his front, his mind obviously untroubled with any shadow of suspicion.

Surprised, they all possibly might be, that the Colonel, in person, should be prowling round at that time and place, but doubtful as to his genuineness they were not.

This was good.

This was great.

This was glorious.

This was worth living for; possibly even worth dying for.

He was about to enjoy one of the most poignantly beautiful episodes of his life; enjoy it to the full; and fill each moment with enjoyment.

"What would it be?" he continued in private but most audible soliloquy. "It is not a dog. It is not a hog. It is not a frog. Yet certainly it is not a man. Or would it after all perhaps be a hog—on its hind legs?" . . .

"But no, it has hands," he observed.

"Would it be an ape of some sort then, a chimpanzee or an orang-outang?" he mused.

33

"Or perhaps a gorilla?" he asked of the circumambient unanswering air—or of the unanswering Guard.

The Guard stared straight to its front.

Not a muscle of the face of one of its members stirred, unless it were just a little one at the corner of the mouth of the bugler, young, foolish and comparatively undisciplined. But though no facial muscle moved, one countenance undoubtedly changed colour; for the fat and pig-eyed face of Sergeant Schumacher grew even redder than usual, achieving an almost betroot hue.

It gave the acting Colonel infinite pleasure, to see this strong man, suppressing powerfully, bravely and silently, some emotion that bade fair to prove even stronger than he.

Surely he must explode or die?

Explode *and* die perhaps. But even on this night of nights, this was probably too much for which to hope.

"Anyway," he decided, as he prodded the Sergeant's bulging chest, "gorilla or goat, camel or crocodile, it is dressed as a man. Yes, in point of fact it is got up in a sort of parody of the uniform of the Legion—with dull straps, dingy buttons, dusty tunic and dirty boots . . .

"And, *Nom de Dieu*, the animal has actually got 'sardines on its legs,' as *mes enfants les légionnaires* would say. Stripes on its arms. . . . Upon my soul, it is actually wearing the *chevron* of a sergeant. . . . To think of such a thing happening in my Regiment!"

And words appeared to fail the Colonel for a moment.

"Well! Well! Well! But that can be remedied. If unfortunately we cannot change its face and its form, or make it keep itself clean, we can at any rate reduce it to the ranks—of those who can."

The Sergeant and the Guard stood firm, those men of magnificent discipline. They even kept their lips firm, though the eyes of some slightly goggled in their heads.

For it is not every day that it is given to simple *légionnaires* to see a well-hated superior humbled in the dust before their wondering eyes. Nor by that Being, usually as remote as *le bon Dieu*, and who was supposed by all good Sergeants—and Sergeant Schumacher was a very good sergeant indeed—to be their prop and stay, the fount and source of all their authority and power.

Removing the silk handkerchief from his left cuff, with the authentic Rochefort flick and flourish, the Colonel held it to his nose.

"The creature is a walking stink," he said. "It is a very horrible creature. A species of pollution. A mass of corruption. . . . *Pah!* But I will assuredly see—and smell—it in Orderly Room to-morrow.

"To what is the Legion coming?" the Colonel asked, as both in sorrow and in anger he regarded the swinish face of the Prussian.

"In the Legion there should be a little discipline. Definitely. And that discipline must be maintained. And primarily by Sergeants who not only know their duties, but set an example. This man evidently knows nothing and knows it all wrong. . . . And though he is, I admit, an example, it is an example of all that should be avoided by a good *légionnaire*."

And as the Colonel was about to turn away on that sad note of disappointment and disillusion, a faint sound was heard, as of a very minor explosion occurring at a great distance, and under what might be termed great difficulties.

The young bugler had been tried too highly. Brave he was as any man, staunch and stout and true, but not as perfectly self-controlled as later he would doubtless become. He had not yet been long enough in the Legion to become a complete automaton.

And, being a bright and merry young Dane, with a highly developed sense of humour, he was apt to laugh at the wrong thing at the wrong time, and in the wrong place. And on this memorable occasion, all three were wrong, or would have been, had "Colonel" Denis Ducros been Colonel Louis Rochefort.

What caused Stevn Knutson finally to explode was the fact that the Colonel's concluding remarks to the Sergeant, were not only couched in the Sergeant's own sort of language, but were the very identical expressions which the Sergeant had two minutes before been addressing to

35

Stevn Knutson—and this did indeed strike this young gentleman as being not only truly remarkable, but very, very funny.

In point of fact, it was not remarkable that the Colonel should have used these particular terms and allocutions, inasmuch as they had, full many a time and oft, been used by the Sergeant to Denis himself.

But funny it was, no doubt, that so very recently the Sergeant should have said to the Bugler:

"You unspeakable species of filth! You walking stink! You pollution! You mass of corruption! I'll have you in the *boîte* to-morrow.

"This is the Legion. And I'll teach you some discipline, you little smell. I'll teach you to keep yourself clean . . ." and so forth, all because Sergeant Schumacher, who did not like the *légionnaire* Stevn Knutson, because he was quick, and clever, and humorous—had imagined that Knutson had laughed behind the Sergeant's back, a crime of which he had promptly and falsely accused him.

And now he really had laughed behind the Sergeant's broad back, for it was so exquisitely amusing to hear the bully told-off in his very own words. But the incident grew even funnier, a little humour going a long way in the Legion, for instantly the Colonel falsely accused the Sergeant of the very offence of which the Sergeant had falsely accused the Bugler!

Sharply turning back, the Colonel again transfixed the purple-faced Schumacher with his cold stare.

"*Ah! . . . Indeed?*" he said, in the authentic tones of Colonel Rochefort. "The little Shoemaker is amused? He laughs, does he? He gives a great, gross belch of drunken laughter, does he? Intoxicated as well as dirty. Possibly a connection between the two states. Dirty because he is an habitual drunkard. Perhaps he is perpetually drunk in an attempt to drown his shame at being perpetually dirty?

"At any rate, it is clear that he laughs because he is drunk; or charitably we will assume that it is so. We should not like to sentence him for gross and intentional insolence to his Commanding Officer. That would be a very serious matter, and not to be settled by a mere reduction to the ranks. No, no. That would be an affair of *le boîte*; a matter of a prison sentence perhaps; a case for a *conseil de guerre*.[1]

"It would seem hard that a man, who had by some mysterious means attained the rank of Sergeant, should be sentenced to eight years' *travaux forcées* in a Penal Battalion, for one indolent laugh. But it would not be for that, it would be for dirt, degradation and the drunkenness that led to the insolence and insubordination."

As the Colonel concluded his harsh and bitter homily, it seemed to the intelligent, if fanciful young Dane, that, for the fraction of a second, the Colonel's cold eye wavered and caught his own with a flicker of understanding.

An absurd idea of course.

With a growl in Colonel Rochefort's lowest register, the Colonel spoke his final words to the apparently stunned and stricken Sergeant.

"See that no *légionnaire* is turned back from his evening walk by reason of his being improperly dressed, dirty or slovenly," he ordered, "for the worst of them could not be as bad as the Sergeant of the Guard.

"I'll deal with you in the morning," he concluded, and turned away.

It may be said that, in a way, the Guard enjoyed the remainder of their tour of duty better than did Sergeant Schumacher, though in another way they did not. For the Sergeant seemed to be angry about something, and was even less affectionate than usual. Never had the bullying ruffian who could courageously face anything except ruffianly bullying, come nearer to the suicide he sometimes contemplated, than he did that night, for his yellow streak, the hall-mark of the bully, though not wide was deep.

And as Denis Ducros turned about and ceased to face the Guard, he also found himself facing a most terrible temptation.

There before him were the great iron gates, symbol of his state of servitude, and of the iron discipline that bound him, and held him, and shut him off from the world of free happy men—and women.

[1]court-martial.

B*

could not possibly look more like a soldier than he already did, for the Legion contained no smarter non-commissioned officer than he. An ornament to the Regiment, a model and a pattern to all its rank and file. Scarcely could he believe his own ears. There must be some mistake; he could not have heard aright.

Never from the days when he was smart, intelligent and ambitious *bleu*,[1] doing his recruits' course, had such words been addressed to him—and then only as a matter of mere form and routine, by a hard-driving Sergeant-Instructor, who said precisely the same thing daily, for the good of his mind, soul and body, to every recruit who passed through his hands.

He must be mistaken!

Such a shocking, unjust and cruel insult . . .

And from the Colonel too, a man who was his *beau idéal* of a fighting soldier and a *Chef de Bataillon*. And who, moreover, had hitherto been so approving and friendly.

He hadn't been at the Depôt for very long, but from the very first he had seemed to realise and to recognise that *l'Adjudant* Buehl was something a bit extra, something a little out of the ordinary, for ability, smartness and discipline, even among the non-commissioned officers of the Legion.

Why, *l'Adjudant* Buehl could have sworn that the Colonel regarded him with exactly the same feelings as those with which he regarded the Colonel.

Try to look like a soldier! What? *He*, of all men, *l'Adjudant* Buehl, with his double row of medals and decorations; his spotless record; his highest rank below that of a commissioned officer; his great reputation as a man-eating disciplinarian; hardest of the hard; smartest of the smart; his high hopes, almost amounting to certainty, of being sent to St. Maixent Military College (for non-commissioned officers selected for training for promotion to commissioned rank).

Try to look like a soldier? What an incredibly cruel, unjust and wicked insult!

And *l'Adjudant* Buehl, who had spent a good deal of the

[1] recruit.

best years of his life in delivering, nay hurling, cruel, unjust and wicked insults at his subordinates, did not himself suffer insult gladly.

It is far more blessed to give than to receive—as both these soldiers in that moment deeply appreciated.

Almost visibly the fine, swaggering, strutting *Adjudant* shrivelled and shrank, deflated by the piercing deadly thrust of the Colonel's sharp and bitter speech. Had the poor fellow but known it, he was for the moment looking, as well as feeling, like one of the wretched *légionnaires* whom it was his delight, if not his duty, to brow-beat, bully and be-devil.

With an almost audible gasp, he lowered his arm from the salute; and with a quite audible chuckle, Denis Ducros dropped his hand from the peak of the Colonel's *képi* as he passed on.

Almost visibly the fine swaggering, strutting Colonel swelled with pleasure, power and importance as he went on his way, pride in his port, defiance in his eye.

That would teach the over-bearing, foul-mouthed swine a little lesson. Do him all the good in the world. The only pity was there couldn't have been a score or two of his victims present to witness the bully's humiliation.

But one can't have everything, and it had been so satisfying. For it is not often, in real life, that one has the opportunity of actually saying the sort of things that, in day-dreams and phantasy, one imagines oneself saying to those whom, with good reason, one hates, despises and fears.

Still, it would have given an even sharper edge to the keen joy of the moment, had there been an audience, if of only one. Michel Aubraine, for example, or the merry and appreciative Stevn Knutson, the bugler.

In point of fact, had Denis but known it, the latter excellent fellow, though not vouchsafed the pleasure of witnessing the discomfiture of the *Adjudant*, was about to enjoy the fruits thereof—and behold a second scourging of the unfortunate Sergeant of the Guard. For, returning to barracks in what could only now be described as a towering rage, and passing through the portal by which the Colonel had so recently departed, *l'Adjudant* Buehl sought a victim upon whom to vent that wrath ere it blew him to pieces.

His eye fell upon the Sergeant of the Guard—also the full weight and violence of his invective—while yet that hapless man still reeled from the blow dealt by the Colonel.

Hard luck indeed . . .

"Mais que voulez-vous? C'est la Légion!" as the Legion says.

Still chuckling, the "Colonel" Denis Ducros went on his way rejoicing, glancing nevertheless with cold hauteur from left to right, and returning, in the Colonel's very own style, the salutes of the soldiers who passed him, grading the movement from the sketchiest raising of a finger, to the punctilious full salute—according to the rank of the individual, which varied from that of *soldat deuxième classe* to brother-officer of field rank.

Ah! . . . And who was this?

None other than the grey-haired, blue-nosed, *vieux moustache* known to his comrades as Père Pinard, *doyen* of his Battalion, oldest soldier, biggest liar, stoutest *légionnaire*, and champion drunk of the Army of Africa. Dear old *Pinard*,[1] who apparently had no other name than that; no other nationality, family or home than *La Légion Etrangère*. A man legendary in his own life-time, a man of tales and stories, those told about him nearly as numerous as those he himself told. A true Soldier of Fortune on whose breast glittered the medals of Tonkin, Madagascar and Dahomey, as well as those of the campaigns of Algeria —not to mention such side-line extras as the bronze cross of the *Croix de Guerre*, and the silver and gilt disc of the *Medaille Militaire*, tinkling symbols of valour and war-like experience, which it was frequently his wont to pawn for wine.

He appeared to regard without pride or satisfaction his almost unique collection of war medals and decorations. It was not so much a case of the contempt that is bred by familiarity, as uninterested acceptance of their existence;

[1] cheap wine.

things that just were—like his grey beard and blue nose. He alluded to them when pawning or redeeming them, as his *ferblanterie*, or tin-ware.

What amused and delighted those lewd fellows of the baser sort, his boon companions, was the fact that wine apparently, indeed obviously, did old Père Pinard no harm, for he could march as far and as fast as any of them; and if occasion should arise on which he had to fight all day and was permitted to drink all night, he would be as ready for the next day's doings, and as bright and early as the youngest of them.

By reason of this curious and lamentable fact he was a living refutation and a walking annoyance to *Monsieur le Médécin-Majeur*, a good *toubib*[1] with strong views on the dangers of alcohol as a cause of *cafard* and many other evils, for soldiers who work, march and fight beneath a burning sun.

It was, to his mind, a very wrong and improper thing that a man who was not only one of the most popular and most distinguished, but also one of the very best of the soldiers in his charge, should be an undeniable and incorrigible drunkard . . .

Père Pinard, magnificently sober on a few bottles of *pinard* and assorted curious spirits of undesirable origin, caught sight of the man whom he supposed to be his Colonel, and saluted with swift smartness and precision.

The heart of Denis warmed to this dear old man, this kindly simple soul, this good soldier who was *bon camarade et bon légionnaire*, to whose wonderful reminiscences drawn from his inexhaustible store of Legion lore, he had so often listened, thrilled and enthralled.

The Colonel halted in his stride.

"Well, *mon cher enfant*, and how goes it?" he smiled benevolently. "Health good, slate clean, and thirst powerful?" Père Pinard, standing at the salute and looking a model of virtue and a statue of military rectitude, concealed his almost unbounded surprise and beamed his almost unbounded gratification.

Bon Dieu de Dieu de Sort! And Name of a Name of a

[1] army doctor (slang).

Hairless Green Monkey! Wonders would never cease. What was happening? Could it be possible that a few bottles of red Algerian wine, a *tasse* or two of cognac, a taste or so of *tchum-tchum*,[1] a few toothfuls of *gènèvre*, and a negligible number of absinthes were making him imaginative?

Was he seeing things?

No, this was the Colonel all right.

Was he hearing things? Voices—like those heard by Jeanne d'Arc? But they had been angel voices, and whatever the *légionnaires* called Louis Rochefort, it was not "angel."

Could it be that he, Père Pinard, was losing grip, could not carry his liquor, was going ga-ga?

Away with such horrible and miserable thoughts. It was not as though he had had a skinful instead of toothfuls, mouthfuls or even bellyfuls. But it was enough to make a sober man think he might be a little drunk; for on former occasions on which the Colonel had given himself the trouble of addressing *le légionnaire* Pinard, it had not been thus that he had spoken.

On the very last occasion of all, and that only quite recently, he had called him, among other derogatory names, a Pillar of the Pot-houses of Sodom and Gomorrah; a doddering, drivelling dreg-drinker, and a tun-bellied, slop-soaking rum-sponge.

Yes, there had been a great deal more *gueule*[2] than endearment, such as this *"mon cher enfant"* stuff. In fact he had alluded to Père Pinard as one whose sole thought and object in life was *se saouler la gueule*,[3] and *se taper la gueule*.[3]

He had roundly averred that Père Pinard was a miserable wreck, an aged ruin whose absolute chronic condition was *ayant la gueule de bois*.[3]

Yes, too much *gueule* about the Colonel's conversation altogether, at that regrettable Orderly-Room encounter.

Quite eloquent the Colonel was apt to be on the subject of poor old Père Pinard's character and habits.

And here he was, smiling at him like a father; and, like a father, was addressing him as *son cher enfant*.

[1] rice spirit.   [2] abuse.   [3] to be drunk.

There was a catch in it somewhere. And Père Pinard must either be drunk, dreaming, or both.

"*Eh, mon vieux lapin*, how's tricks?" continued the Colonel, smiling with a bright and charming kindliness, as the aged reprobate grinned and wagged his beard in lieu of tail.

Lapin!

He was the Colonel's *vieux lapin*[1] now, was he?

Only the other day, it had been rather a case of *ne pas valoir un peu de lapin* (his not being worth a tinker's damn), and of less use and value than the butt end of a dead bed-bug, as the Old Devil had clearly expressed it.

Quite good at phrases, the Colonel was; well up to his job at *fichant un poil à quelqu'un*[2] when he felt like it.

"Still no gold stripe, I see," continued the Colonel. "Not even a worsted one. How's that, now? Come, come. We can't have it. Not with that fine show of *ferblanterie*. It wants stripes to set it off.

"Only *soldat première classe*. No. We can't have that," he said again, smiling even more warmly. "Not with a *vieux moustache* who has served France faithfully, man and boy, for nearly half a century—Line, Marsouins, Legion and all . . .

"We must see about it, *mon ami*. We must do something about it, mon gars.

"Yes. Tell Sergeant-Major Lorraine that I shall want a word with him about it to-morrow. . . .

"It is a disgrace to the non-commissioned officers of your Company that your name has not been put forward before this. Rank injustice and the old grudge-and-favouritism somewhere."

And the Colonel shook his head sadly.

"*Mon Colonel!*" murmured the abashed Père Pinard, shaken between joy at such wonderful words and fear at such apparent sarcasm.

"And I'll have a word with Captain de Grandeville about it," added the Colonel; and, with a playful tap of his cane, a kind of accolade and blessing, bade the old soldier be of good cheer, and have a night of good cheer, too, in celebration.

[1] old rabbit.   [2] giving anyone a dressing down.

As he passed on, the Colonel left the good Père Pinard trembling with alcoholic emotion, and fully prepared to subscribe to the belief that the day of miracles was not passed and that the millenium must be very close at hand. In a fog of happiness and wine fumes, the elated *ancien* made his way back to barracks and to bed, resolved to lead a higher and better life. He would make a fresh start, begin again, and turn over a new leaf.

After all, he was only seventy.

And what wonderful things he could do if he were promoted Corporal, and then Sergeant. How enormously he could help all his friends, and prevent their enemies in all their unkind doings.

He would be a model Sergeant; the beloved father of his *escouade*, the admired and trusted shepherd of all black sheep . . .

Meanwhile, a few yards further on, the Colonel was aware that Mademoiselle Angélique, a Polish and polished young lady, who appeared to have no other name save Oui-Oui, was crossing the road and coming in his direction.

Little friend of all the world and of most of the half-world, she still could not claim acquaintanceship, much less friendship, with the austere and rigidly virtuous Colonel Louis Rochefort, *homme toujours très sérieux et comme il faut.* And she lowered her eyes modestly, as she stepped on to the pavement in front of him.

That Great One had nothing to say to such people as the *petites Angéliques* and *Oui-Ouis* of this world, she well knew.

Judge then of her surprise when, swift as a little bird and light as a little tickling feather, the Colonel's ungloved hand shot up from his right side and chucked her under the chin.

But what in the name of kind Saint Louis, patron Saint of all good little naughty girls, was this?

Mademoiselle Angélique Oui-Oui could scarcely believe the evidence of her own chin.

Oh, la, la! M'sieur le Colonel himself. That grim man, so cold, so severe, so disapproving. It was as though the virtuous Saint Anthony himself, promenading the Golden

Street, had suddenly and playfully tickled a demure little angel passing by.

But there, they were all alike under the skin—and still more so under the rose!

And Mademoiselle Oui-Oui, smiling bewitchingly, raised her sparkling dark eyes to those of the Colonel.

"Qu'elle est ravissante," he sighed aloud, as to himself.

"Bon jour, ma chèrie. Comment ça va?" he greeted her in the tone and manner of an old friend and ardent admirer. And this latter, indeed, the humble *légionnaire* Denis Ducros had long been—from a distance.

Not for him, *soldat simple* that he was, the friendship of the fashionable Angélique Oui-Oui, who indeed only shed the light of her countenance and the charm of her conversation upon lonely shoulders of commissioned rank.

Should such an obscure person as Denis Ducros, *légionnaire* and officer's servant, ever feel that the austerities and asperities of the monastic life of the celibate warrior needed the kind amelioration of feminine society, conversation and charm, he could get him to *le village Nègre* and seek it there. The romantic companionship of Arab and negro women was there available for the bold Romeo who bravely sought it. But he must not be of the fastidious, hypercritical and too discriminating type of traveller in the *pays du tendre*.

But the ha'penny-a-day *légionnaire* might just as well sigh for the moon, or a champagne-and-oyster dinner, as for the pleasure of the society of the famous Angélique Oui-Oui, *belle* of Sidi-bel-Abbès.

Yet here he was, *légionnaire* Denis Ducros, smiling upon her paternally, patronisingly indeed, and speaking to her, not as a mere suppliant, not as an equal, but positively *de haut en bas*.

"Oh, M'sieur le Colonel!" she murmured, very much as Père Pinard had done; and, although not looking in the least as Père Pinard had looked, feeling nevertheless much as he had felt on receipt of such signal honour as the kind and approving notice of stern Colonel Louis Rochefort.

"Oh, M'sieur le Colonel! Comme vous êtes gentil!"

"A happy chance! A most fortunate meeting," smiled

47

the Colonel encouragingly, as he patted her hand. "I have for some time been meaning to call and pay my respects. I must give a party in your honour."

Mademoiselle Angélique did her utmost, by means of a private and peculiar process of her own, to blush becomingly. It was not easy, as it involved holding the breath for a rather prolonged period, and there was already a quite considerable and permanent blush established and in evidence on her rounded cheeks.

"Yes. Most certainly we must have a party," continued the Colonel. "You must bring along some nice girls, and I will bring my boys . . . All the brightest and the best of them.

"Now where shall we have it? *Chez Mademoiselle Angélique?* Or what about a moonlight picnic, a *fête champêtre*? No. I know what we'll do. We'll have a gala dinner at the Grand Hotel."

"But how delightful," murmured Mademoiselle Angélique.

The Colonel beamed in most friendly fashion.

"M'sieur le Colonel est très gentil," she faltered, looking up a little more boldly into the kindly and affectionate eyes that gazed into hers.

"Well! Well! . . . What a world we live in," she reflected; and, again like Père Pinard, decided that wonders would never cease.

For in a life not devoid of surprises, this was a surprise indeed.

Usually of quite adequate fluency, and as ready of wit as of speech, Mademoiselle Angélique Oui-Oui was positively dumb.

Monsieur le Colonel Rochefort himself! Who next? And it was with something very nearly resembling a genuine blush that Mademoiselle smiled her joyous gratification as the Colonel patted her hand in the manner of a fond parent.

Fond certainly, if not quite parental.

"Au 'voir donc, chère Angélique," concluded the Colonel. "I'll send you the invitation-cards—or, better still, I'll bring them round myself," and in his most gallant manner,

or Colonel Louis Rochefort's most gallant manner, he brushed with his moustache the fingers of her right hand.

Wafting Mademoiselle Angélique an airy kiss, he then saluted and turned to resume his stroll, a warm glow around his heart, a kindly sense of something accomplished, something done to earn someone else a little pleasure, if not repose.

But scarcely had he turned to go, when a new idea illuminated his receptive mind.

Why let this charming encounter with such a nice girl be so brief? Why should it not be prolonged a while? He could hardly ask her to promenade around the town with him, for her company would rather tend to cramp his style, and his society would sooner or later be something of an embarrassment and hindrance to herself.

But he could suggest her accompanying him to the Grand Hotel for an *apéritif* and the making of all arrangements for the party.

It would give her great pleasure to walk with him, to have a drink with him, to enjoy with him the ordering of the dinner and making all arrangements for the gala, he felt sure.

It might be but a dream. It was, of course, a dream, a rosy illusion. But Angélique was unaware of that cold hard fact. She would live for a few days, or at any rate, a few hours, in a state of illusory but warm and joyful bliss.

Illusion, alas! But is not illusion finer and greater than reality?

What was it that buoyed men up, through the rough and stormy seas of life, but hopes—usually destined to remain for ever unfulfilled.

And if hope springs eternal in the human breast, let illusion also shed its soft and comforting light upon the darkness of the human path . . .

And for the space of a minute or so, such of the cosmopolitan public of Sidi-bel-Abbès as was on the spot, was treated to the stimulating and intriguing sight, as it supposed, of Colonel Louis Rochefort in hot and hasty pursuit of the well-known form of Mademoiselle Angélique Oui-Oui.

"Ah, Mademoiselle," said Denis as he overtook that young lady, "it just occurs to me . . . Shall we proceed at once and together to the Grand Hotel to order our dinner and make our little arrangements?"

"*Oh, Monsieur le Colonel!*" smiled Angélique happily. "Such an honour! But how charming! . . ."

Well! Well! Well! The good Saint Louis was going it! To think that she should live to walk down the most fashionable and popular boulevard of Sidi-bel-Abbès with the distinguished Colonel Louis Rochefort, that Monsieur so correct and impeccable, and he married too, and notoriously a model of strict domestic virtue.

Was he tired of it all?

Personally she had never tried it, but she could imagine the practice of strict virtue to be a boring pursuit and a great nuisance.

Anyway, if *Monsieur le Colonel* was contemplating a brief excursion from the strait and narrow path, she would be more than willing to accompany him into the flowery woods and dells of the realms of Romance.

And those observers who had seen the Colonel turn about and pursue Mademoiselle Angélique Oui-Oui, now, with astonishment and with breath that would not long be bated, saw him walk off beside her in pleasant fellow-ship, chatting and laughing with an ease that was almost abandon.

And through the portals of the best hotel of Sidi-bel-Abbès, those whose eyes followed, and they were not few, saw the adventurous couple about to disappear.

Not among these busy-bodies, but coming from the opposite direction, was Madame de Beauchamp, the wife of Major de Beauchamp of the Spahis, and an intimate friend of Madame Rochefort, the Colonel's extremely proper and serious-minded wife.

On one point, at any rate, Colonel Louis Rochefort and Acting-Colonel Denis Ducros held identical views. They both cherished a regrettable detestation of Madame de Beauchamp, that *maîtresse femme*, who considered herself the leading lady of Sidi-bel-Abbès, appointed herself its censor and the judge of its morals, was charitable to no man, still less to any woman, and was generous in nothing but rebuke.

In the opinion of Colonel Rochefort she was a most unpleasant and uncharitable person, who, in her dealings with Society, hoped for the worst rather than expected the best.

In the opinion of Denis Ducros she was just a plain *biche.* One of the plainest he had ever seen.

As the happy couple were in the act of turning to go into the hotel, they came face to face with Madame, and to both of them it was evident that, though it might be for the first time in her well-spent life, the great and good woman was wholly unequal to the occasion.

She had no words. Nothing but a gasp wherewith to reply to the Colonel's polite,

"Ah, ma chère Madame de Beauchamp! What good fortune! I wonder if you have met my friend, Mademoiselle Angélique Oui-Oui? . . . No? Permit me to present you to . . ."

But if Madame de Beauchamp could not utter, she could totter. Removing her horrified, indignant gaze from the Colonel's bland face, she stabbed Angélique with a viciously contemptuous stare, and made to pass on. But the deep inhalation, with which she recovered her breath after her gasp of wrath and horror, wrought evil as well as good.

Madame was large, and Madame was inclined to mitigate the appearance, if not the fact, of a slightly excessive *embonpoint,* by means of a sartorial discipline of which the key-note was tightness. Everything she wore was tight, tight almost as her compressed lips; and the deep breath which she drew through angrily inflated nostrils made everything tighter.

Too tight indeed for one terribly important button.

She felt, though none might hear, a definite and horrifying pop.

She took but a step . . . she faltered . . . halted, clutched and shuffled.

"Permit me," said the gallant Colonel, swiftly stooping, as Angélique's peal of merry laughter rang out unabashed.

51

Ignoring the outstretched hand and the silken pinkness which it proffered, Madame de Beauchamp recoiled, and still without a word, recovered her poise sufficiently to go on her way, without rejoicing.

"But what shall I do with them, Madame?" enquired the Colonel loudly of the broad back of the retreating Madame de Beauchamp.

"One would say the old dear is deaf," laughed Angélique, in her high and all-too-audible voice.

"Quite," replied the Colonel seriously.

"I apologise, my dear," he said. "I thought it was a lady . . . A lady of my acquaintance in fact . . . and these are undoubtedly her property."

Madame's back appeared to shudder.

"Well, if she doesn't want them . . ." smiled the practical Angélique, and swiftly performed a small miracle of folding and compression.

A moment later, laughing happily, the two passed through the swing doors into the foyer of the Grand Hotel.

Hastily a Franco-Spanish-Arab servant fled to inform the Management that an army officer of high rank, accompanied by a lady, had entered the hotel. Swiftly the Management hurried from the little office in which it lurked, and, bowing low, smiling toothfully, and apparently cleansing its hands of all stain of sin, hurried to welcome the Colonel and to beg that he would honour it with his commands.

The Management, widely and deeply acquainted with Life, especially as it is lived in provincial towns of Northern Africa, was certainly not shocked, but was undeniably a little surprised, to discover that the lady who accompanied Monsieur le Colonel Rochefort, Commanding the Depôt of the French Foreign Legion, was none other than Mademoiselle Angélique Oui-Oui, with whom he was not unacquainted.

In fact, only the previous night, which included part of the morning of that very day, Mademoiselle Angélique had been the bright particular star of a little party at which the Management had permitted itself to relax from the anxieties and cares of Management.

But the Management's face was bland, placid and inscrutable; and the bow with which he honoured Mademoiselle—now by a strange turn of Fortune's wheel, his patron—was one of the deep respect due to a distinguished stranger.

Slightly to the Colonel's rear and right, Mademoiselle politely acknowledged the Management's deep bow with a gracious inclination of the head, and a swifter one of the right eyelid.

But neither a nod nor a wink is necessary to a clearsighted horse, and the Management thought that Mademoiselle might, without sign or signal, have trusted him to act with the utmost discretion. However, doubtless the nod and wink were but the outward and visible sign of little Angélique's girlish levity. The wink but called upon him to regard her; to note that it really was she; to observe the social heights to which she had risen; and also to share the joke.

And the Colonel spread himself.

In a vision he also spread a table of good things, the sort of dinner of which the *légionnaire*, who has lived for years upon an unchanging diet, dreams as he sits down to his mid-day meal of *soupe* and bread, and again to his evening meal of—*soupe* and bread.

It was not that Denis Ducros, since becoming a batman, had anything of which to complain in the matter of food and drink, but he would have loved to sit down to a grand dinner more costly, more copious and more varied than those at which he served when Madame Rochefort gave a party.

Nor was it a dinner of quite that type that he wanted. He wished to provide a sort of feast that would appeal to his austerely and monotonously fed *copain*, Michel Aubraine, and his good friends Hans Müller, Ivan Dobroff, Père Pinard, MacSneeze, Ramonones and the others of his *escouade*.

That neither he and his friends, nor the lady friends of Angélique would ever sit down to any such feast at the Grand Hotel, troubled him not at all.

It was neither here nor there.

He was an artist; and, at the moment, he was giving full rein to his artistic imagination in the matter of arranging a sumptuous, beautiful and happy evening for the friends he loved and the strangers he was fully prepared to love.

He was also enjoying to the utmost the sense of power, that, in imagination, he could command.

He was enjoying too, and even more, the moment in which, and for which he lived, with its actual if brief sense of genuine reality. It was not illusion; it was not merely in his imagination that this fat *pékin*[1] was bowing before him, assenting with the utmost respect to his every suggestion, and taking his orders as does a . . . as does a . . . batman, the orders of a Colonel.

"As to the numbers, now," enquired the Management. "If *Monsieur le Colonel* would first of all kindly fix the . . ."

"Oh a score," promptly interrupted the Colonel. "Ten officers and ten ladies.

"Besides ourselves, of course," he swiftly amended.

A far-away look o'erspread the ingenuous countenance of Mademoiselle Angélique Oui-Oui who was making a rapid calculation. Herself and ten more of *les girls*? Were there ten just women in all Sidi-bel-Abbès? Just the right sort, so to speak; quiet, discreet, well-behaved, and in all respects worthy? . . . There would have to be.

And if she could not raise a full team from among her personal friends and acquaintances, she could call at Madame de Beuglant's School for Young Ladies and enter into negotiations for the loan of one or two of her pupils. Nicolette, for example—and a good example.

What a lovely evening it would be. Such an event in her quiet life! Such a change!

And Mademoiselle Angélique Oui-Oui loved change. The more the better. She fully subscribed to the belief that variety is the spice of life, and she had a marked *penchant* for spice. . . .

And was there any special *plat* to which Mademoiselle gave preference? If so, she had but to mention it.

The Colonel recked not if she should mention oysters,

[1]civilian.

lobsters, whitebait, and caviare.   Nay ortolans, larks'
tongues, Strassburg pie, and *paté de foie gras*, things in
season or out of season.

Mademoiselle had many preferences and mentioned
them all.

Good! The more the merrier.

The Management scribbled hard in its little pocket-
book.

And talking of merriment, what of the wines?

That was a subject quickly settled, in so far as Mademoiselle Angélique was concerned.

Sweet Champagne to begin with. Sweet Champagne to
go on with. And sweet Champagne to finish with.

And after dinner some sweet Champagne.

In its little book the Management scribbled, *Asti
Spumante pour Oui-Oui et les girls.*

Smiling tolerantly at so truly Angelic a preference, Denis
gave joyous rein to his imagination, and once more spread
himself.

His knowledge of wine was not negligible. He knew
what *Messieurs les Officiers* drank at the *Cercle*; he knew
what wines went with which courses; and he knew, both
by hear-say and by study of prices in the Club wine-list,
which were the noble wines of France.

In the light of this knowledge he now spoke of a light
dry sherry *apéritif*; a rich brown sherry with the soup, a
fine Chablis with the fish, a noble Burgundy with the
entrée; a great Champagne, just twelve years old, with the
joint; a generous port thereafter; and the Management
must see to it that the Cognac which accompanied the
coffee should be at least Napoleonic, if not real Napoleon
Brandy.

And if, as he spoke of Napoleon, a shadow of his own
Waterloo crossed the glowing soul of Denis Ducros, he
ignored it bravely and utterly.

Was he not enjoying himself marvellously?

And was he not giving great pleasure to himself, to
cette chère petite Angélique, and to *ce gros Monsieur*, the
Management.

He was indeed.

For the joy of the Management was even greater than its amazement, which was great indeed. How he had misjudged this gallant Colonel, especially in the matter of gallantry.

What had come over him? Anyway, La Oui-Oui had over-come him, and to some purpose.

What a dinner!

The best of everything, and apparently without stint, or thought of cost. Better to be on the safe side though. And if, as apparently was the case, the sky was the limit, the fact had better be mentioned.

Did the Colonel quite realise the cost of one or two of the items so airily mentioned?

That Nuit St. Georges *par exemple*? That Mouton Rothschild? That forty-year-old Château Yquem for those who preferred it.

"Would *M'sieur le Colonel* prefer to see the wine-list?" the Management asked deferentially.

That would give him some idea of what he would be letting himself in for.

No, the Colonel did not wish to see the wine-list. He merely wanted his orders fully and accurately carried out.

The Management bowed, while mentally rubbing its chin.

And would *M'sieur le Colonel* like an estimate? *Monsieur le Colonel* would not. As he had indicated, he required the best that the Grand Hotel could provide. The best would have to be good enough; and *Monsieur le Colonel* would look to the Management to see that it was the best.

As to the cost, *Monsieur le Colonel* expected it to bear reasonable ratio to value, and to be a fair and proper charge for wine and food of the very finest quality. It was to be a gala occasion, and its cost was not the prime consideration.

"Good enough," smiled the Management to itself, and had a bright idea.

"*Monsieur le Colonel* would of course desire that the ladies should have gifts, as is usual upon gala occasions?"

"But of course! . . . Of course! . . . I was coming to that," replied the delighted Denis, concealing his pleasure and enthusiasm at receiving this admirable suggestion.

This Management was a good fellow, unprepossessing as he looked. He might have a pendulous lip over which the tip of a red tongue continually flickered, a pasty, greasy skin, a boiled eye, and a protuberant paunch, but he had ideas.

Freely Denis admitted that but for this fat civilian he would never have thought of gala presents for the ladies.

Splendid. It gave even wider scope . . . And they should be noble gifts. Something worth having. And what was more, there should be something for *les messieurs* as well as for *les dames*. A good solid silver cigarette-case for each of the men, and for the ladies? . . .

His imagination began to run joyous riot.

What a lovely game this was.

A different kind of cigarette-case for the ladies? Smaller? Daintier?

No. Rather banal; some of them might not smoke.

What did one give girls upon a gala occasion? Would jewellery be a little excessive? Rings . . . bracelets . . . wrist-watches . . . That sort of thing?

He did not want to be vulgarly lavish of course, although he wanted everything to be of the best, and no reasonable expense spared.

But, of course, Angélique would know the sort of thing; and it would rest with him to decide the sort of quality and value.

"If I might be permitted to make a suggestion," continued the Management, "perhaps *Monsieur le Colonel* and —er—Mademoiselle would care to glance at the show-case."

"Oh, you have a stock of—ah—such things, conveniently on the premises?"

"Yes, *Monsieur le Colonel*."

"*Ah! . . . Indeed?*" replied Denis in a tone and manner that would have fully persuaded Colonel Louis Rochefort that he was both hearing and seeing double; and which suddenly reminded the Management that there was more than one side to the character of this distinguished and versatile officer.

If *Monsieur le Colonel* and Mademoiselle would kindly

step this way, suggested the Management, waving a large persuasive hand in the direction of a corridor.

With a brusque unkindly murmur that he had never yet learned to step in just that way, the Colonel nevertheless turned and followed the Management to where glittered a jeweller's show-case, elegant and attractive, beneath the electric light.

"*Oh-h-h*," whispered Angélique, feasting delighted eyes upon its contents, "*Chez Tiffany, Cartier et Cie*," for such were the names modestly adopted by the gentleman of Hispano-Israelitish extraction who kept the leading jeweller's shop in the *Place Sadi Carnot*.

"I will get the key if *Monsieur le Colonel* will excuse me," murmured the Management, and disappeared into his office.

"I thought of giving the gentlemen cigarette-cases, all alike," stated the Colonel decisively. "Something plain, but very good; with just the date and a little inscription. A trifling, but lasting and useful, memento of . . ."

"And the ladies?" interrupted Angélique almost impatiently.

"Ah! There you can help me, *chèrie*," smiled the Colonel. "Suppose I leave that to you."

"*Ah-h-h*," breathed Angélique.

This was indeed a man. A great and good man, who, praise Saint Louis, was not so good as all that.

"But with the greatest pleasure," she said. "To do *anything* for *Monsieur le Colonel* would be a pleasure."

It would indeed—to do anything of that sort especially; and Angélique made rapid mental calculations. Ten girls beside herself. A little commission from the jeweller on each, and a very distinct understanding with each of *les girls* beforehand.

And something rather extra special in the way of gala gift for Mademoiselle Angélique Oui-Oui.

"I have an idea, *Monsieur le Colonel*," she whispered, as the Management opened its door. "Let us go to *Tiffany, Cartier et Cie*. There will be more choice at their shop. This is but a small selection."

"Excellent," replied the Colonel.

And so it was. Truly excellent. Fancy entering the

58

finest jewellers' in the whole place with a pretty girl, and giving her *carte blanche*.

What a night he was having!

And how one thing led to another! Heaven knew what it would lead to in the end; but it is the travelling, not the arriving, that makes the joy of travel. To reach the end is but to reach an end; but to go on for a long strange journey into unknown regions, *that* was to live and to savour life.

And this was a long strange journey into unknown regions, as *le bon Dieu* could testify!

"Look," said he, as the Management made to unlock the glass door of the case, "I'll have a set of those cigarette-cases, all alike if possible. If there isn't time for that, have them all about the style and size of that one . . . I won't choose the ladies' presents here. I think I shall go along to *Tiffany, Cartier et Cie*, and have a look at what they've got there."

"I will ring them up at once and tell them to have ready the sort of article *Monsieur le Colonel* might think suitable," the Management assured him helpfully.

He would indeed ring them up, both Tiffany and Cartier, not to mention *Cie*, and point out that any sales effected in the shop would count for commission on precisely the same terms as those made from the show-case in the hotel. And there was to be no nonsense about it either . . . Indeed, in view of the grandeur of the grand total, an extra five per cent. was most obviously indicated.

More happiness.

The gentleman who was *Tiffany, Cartier et Cie* was promptly rendered as happy as was the Management itself, and Mademoiselle Angélique Oui-Oui herself, though none of them naturally was as happy as Denis Ducros, the Dispenser of Bliss.

Quickly thereafter, the business of arranging the gala dinner being now concluded, the moment for relaxation and refreshment arrived.

An *apéritif* seemed to be indicated.

What did Mademoiselle Angélique fancy, by way of a little stimulant, at this time of the day?

At this time of the day, and in point of fact, at any other time of the day or night, Mademoiselle fancied a little sweet Champagne. And her preference being made known, the Colonel bade the Management produce a bottle of its best. Or no; on second thoughts, a half-bottle of its best, of that sort, for Mademoiselle; and a bottle of the High and Dry for himself.

If the Colonel would give himself the trouble to cross the foyer to the *fumoir*, the Management would itself see to the exact fulfilment of the order, and see that the wines were of the desirable degree of coldness. As a connoisseur, Monsieur le Colonel would realise that none of such a wine as he had mentioned was kept permanently on the ice.

With but a wave of his hand, the Colonel accepted the Management's assurance, and with a gentle pressure of the other upon the bare arm of Mademoiselle, he escorted her to the *fumoir* and a comfortable couch in a quiet and discreetly screened corner.

As he and his attractive companion crossed the broad expanse of carpet, a girl with a sudden start, seized the arm of her companion, a smart young officer of Spahis, and at the same time lowered her head so that the shady brim of her hat concealed her face.

"Mon Dieu! . . . Mon père! . . ." she whispered in horrified astonishment as the Colonel and his friend, in seating themselves upon the divan in the corner, disappeared from view behind a screen.

"Well, Beloved of my Soul," drawled the young officer, "I, of course, knew you were of the most divine origin, but . . . a daughter of Heaven?" . . .

"What do you mean, stupid? Don't you see?"

"No, I only heard. You seemed to be claiming *le bon Dieu* as your parent . . . But after all, of course . . ."

"Don't be an ass, Henri. Didn't you see who that was?"

"No. The blinding dazzle from the head-lights that you have for eyes . . ."

"Oh, shut up, idiot. Didn't you see two people just come over from the foyer and go across to that corner?"

"Darling, I see nothing, absolutely nothing but you, when we are together."

This, alas, was a deviation from the truth, for glancing up, Henri had seen, smiling full upon him, the well-known face of Mademoiselle Angélique Oui-Oui, and swiftly he had glanced down again.

Angélique was a good girl, and the soul of discretion; but she was smiling like a cat that has just had a saucer of cream; and when she looked at him, grinning like that, anyone might think that she was a—er—friend of his.

So she was, as a matter of fact; but an even closer and more intimate friend of his friend Lieutenant Pierre de Pont-Chatelrie.

And of course it would be silly and awkward to have to explain to Rochefort that the lady with whom he had exchanged smiles was but the friend of a friend, and an almost total stranger.

It would not be convincing.

And he had looked away so swiftly that he had not so much as glanced at her companion.

But *what* had Marguerite said?

Her actual words had been,

"Mon Dieu! Mon père! . . ." in tones of the utmost consternation and alarm.

Nonsense!

Colonel Louis Rochefort of the Legion?

With Angélique Oui-Oui?

In the Grand Hotel?

Lurking in a corner behind a screen?

Rubbish!

It is a wise child that knows its own father, no doubt; but one might assume that Marguerite knew hers when she saw him . . .

Yet old Rochefort was about the strictest and most strait-laced officer in the Nineteenth African Army Corps, or any other. From taste and conviction too. It wasn't that Madame Rochefort saw to it that he was a model of propriety and virtue, for Colonel Louis Rochefort ruled the domestic roost as he did his official one, or any other in which he might find himself.

Colonel Rochefort—*Père Fait-en-fer*—as they called him, was about as likely to be behind that screen with

C

Angélique Oui-Oui as to be on the throne of France or the backs of two elephants.

And a good job too!

For Lieutenant Henri de Valaubon had not the faintest desire to be introduced to Colonel Louis Rochefort in the present circumstances and environment. From what he had heard of the Colonel's views and opinions, manners and customs, he did not for one moment believe that he would look with favour and admiration upon the young officer—or anybody else—who took Mademoiselle Rochefort to the Grand Hotel and sat in a quiet corner of the *fumoir* of that place of resort, drinking cocktails with her before taking her in, or out, to dinner.

The probabilities seemed greater that he would look upon him with an ice-cold eye that would suddenly turn to one of scorching flame, ere withering the offender to dust or blasting him to ashes.

What an appallingly narrow escape!

And the young gentleman, who was by no means lacking in courage of a high order, felt the effusion of a gentle but cold perspiration upon his reasonably lofty brow.

What about a strategic movement to the rear, as a preliminary to a complete withdrawal from this overcrowded field of love—and war? Why, he had suggested the meeting with Marguerite here at the Grand Hotel as being the one place in Sidi-bel-Abbès where they would be absolutely safe; and where he would not run the slightest risk of encountering the terrible Colonel in circumstances so compromising!

When he did meet him—and that would be when he could no longer postpone the painful pleasure—he would prefer it to be in circumstances very different from these. He was madly in love with Marguerite, and it was his highest hope and ambition to marry her, but he realised that he was already sufficiently handicapped by impecuniosity, lowly military rank, and a certain reputation for—er—wildness, recklessness, and lack of balance and discretion, without adding to that handicap by so appalling a misdemeanour as this.

Why, Colonel Rochefort probably thought that Marguerite had never set foot in a place like this in the whole of her young, innocent life! . . .

In point of fact, it was the *bons Papas* who were innocent nowadays—and that wouldn't help him at all if the Colonel caught them here . . .

But—wait a minute! . . . What exactly was the Colonel up to? . . . Wouldn't he be just as dumbfounded and knocked all of a heap—at being caught in here with Angélique Oui-Oui—as would be Henri de Valaubon, at being caught in that shady (oh, entirely shady) retreat, with the Colonel's daughter?

Doubtless! And would that make him love Henri more? Henri, the brazen scoundrel who had decoyed the innocent Marguerite there, and had added to this crime the greater one of having caught Marguerite's father there too!

Definitely time to withdraw in good order, and pray that they may not be taken in flank while crossing the enemy's front.

" '*Two people*,' darling?" he murmured. "And one of them your father? . . . Who then was the other?"

"I did not notice," replied Marguerite. "I saw Father—and that was enough for me! I nearly fainted!"

"A very interesting situation," reflected the young man. "Also an interesting speculation—as to what would have happened had we all simultaneously recognised each other."

"Yes, but who could it have been?" wondered the girl.

"Who *can* it be? It couldn't be Mother. I should have known without looking at her, so to speak. Besides, she'd never come here. And if she wanted to, Father would never bring her."

"Why not?" expostulated Henri. "There's nothing very terrible in . . ."

"Oh yes, there is, *mon cher* . . . You ask them."

"Shall I go over and ask the Colonel now?" smiled Henri.

"Yes," laughed Marguerite softly. "You go over and ask him if it is not a terrible thing that he should be making assignations at a place like this."

"And if he says '*No, certainly not*,' I'll reply '*Splendid, Sir, just what I said to Mademoiselle Marguerite. And here we are*.' "

Again Marguerite laughed softly.

All very well, and all very funny no doubt, but Henri should not be so terrified of Father . . . She herself was, of course, but that was different. She was only a girl, and fathers are very terrifying animals; and, among them, *ce bon Papa* must surely hold the record.

And she had to live with him . . . For the present, anyway.

Yes; right and reasonable enough for her to go in fear and trembling, but Henri was a man—and didn't have to live with him.

Marguerite Rochefort did herself no little injustice. For, far from being a timid and nervous person who went in terror of her redoubtable sire, she was as much his true and worthy off-spring as she was that of Madame, his wife. Rather more so, in point of fact. As Colonel Rochefort frequently and a little wistfully remarked (behind her back, *bien entendu*), she was a chip of the old block and ought to have been a boy.

Nevertheless, she had a very wholesome respect for her stern strict father, and an irrepressible urge to stand from under when trouble appeared likely to fall upon her from that direction.

So while she could, to a certain degree, sympathise with Henri's feelings with regard to the Colonel, she had no intention whatsoever of admitting the fact.

Henri loved her and she loved Henri.

Henri would give his right hand to marry her, and it was time he gave her father some slight inkling of the fact. True, he was not exactly an eligible *parti*, though by no means an obvious detrimental. Indeed, had he any money on which to marry, there was no very apparent reason why they should not do so. Still, it would be rather a strong card in her father's hand, if, on being asked for her own, the Colonel said,

"You wish to marry my daughter? *Ah! . . . Indeed?* And on what do you propose to keep her? On your pay?" and Henri had to admit that the Colonel had guessed it, the first time.

Father would scarcely trouble to answer Henri's modest request, save with one of those looks—the kind that is said to speak louder than words . . . and you could easily supply the words yourself.

Nevertheless, Henri must arise above the Colonel's horizon; become a star, however tiny, in his firmament.

Father must certainly be made aware of him, though perhaps not just yet, in the *rôle* of aspirant for the honour of membership of his family.

A tinkling of glasses and a tinkling little laugh floated across, from behind the screen.

No, definitely this was not the moment for Henri to introduce himself.

But then again, might it not be the very identical moment? Might it not be the moment auspicious and fortunate beyond belief? The moment for making an unwritten, indeed unspoken, pact with Father? . . . Something like,

"You be nice about Henri, Daddy, and I'll be nice about . . . Whatever it is that's going on."

But what could be going on? Father never went on.

"Henri," she said. "On second thoughts, don't you think it might be a good idea if we put a bold face on the matter?"

"Not if you're the matter, darling. I should hate to see a bold face on you. Besides, I loathe second thoughts. Generally worse than first. Now third thoughts . . ."

"Listen, mannikin. Don't you think it would be a good idea if we summoned up just a little courage, and frankly showed ourselves to Father, and . . ."

"But, darling, he's seen you lots of times, and I'm sure he doesn't want to see me."

"In fact you're afraid of him, and . . ."

"Of course I am, darling. Terrified to death of him."

"Then when do you propose to make his acquaintance, my dear Henri?"

"Not while he's over there," replied Henri firmly. "Let me grow a bit bigger and stronger. You know . . . finer chest . . . more presence."

"Well, do you know, it occurs to me that while he is over there is just the time, a Heaven-sent opportunity."

"Oh darling, don't bring Heaven into this. I am sure

it is no place for *le bon Dieu*. Besides, my Angel, really . . . I mean to say . . . It would be so embarrassing to barge in like that. Why, it would almost have a faint suggestion of implied blackmail about it."

"Yes, just what I thought," agreed Marguerite. "Sort of '*Oo—Daddy, aren't we naughty boys and girls? Haven't we caught each other out nicely? . . . Now we'll all be so nice to each other, and live happy ever afterwards.*'"

Henri gave an exhibition of horror that was scarcely exaggerated.

"My precious child! The clean potato, I beg."

And Henri reflected that completely innocent and honourable young ladies can contemplate a line of conduct quite barred to wicked men, such as himself.

How different is the feminine mind, bless it.

Now to any decent man this was the one occasion upon which the Colonel must not be discovered. Not on any account whatever. But to Marguerite, it was the opportunity of a life-time, a glorious gift from Heaven itself, and to be exploited to the utmost.

Terrible idea! . . . What they'd better do was to go while the going was good.

There came a sound of movement from behind the screen in the opposite corner, and the Colonel and his companion reappeared, he laughing heartily and Angélique smiling the smile of a completely successful and happy woman.

Lieutenant Henri de Valaubon bent swiftly down, drew his handkerchief from his cuff and flicked the immaculate toe of his boot.

Mademoiselle Marguerite Rochefort equally quickly bent her head slightly, so that her large tilted hat hid her face from view. But her own view from her left eye remained almost unobstructed.

"Good Heavens!" she thought. "Where did Daddy find *that*? Well, well, well! You never know. Of all people on this earth! . . . I shall be catching Mother out, next."

And without taking much risk she peeped at her erring parent.

Poor dear old Daddy! She had never in the whole of her life seen him look so happy, so care-free, young and jolly. He *was* enjoying himself!

But at that very moment, Denis Ducros, who was indeed feeling happy, care-free, young and jolly, *and* enjoying himself, laughed even longer and louder at a whispered *mot* from his dear little Angélique; and Henri thought he felt Marguerite suddenly stiffen.

He was right, and well might Marguerite do so, for she had received a further shock.

That might be her father's face and form and figure, his style, manner and bearing. It might be his uniform, but it certainly wasn't his laugh.

And indeed, so great was his happiness and joy at his marvellous success, that Denis was growing careless. Had he had the slightest idea that among his audience would be Mademoiselle Marguerite, he would have made a better job of it. He would have laughed differently, would have laughed exactly as the Colonel did, on those rare occasions when laughter overcame him; and, wonderful mimic that he was, might very well have got away with it.

But he was laughing naturally now, and the spontaneous and natural laughter of Denis Ducros was something quite different from the Colonel's laugh.

In his innocent joy at giving pleasure, he was not so much forgetting himself, as forgetting the Colonel whom he was impersonating.

Homer nodded—and Denis Ducros laughed.

He laughed as he did when sharing a joke with Michel Aubraine or fat Natalie. And that laugh did not fully consort with the dress and dignity of Colonel Louis Rochefort. It was a lovely laugh, joyous, care-free, and straight from the honest heart of a happy man. But it was not Colonel Rochefort's.

And Marguerite knew it was not.

Quickly she looked up, with a swift searching gaze, at the face of the man who was passing in front of her.

Amazing!

It was her father . . .

Very nearly . . .

No, it was not quite *le bon Papa*.

Or was it?

A truly wonderful likeness, and if it were not her own respected parent, who on earth could it be?

Of course it must be Father. She must be imagining things. When the Colonel was not solidly *en famille*, and *was* feeling happy, gay and care-free, he probably did have a different laugh from the one to which she was accustomed.

What was that proverb that she had learnt at her English finishing-school in London?

"*A smile abroad is oft a scowl at home,*" was it? Yes. Daddy certainly scowled a good deal at home. Perhaps this was how he laughed abroad.

In the act of passing Marguerite and Henri, the Colonel, his attention completely engaged by Angélique, smiled, brushed upward the right-hand side of his moustache, and drawled,

"*Ah! . . . Indeed?*"

Yes, that was Daddy all right; but it was a different Daddy, so different indeed that one might expect his actions and reactions also to be different.

If it were her father, something ought to be done about it—in her own interests and those of Lieutenant Henri de Valaubon: if it were not her father, still more should something be done about it.

An extremely quick-witted girl, Marguerite changed her plan of campaign on the spur of the moment.

As the Colonel and Mademoiselle Angélique Oui-Oui passed from sight in the direction of the hotel-entrance, she nudged the still bending Henri.

"All right, cowardy," she said. "Come out of hiding."

"*Phew!*" breathed Henri, sitting up. "My nerves are not what they were when I was young."

"Your nerve isn't," replied Marguerite, "but it'll have to serve, for you are going to meet Father. You are going to be presented to him as my Boy Friend; and you've not only got to be brave and play the part of a man, but to play the part of my Young Man."

"I am only a simple soldier," murmured Henri, "but beneath this tunic beats a . . ."

"Listen, Henri, instead of talking. Do you wish to marry me?"

"It's the only thing I do wish, darling."

"At once?"

"Sooner than that."

"And if Daddy gave us his blessing?"

"We would fly . . ."

"Where to?"

"Well, at least as far as old Père Tiffany-Cartier."

"Oh, *Henri*!"

"And we'd come out of that Robbers' Cave with the finest ring they've got in the place."

"And then, Henri?" smiled Marguerite, slipping her hand in his.

"And then we'd go and call on every friend we've got, and tell them the great news."

Marguerite rose to her feet.

"Come along, my lamb," she said.

And the lamb went meekly and bravely to the slaughter. Colonel Louis Rochefort, *pardieu*!

"We'll follow them," she said, as she and Henri passed through the still swinging door, inside which the Colonel had paused to light the magnificent cigar respectfully offered by the Management. "He's bound to say farewell to his girl friend in a minute or two, and then we'll pounce. We'll catch him while he's still feeling all gay, and . . ."

"Guilty," murmured Henri, who privately doubted whether, if he knew his Angélique, the moment of farewell was at hand. But perhaps the Colonel had a technique of his own for use for these occasions. Evidently a dark horse. Well, well, well!

"Look, he's grabbed hold of her arm again," said Marguerite.

The Colonel had indeed taken Angélique delicately by the elbow.

"Here we are, my dear," he said, with a gaiety surprisingly bright and youthful for a hard-bitten veteran of so many cares and responsibilities; threw open the net-

69   c*

curtained door of the brilliant emporium owned by Messrs. Tiffany, Cartier *et Cie,* and entered what was to him Aladdin's Cave of Enchantment.

From behind a black velvet portière appeared, as doth the prompt attentive spider, the stout and somewhat oriental-looking gentleman who was a host in himself, being not only two men and a *Cie* in one, but a most kindly host to all who walked into his parlour.

And Denis Ducros settled down really to enjoy himself . . .

Power and Glory!

He felt as though all the Kingdoms of the Earth were at his feet.

And scarcely less happy was the excellent Angélique of whom Henri's friend, Pierre de Pont-Chatelrie, was wont to testify that her kind good heart was even better than her morals.

"Now now choose just what you like, my dear," said the Colonel. "You will know better than I what will please your little friends." And to Messieurs Tiffany, Cartier *et Cie*, he gave a stern brusque order that he should put himself entirely at the lady's disposal and endeavour to give her every satisfaction.

Messieurs Tiffany, Cartier *et Cie*, concealing with a skill that equalled that of the Management of the Grand Hotel, whatever emotions he may have felt, assured the Colonel that it was his sole remaining ambition.

And promptly the kind good heart of Angélique manifested itself, both in the loving forethought with which she selected suitable little gala-tokens for her ten girl friends, and the kindly consideration with which she spared the Colonel's pocket. So far as the ten just women were concerned, *bien entendu.*

"And now, my dear," smiled the Colonel, when ten nice little *articles de Paris* had been selected, "you have neglected yourself. We can't allow that, you know. Something rather special for my kind little hostess."

And the Colonel's unwontedly smiling face positively glowed with generous satisfaction.

So did the heart of Messieurs Tiffany, Cartier *et Cie*,

though the sharp edge of his acute mind was almost dulled with wonder.

Colonel Louis Rochefort . . .

Mademoiselle Angélique Oui-Oui . . .

Something rather special for his dear little hostess! Now just how special, and how dear?

But when it came to the selection of her own trifle, the girlish face took on a look that perhaps was rather more of the ingenious rather than the ingenuous.

"Oh, just something quite small," she murmured, with a flicker of long eye-lashes in the direction of Tiffany, Cartier and every one of the *Cie*.

Again a nod was even better than a kick in the ribs to a sharp-eyed horse.

And, as though by magic, there appeared on the black velvet cushion that rested upon the glass-topped counter, something "quite small," that seemed, to the delighted eyes of the Colonel, to sparkle more brightly than the electric lights themselves.

"Ah!" said he. "A little ring, one perceives. How elegant."

Tiffany, Cartier *et Cie* agreed that it was indeed of an elegance. A diamond, in short, of the very first water.

"Water? More like Champagne," laughed the Colonel merrily, and Tiffany, Cartier *et Cie* agreed that a noble wine was indeed more worthy of mention than mere water in connection with so beautiful a stone.

"It is real?" breathed Angélique in pretty wonderment.

Tiffany, Cartier *et Cie* agreed that the jewel was indeed of a realness.

A brief silence fell on the little group.

Angélique regarded the diamond; Denis regarded Angélique; and Tiffany, Cartier *et Cie* regarded both of them, and the diamond.

Angélique forbore to ask the price of so beautiful and valuable a thing.

The Colonel forbore to ask the price of such an obvious trifle.

And Tiffany, Cartier *et Cie* forbore to mention the price,

lest it prove a bomb-shell that should blow the Colonel right out of the shop.

In his previous professional encounters with the Colonel, Messrs. Tiffany, Cartier *et Cie* had found him a very exigeant and careful buyer, prone to affect contempt for the article he was examining and incredulous horror at the price asked for it.

But this was a different man from the Colonel whom Tiffany, Cartier *et Cie* had hitherto known, admired and respected.

"*Love! . . . Love! . . .*" whispered the *Cie* in the dark depths of its experienced bosom. What won't Love do?

One thing it would do evidently, was to turn a middle-aged military tiger into a silly old goat.

Well, well, well!

Sad, sad, sad!

And what about another five hundred francs on to the price? To a man in the Colonel's present frame of mind such a difference between one sum of money and another would be scarcely perceptible, and if it were it would be negligible. And if it were not, he could, to show his great generosity, sympathy and commercial honesty, simply knock it off again.

Drawing toward him a little pad to which a pencil was attached, he wrote upon it the amount at which the ring had been assessed, enriched by the imperceptible or negligible sum. Discreetly he displayed the figure in such a way that the Colonel, not to mention Angélique, might have some idea of the spaciousness of the business upon which he was embarking.

With a typically Rochefort wave of his hand, the Colonel acquiesced in the financial suggestion, and dismissed it from parade.

He was not interested.

Angélique was.

And the message of her bright brown eye was to Tiffany, Cartier *et Cie* as comprehensible as it was direct.

"Yes, yes, my child," he replied, without the use of spoken words. "That's where the extra five hundred francs come in."

72

Angélique again fondled the jewel with her eyes and her fingers.

"And so you'd like that one, would you, my dear?" said the Colonel.

"Oh, *M'sieur le Colonel*!" breathed Angélique, words almost failing her, but not quite; for, after another brief period of wrapt contemplation, she added, almost breathless with joyful excitement,

"Might I . . . Might I . . . take it *now*, and keep it till the party?"

For an imperceptible moment, the Colonel appeared to hang in doubt, as the cold spectre of Reality tried to materialise in the rosy mists that floated about his glowing landscape of golden Illusion.

He only wished to be happy, and to make others happy; to taste the heady draught of authority, rank and power; to act the great man, greatly, if but for an hour, and to act it flawlessly, with all his little world his stage.

But he didn't want to do any harm; anything really wrong. He was an honest man, and although he and Michel Aubraine had got up to some rare tricks, and had supported each other in divers remarkable escapades, they had never done anything criminal or incurred a punishment they could not take in their stride, or received a sentence they couldn't do on their heads, as they phrased it.

No, he was no gaol-bird, and he had no desire to become one, and it rather looked as though *cette petite* Angélique Oui-Oui was leading him from the path of virtue.

That might be her business. But it was his to remain on it—within reason *c'est à dire*; and, at any rate, not suddenly to turn off at right angles.

And this would be the wrongest of right-angles—obtaining a valuable diamond ring under false pretences.

To masquerade as the Colonel for fun, for his own diversion and that of his friends, and to satisfy a tremendous urge to strut for a brief hour in the limelight, was all very well; but to rob a jeweller was quite another thing—all very ill.

Yes, the little Angélique had put him in a rather difficult position; spoilt the game a little; and . . .

But no. Not a bit of it. No positions were difficult for Colonel Louis Rochefort. Or, if they were, he would very soon turn them into easy ones.

"Oh, but *ma chère amie*," he replied almost at once, on a note of amused expostulation. "No, no, no. That would never do. Why, it would spoil all my pleasure in giving you the little token, and most of yours in receiving it— surely . . . No, No. It's a little gala gift to grace a gala dinner, and . . ."

"But of course, *M'sieur le Colonel*," agreed Angélique, who realised that if a bird in hand was worth two in the bush, a bird selected, tied up and paid for by Colonel Louis Rochefort, might be regarded as being in the hand. On the finger practically.

Ah! That was better, breathed Denis. That marched. Back once more into the beautiful dream—of lovely jewels, fair women, and distinguished officers whose whim, pleasure and delight it was to present the one to the other.

"Well then, that's all, I think," said the Colonel, desirous of concluding the business on this pleasant, safe and satisfactory note.

"Now will you send those things round to my house some time to-morrow?" he said to Tiffany, Cartier *et Cie* . . . "With your bill, and without fail. Colonel Louis Rochefort, Foreign Legion."

Tiffany, Cartier *et Cie*, with deferential delight assured *Monsieur le Colonel* that he would indeed send the selected ten *articles de Paris* and the diamond ring to the Colonel's house by special messenger (whose duty and pleasure it would be to await the Colonel's signature of receipt), definitely on the morrow, undoubtedly with the bill, and assuredly without fail.

And with a brusque and condescending, "*Bon*," the Colonel turned, opened the door for Mademoiselle Angélique Oui-Oui, and—Mademoiselle Marguerite Rochefort pounced.

CHAPTER III

THE COLONEL'S DAUGHTER ADMIRES THE UNIFORM

"WHY, *Daddy*!" she said in accents of surprise which gave no hint of the fact that, for at least half an hour, she had strolled, promenaded, and shop-window gazed, in the close neighbourhood of Tiffany, Cartier *et Cie*, with one eye upon its discreet door, and one hand metaphorically upon the leash at which Henri undoubtedly strained.

For, ardent and honourable lover as he was, Henri did not wish to encounter the Colonel just now—in such circumstances (to call Mademoiselle Angélique Oui-Oui a circumstance); in the street; in Marguerite's company; nor in the *rôle* of Marguerite's would-be fiancé.

The Colonel started, a trifle guiltily—as well he might, thought Henri—and then rose to the occasion as a Rochefort should, with a fond parental smile.

Mademoiselle Angélique Oui-Oui understood perfectly, and behaved as a nice girl should in all such cases. With a charming smile, a polite bow, a soft murmur of thanks, and a discreet word of farewell to her kind patron, she effaced herself, fading away as easily as fades a dream at day-break.

"This *is* fortunate," continued Marguerite, with a kindly enigmatic smile. "I have been meaning for some time to present to you my friend Lieutenant Henri de Valaubon of the Spahis. I met him in Paris, you remember, at Madame Lecamier's, and he has just come here from a course at Saumur of Saida or somewhere . . ."

"Why, of course!" smiled the Colonel in the most urbane and friendly manner. "You told me, I remember . . . And now the Lieutenant has rejoined his regiment here . . . You must bring him to meet your mother, at the earliest opportunity."

Denis Ducros felt that this was the right line.

Must be.

What was it that fat Natalie was saying, only the other day? Something about the Colonel being an absolute

ogre where young men were concerned; and that if
Mademoiselle didn't soon take matters into her own hands,
including a young man or two, she'd die an old maid yet,
pretty as she was . . .

Yes, the right line . . . the right line . . .

Must be . . . But for how long could he hold that
line? . . . Was this the end of the little escapade that had
been such an unqualified success. He knew *la petite
Mademoiselle* Marguerite well enough, and surely she knew
him? No disguise could be good enough, no acting clever
enough, to deceive a daughter; to persuade her that a
man, who was not her father, was her father, surely? At
a little distance, and in a poor light, perhaps . . . Say
from the other side of the street, at dusk . . . But close
up like this, face to face? Not a hope.

Moreover, the voice, . . . every nuance of expression.
Absurd.

If one, expecting to see a member of one's family, one's
daily household company, *sees* what one expects to see,
instead of what is actually there, the same would scarcely
apply to hearing, surely?

A clever mimic can copy another person's social
mannerisms and turns of speech—but a voice, after all,
is a voice; and surely a daughter knows her own father's
voice, and, moreover knows when a voice that is not her
father's tries to imitate it.

An order, a familiar phrase, a wonted remark, yes,
perhaps—but not a conversation.

And yet, here she was, actually holding a conversation,
and giving no sign that she had any suspicions whatsoever.
Unless that smile really were enigmatic and ironical, and
not merely made to appear so by his guilty conscience.

Henri de Valaubon made suitable sounds, a confused
and murmured expression of gratitude and delight. It was
not often that he was, however briefly, deprived of his
nonchalance, his air of complete social equanimity, but he
was on this occasion, completely taken aback, and, as
later he phrased it, he was knocked clean off his perch.

Could this be the grim and unapproachable Colonel
Louis Rochefort? A man with a reputation, and an un-

pleasant one, for being difficult whenever it was possible, and as difficult as it was possible to be.

It was also well known that anyone who approached his daughter with covetous eyes, might as well covet his wife, his house, his man-servant or his maid-servant. He had no ox or ass.

No. It was generally supposed that it would be dangerous sport to attempt to steal the Colonel's daughter.

Yet here he was, positively beaming; one might say radiating affability and geniality.

And he, too, asked himself, though merely rhetorically, could *this* be the famous Colonel Louis Rochefort?

Well, he knew it was. But what a surprise!

Marguerite, on the other hand, knew it was not. But what a surprise!

Who *was* the man, and what was the game?

Well, whoever it was, the game should be hers while it lasted—and it should last, at any rate, until it had served her purpose.

And what an amusing game it would be if it were properly played. She'd play her part all right—that of the innocent person completely deceived. This for Henri's benefit—and ultimately her own. It was of course, absurd to suppose that the impostor should really think he was deceiving the Colonel's own daughter, clever actor and impersonator as he might be, and undoubtedly was.

What fun to fool him that she was being fooled; to lead him on and keep him guessing—guessing at what her game might be, and yet at the same time wondering all the while whether he was actually getting away with it, and, if not, when and where she would decide to denounce him.

Who could the fellow be? And was it a daring if dubious joke for a bet, or for the sake of the tremendous *réclame* inevitably consequent upon the remarkable feat of pulling the unpullable leg of Colonel Rochefort?

Probably some wild spirit among the officers of the garrison; but it was no boyish prank, for the man was obviously every day as old as the Colonel himself.

But it *must* be Father.

Of course it wasn't.

77

The uniform; the face; the bearing; the manner and mannerisms, might all be those of Colonel Rochefort, but the voice wasn't—quite. Not all the time. Something in the *timbre*. And the laugh was not his. And it was more than not-quite. Daddy didn't laugh—much; and, when he did, it had little connection with amusement or any feeling of gaiety.

Daddy was not amused, nor gay.

And if it had been his voice and his laugh, it certainly wasn't his behaviour. He would not have been at that hotel. He would not have been with that woman; and most certainly he would not have been with her in Tiffany, Cartier's shop.

Those were things Daddy would not have done; and one or two that he would have done would have been to bite Henri's head off and to enquire what the devil she was doing here at this time of the evening.

He would not have been affable, genial and friendly. He would have been extremely rude, overbearing, and ferociously parental.

No, she did not know who this masquerader might be; but he certainly was not her father.

Nevertheless, he was going to play a father's part, since he'd assumed that *rôle*; and he was going to play the part of a father-in-law-elect if she had any luck at all and if she were clever enough to prompt and guide him in both these manifestations.

"And where are you off to, my dear?" enquired the Colonel, having graciously accepted Henri's respectful and grateful greetings.

"Well, to tell you the truth, Daddy, we were thinking of having a little dinner, together, at the Grand Hotel," replied Marguerite brightly.

"*Ah! . . . Indeed?*" said the Colonel, brushing his moustache, as he smiled sardonically; and so authentic were the intonation of his voice and the gesture of his hand, that Marguerite's own faith was shaken to its foundations, and she all but quailed.

Henri was suddenly aware of the firm pressure of Marguerite's elbow against his own.

78

Henri was a soldier, one of those who seek the bubble reputation in the cannon's mouth or even in the Colonel's mouth, and whose trade, profession, vocation, and calling it is to step into the imminent breach. This looked like an imminent breach, all right, and into it Henri stepped with both feet.

"I wonder if you would do us the great honour of joining us, Sir," he said, wondering at his own temerity. What would happen now?

"*Do*, Daddy," seconded Marguerite. "We should love it."

Again, Denis Ducros rose to the height of the occasion in true Rochefort style.

Fate appeared to be in most friendly mood; his luck to be most unwontedly in; and if Fate chose to give him the opportunity of dining in style at the Grand Hotel with a daughter of his own, and with a Spahi Officer, her fiancé, who was he to refuse that opportunity?

Vogue la galère!

How marvellously one thing was leading to another. And what another!

But this piquant, charming and lovely girl!

Was he, Denis Ducros, as clever an actor as all that?

It was clearly one of two things. Either he had deceived her, or else she was attempting to deceive him, for some reason best known to herself.

Anyhow, she hadn't denounced him to this Spahi Officer, and presumably did not intend to do so—for the moment. And until she did, he would play his part as perfectly as it lay in his power to do.

On with the game!

The Colonel glanced at his wrist-watch in the Rochefort style. A tap on the right cuff with the left hand exposing the watch, a closing of the right eye and a fixing of the watch's face with a stare through the monocle (*and*, noted Marguerite, that *is* Daddy's watch. Curiouser and curiouser).

"Well," said the Colonel, "I should love to, but . . ."

"Oh, you must, Daddy," interrupted Marguerite, and held the Colonel's eye with a cool and compelling stare.

Not menacing, threatening or blackmailing, of course; but somehow it carried a message, and Denis hastened to assure the young lady that he had merely been going to say that he wouldn't be able to give them his whole evening, much as he would like to do so.

"Never mind, darling," replied Marguerite, who was not in the habit of thus addressing her formal and austere father. "We'll just have a quick dinner if you've got other engagements. That will be long enough for Henri to tell you something."

Henri made a curious little movement; again felt the firm pressure of a determined elbow; opened and closed his mouth as doth the gold-fish, and like the gold-fish, was dumb.

"Delighted . . . Delightful . . ." responded the Colonel, equally full of wonderment, not to say consternation, despondency and alarm, as was Henri, but far too good and conscientious an actor to permit his features or manner to register these awkward feelings.

"*En avant, donc!*" he said gaily, turned with the others in the direction of the Grand Hotel, and Sidi-bel-Abbès, like Linden, saw another sight to which it was wholly unaccustomed.

It was that of the unsociable and exclusive Colonel of the French Foreign Legion, walking, in bright merry converse with his daughter and a gay young subaltern of Spahis—a less *épatant* sight than that of the Colonel strolling with Mademoiselle Angélique Oui-Oui, but every whit as remarkable and rare.

In point of fact, both sights were unique. And those who that night beheld both, felt that here were strange portents, and that old familiar landmarks were slipping indeed.

On the way to the hotel, Marguerite took charge of the conversation, and, as Denis soon realised, did so with a kind of light and bright malice that was rather disturbing. Could she, realising that he was an impostor, be leading him to the scene of his public exposure, disgrace and humiliation? Was he to be held up to the contemptuous ridicule of the habitués of the Grand Hotel, and the angry derision of the Management and his staff?

If so, let him like a soldier fall, when they drew him out on his ear.

Let him die game.

And let him hug to himself the satisfaction and joy of having so wonderfully fooled them; and of having had his bright, brief crowded hour of glorious life.

His Hour of Glory.

But somehow he felt that this managing young woman had some other end in view. Had she been merely leading him to the scene of his downfall, she would hardly have troubled to select and follow so persistently the subject of the manifold virtues of this probably admirable, but apparently quite ordinary, Lieutenant of Spahis.

Doubtless he was the military marvel and compendium of virtues that Mademoiselle Marguerite described him to be, even if he possessed nothing in the world but the beautiful uniform in which he stood up. But he seemed, with commendable modesty, to hide his light quite successfully.

There was one thing, no-one could say that he talked foolishly, for he didn't talk at all.

And there was another thing. Whatever the young woman suspected, thought or knew, there were no doubts in the mind of her young friend. If he were sure of anything in this uncertain world, it was that his distinguished companions were not only the Colonel's daughter, but the Colonel himself. He did not give the impression of being a young man who was easily daunted or disconcerted, but definitely he gave the impression of being a daunted and disconcerted young man.

So far, so good; and if nobody penetrated the disguise of Denis Ducros this night, save the daughter of the man he was impersonating, then it would not have been a bad job of work on the part of Denis Ducros.

There might be bad results, but the work wasn't bad; in fact, it would be its very goodness which would be its chief offence.

He began to feel a little sorry for the over-awed and tongue-tied young man. He must take his part against this over-confident daughter of his, and put him at his ease.

Lieutenant Henri de Valaubon responded sensitively and gratefully to the Colonel's kindness and condescension. Gradually he grew less uncomfortably diffident; and by the time the party reached the hotel, he was chatting freely though respectfully, with Marguerite's redoubtable and awe-inspiring father.

So, for the second time in one evening, and for the second time in his life, Denis Ducros entered the lofty halls, of faded gilt and dusty velvet, of the *Grande Hôtel d'Algérie et de Maroc*, and trod their creaking boards with the firm and confident step of one accustomed to such splendour and luxury—or of one who was an actor of real genius, thoroughly enjoying the part which he was playing. The true Rochefortian manner in which he drew off his gloves, and arrogantly thrust *képi*, cane and gloves at the hovering menial, made Marguerite marvel again, and mentally award his performance the meed of grudging yet unstinted praise.

She was in excellent form, and particularly alert in mind. She was also going to have some fun, and very profitable fun too—with a little luck and a little innocent deception of poor dear Henri.

"Will you order dinner, Daddy?" she said, when the three sat down at the table selected by the Management as the most desirable for this most distinguished but most incredible party.

(Really! The spartan and unbending Colonel Rochefort, who did not enter the place twice in a year, coming in twice in a night—and, moreover, first with the Belle of bel-Abbès, and then with his own daughter and a very junior young officer. Had it not been that the young lady indubitably was Mademoiselle Marguerite Rochefort, it would have been almost enough to make the Management doubt either the evidence of its senses or the genuineness of the Colonel Commandant!)

Promptly the Colonel excelled himself.

If he couldn't run a depôt, he could order a dinner; and it was with genuine respect for his gastronomic knowledge and understanding that the Management took his orders, and, with deep regret, had occasion to point out that delightful and desirable as certain suggested items might be, they were, alas, unprocurable. In the end it was clear that, should the dinner fall short of perfection, the failure would be in the hotel's resources rather than in the Colonel's competence and hospitable spirit. Nevertheless, it was, all things considered, an admirable dinner; and partaking of it gave Denis Ducros almost as much pleasure as he had had in ordering it.

And that had been a great moment, one of the best of that great evening. As in the case of the gala dinner, the wines were most expertly chosen. Not the wine-steward at the *Cercle Militaire* himself, could have displayed a finer knowledge of vintages than did Denis, who was interested in the subject, and who had heard so much talk of wine as he waited at Mess and private dinner party.

With the affable kindliness of the older man, sympathetic and understanding, who wishes to put his young guest at his ease, he consulted Henri, who, flattered yet diffident, gratefully admitted, what was the simple truth, that his host knew far more about wine than he did.

And as the generous ichor warmed his veins, Denis again expanded, completely throwing off the slight sensation of doubt and constraint which, beneath the cool eye of the Colonel's daughter, had threatened to cramp his style and freeze the genial current of his soul. Quickly he regained completest confidence, lost every trace of diffidence, and not only played, to the life, the part of Colonel Louis Rochefort, but *was* the Colonel.

Marguerite admitted it. The only fault she had to find with the impersonator was that he was better than the original. So infinitely kinder; so much more human; so . . . lovable; and so very, very nice to Henri.

And *how* he became the Colonel's uniform; and how the uniform became him!

This was a Dream-Daddy. The sort of father she had sometimes, in fantasy, imagined as her own. Strong and all-wise, of course, but yet gentle, courteous and encouraging. Surely the truly polite man was as polite to his wife and daughter as to anybody else. Courtesy, like charity, should begin at home. But though Daddy was funda-

83

mentally a good husband and father, no-one could say he was a kind or pleasant one.

This man might be an impostor—of course he was an impostor—but how nice if she could wake up, rub her eyes, and find that this was her real, original and genuine Father! What a Father to whom to present Henri!

What a reception for her Henri to receive!

And what a blessed vista of bliss to be opening out before her now.

Who could he be? Why was he doing it?

He didn't appear to be doing any great harm, and there seemed to be no urgent reason for her promptly to expose him, the moment he had served her purpose. So long as he wasn't doing any serious or irreparable damage, there seemed no good reason why the joke should not go as far as he chose to carry it. Not that that could be very far, of course.

He was bound to come a cropper sooner or later, and, at most, the little game could only be played for that evening.

He could hardly go on parade in the Colonel's uniform.

Probably, had she been the ideal *jeune fille* and perfect daughter, she would have denounced the wicked man as soon as she realised that he was a fraud. But she had never professed to be that, and until she discovered real and serious harm in it, she was quite disposed to regard the joke as a joke.

And to think of a joke—on Father, of all people in the world!

But wait a moment! What about that jeweller's shop? Might he not have stung Daddy pretty badly? Of course, if it were a common swindle she'd have to do something about it. Do that Duty, with a capital D, of which Father was so fond of talking.

Yes, later on she'd have to go along to the jewellers and make a few enquiries. The joke mustn't be carried too far, and though she began to think this bogus Father was a real dear, she was, after all, her real Father's real daughter.

Meanwhile she had never enjoyed a dinner-party more, for the situation appealed tremendously to her Gallic and impish sense of humour.

The sight of Henri, respectful; humble, on his best behaviour, making the politest of deferential conversation, and behaving like a school-boy in the presence of his headmaster, was delightful.

And to see this Unknown playing Colonel Rochefort simply fascinated her.

It was a finished performance. He was so clever—*and* so nice.

It gave her, moreover, a rather delightful sense of power, to play just a little of the cat-and-mouse game with him, and to feel that, at any moment, she could bring him up with a round turn.

The whole affair was most extraordinarily piquant and most devilishly puzzling.

And if Marguerite was puzzled, so was Henri, for a different reason.

Untroubled by the shadow of a doubt as to the *bona fides* of the Colonel, and naturally supposing him to be the person Marguerite obviously knew him to be, Henri's puzzlement was due to the amazing discrepancy between the descriptions he had heard of Colonel Louis Rochefort and the man himself. . . .

Rude?

Surly?

Sarcastic?

Unapproachable?

Unfriendly?

Unsociable?

Inhuman?

Why the man was geniality personified.

Rude? He was most courteous.

Surly? He was urbane.

Sarcastic? He was of a delightful simplicity and transparent kindliness.

Unapproachable? He was a living invitation to easy intercourse and pleasant confidence.

Unfriendly? He, Henri de Valaubon, had never met a friendlier person; never got on more delightful terms in shorter time. He already felt that he had known him for years.

85

Unsociable? He was the soul of hospitality. The perfect host. Fancy anyone using the word unsociable in connection with a Colonel of that seniority who could so swiftly and completely put a young subaltern at his ease and make him feel that, for the time being, there were no barriers of rank between them.

Inhuman? He was the most warmly human person he had ever met. Look at his attitude to his daughter. Look at him now, patting Marguerite's hand. Look at Marguerite laughing up into his face.

Had she been pulling his leg with these cock-and-bull tales of a stern parent who was a cross between a hungry tiger and a sore-headed bear?

He'd have a word with the young woman about this. Why, he might have gone to this father long ago—and he'd tell her so.

On the other hand . . . Wait a minute . . . What she'd said on the subject of the Colonel was a good deal less than what everybody else said. She had loyally defended him to the best of her ability, but, at the same time, had admitted that he wasn't exactly the sunshine of the home; that she didn't positively tie him round her finger; and that Henri had better lie low, walk warily, stand from under, and generally keep out of the Colonel's way until the propitious hour struck and she gave the word to him to emerge from the depths of that profound obscurity in which junior subalterns lurk unseen, unheard.

Well, it just showed how utterly false and unreliable gossip was.

Lies. Talk about rumour being a lying jade! They were an ill-natured lot in Sidi-bel-Abbès. But there . . . no doubt all garrison-gossip was alike.

Colonel Louis Rochefort was obviously one of the very best, and, so far from being repellant and intimidating, gave one the impression that it would be quite a simple matter, if not indeed a pleasure, to present oneself to him in the *rôle* of Marguerite's suitor.

And the Colonel's thoughts at that moment were curiously and beautifully reciprocal.

Seen through the rosy haze of the fumes of excellent

86

wine, the young man seemed in every way admirable, charming and worthy—worthy to be the fiancé and, ere long, the husband of his beautiful and attractive Marguerite.

Whatever lay in his power to do, should forthwith be done to encourage their hopes and facilitate their fulfilment.

How delightful a thing, to be able in some measure to avert that malign Fate so powerful and malevolent as to make it proverbial that the course of true love never does run smooth.

He turned his benign gaze upon the fascinating girl to whom he stood *in loco parentis*.

Never until this moment had he recognised and realised her irresistible charm. But then, of course, he had never hitherto smiled at her across the rim of his eighth glass of noble wine.

But let it not be thought that though he saw her clear, and saw her whole, he saw her double.

Denis was uplifted.

Denis was beside himself.

But Denis was not drunk. Not physically drunk, that is to say, with material nectar distilled by mortals, but intoxicated with the ichor of the gods, the heady draughts of Power, that most intoxicating of all immortal drugs. Sober as a judge and a model of deportment, he yet lived and moved and had his being in a world of fantasy and unreality.

He was now no masquerading servant. He was a king, a Midas, an Alexander the truly Great, and still more an Oberon, a King of Fairyland.

No, he had never realised how wise and wonderful, witty and womanly, appealing and precious a girl was this daughter of his, long as he had known her.

She should be happy. He would make her happy, bless her lovely smiling face . . . and dear little tricks.

And the boy, too. Splendid young fellow. And all his life with its joys and sorrows, victories and defeats, still before him. He would give him a victory and a joy that would o'ershadow all others, and make him, on the very

threshold of his fine career, a happy and delighted man
. . . fulfilled.

He, Denis Ducros, would be that fairy godfather.

What glorious thing is Power—when rightly used.

He turned his warm and benevolent, but by no means
vinous, gaze upon the object of his thoughts, and smiled
kindly, understandingly; almost, it seemed to Henri,
affectionately.

"Sir," he began nervously, "there is something I want
most respectfully, most humbly, to say to you. It is about
M . . . M . . . Marguerite and . . ."

"I know, my boy, I know!" interrupted the Colonel,
with a smile of the most paternal. "I know. You love her.
She loves you. You want my consent. You have it."

Henri was overcome with relief, gratitude and joy.
Springing to his feet, he wrung the Colonel's hand in an
access of emotion almost too powerful for expression.

"Sir!" he stammered. "I do not know how to express
my feelings, my joy and gratitude. I can only . . ."

And as, most warmly, he returned the ardent grip of
the young man's hand, Denis Ducros again touched the
heights and wandered singing among the shining stars
that also sang.

It was a great moment.

Almost the greatest of that great evening.

Marguerite showed immense control of her emotions,
whatever these may have been. Obviously they included
happiness, while not appearing wholly to exclude amusement. But then she had always been an unusual girl, who
took a line of her own and cared little if it were not the
one she might be expected to pursue.

And, amused or not, she thanked the Colonel prettily,
but refrained from kissing him, a thing which Henri himself had scarce forborne to do.

But although she was not fluent in the expression of
her feelings, she quickly gave signs that she was far from
being placidly unmoved.

"And you really mean that Henri and I can now consider ourselves engaged?" she said.

"Most certainly, my pet," replied the Colonel. "Why

not? Why not, indeed, from this very moment? Have I not only given you my permission, but my unfeignedly heart-felt blessing? I hope and pray that, from this moment, you may both henceforth walk in a fairyland of happiness without one cloud to darken the brightness of your path. . . . Engaged? Most certainly."

And as a demure eye strayed in the direction of Henri's beaming face, Marguerite asked softly,

"And may we announce it, Daddy? At once—to all our friends? Tell them we are to be betrothed? And may Henri give me a ring? And may I wear it from now?"

"But of course, my child. Tell everyone. Let Henri take you straight to the jewellers'. Come out of the shop with his ring on your finger."

And Henri, no laggard in Love, as no laggard in War, again sprang to his feet.

"We'll go to that same jewellers' that you yourself visited this evening, Sir. I suppose they're the best in Sidi-bel-Abbès?"

"Yes," agreed Marguerite. "By the way, Daddy, what were you buying at the jewellers' to-night?"

And Denis Ducros was brought for a moment, back to earth, as a straight and level gaze met his.

"I, my love? Well, since you ask, I was buying a rather nice little present for your dear Mother. In fact, a *very* nice one . . ."

That was a good lie.

And he could add to it and improve upon it.

"For *Mother*?" replied Marguerite, completely taken aback; for giving valuable gifts to his wife was certainly not one of the most noticeable of Colonel Rochefort's habits.

"Yes, my child. And how amazingly *à propos* and timely it turns out to be. Do you know what I shall quite unashamedly tell her? . . . Why, that it is in commemoration of *this* great occasion."

"What is it?" asked Marguerite bluntly.

"Curiously enough, my child, a ring. Rings are very much on the *tapis* to-night, aren't they?" he laughed easily. "Yes, it will not only celebrate your engagement, but commemorate our own. She will be quite touched when she receives it to-morrow."

"She will indeed," agreed Marguerite thoughtfully.

"You feel, Sir," asked Henri hopefully, "that Madame Rochefort will be as kindly disposed and acquiescent as yourself?"

"I am sure she will, my dear boy. I am sure she will," the Colonel assured him.

"If I say so," he added, out of his considerable knowledge, both deep and wide, of Colonel Rochefort's habit of "saying so," and his wife's custom of prompt agreement.

"Oh, yes, Mother will be glad," said Marguerite. "If only because Daddy is. She wouldn't dream of raising the slightest objection—*when she hears we've told everybody in Sidi-bel-Abbès to-night that we're engaged*, and she sees me wearing your ring.

"Come on, Henri darling," she begged. "I'm too excited to sit still another minute."

Rising to her feet, she gave the Colonel, who also rose, a long and searching look.

"Thank you," she said. "Thank you for all your wonderful help. You have made us very happy, and have made it—er—possible for us to have a life-time of happiness together. And I *do* admire your uniform, Daddy."

Bending quickly forward, she impulsively kissed the Colonel on both cheeks; and the heart of Denis Ducros nearly burst within him.

A minute later she and Henri had departed, and the Colonel was on his way to the telephone.

"*Hullo! Hullo!* Is that Tiffany, Cartier *et Cie?*"

"*Oui, Monsieur,*" replied the suave voice of the firm.

"Colonel Rochefort is speaking."

The voice of the *Cie* became even more suave. It became warm, respectful and ingratiating.

"You know that little parcel of odds-and-ends I ordered this evening?"

The firm did indeed remember it. It would never forget it. It had given it the very greatest pleasure of a life-time to be privileged to . . .

The Colonel cut short the oily flow of compliment.

"Well, look. There was a ring, wasn't there? I've changed my mind."

Tiffany, Carter *et Cie* groaned almost audibly.

There was indeed a ring. A *pièce de resistance*.

"Well, I want the ring directed to Madame Rochefort instead of to myself. The bric-à-brac can be sent to me under separate cover.

"My daughter is just coming along with her fiancé."

An ecstatic sound escaped from Tiffany, Cartier *et Cie*, and was quite audible at the Colonel's end of the telephone.

"Should she make enquiries about that ring, and say that she would like to see it, I have no objection. Understand? . . . The ring . . . To Madame Rochefort . . ."

Possibly for the first time in its life, Tiffany, Cartier *et Cie*, permitted a falsehood to escape its lips, and most emphatically declared that it understood.

Fully. Perfectly.

Whereas it was extremely puzzled; and it entirely failed to understand why a valuable diamond ring, purchased with and for Mademoiselle Angélique Oui-Oui, should now be sent to Madame Louis Rochefort!

Shrugging his shoulders almost to his decorative ears, while raising eyes and palms of wonderment, Tiffany, Cartier *et Cie* permitted himself the ghost of a chuckle, and replaced the receiver as the Colonel rang off.

What a man! What a man!

To get little Angélique Oui-Oui to choose, as for herself, the ring that he intended for Madame, his wife!

Outside the telephone-box the Colonel paused a moment in thought.

Excellent. It was high time Colonel Louis Rochefort gave his wife a present. And if he didn't like the ten *articles de Paris* with which on the morrow he would be enriched, he could say so.

Doubtless he would.

Smiling to himself, Denis strode to the foyer, accepted his *képi*, stick and gloves from the obsequiously hovering attendant, and turned his haughty gaze upon the head-waiter, who with many bows, ventured to approach, bearing a discreetly folded bill upon a plate.

"Pencil," he growled, and the head-waiter having in the manner of a conjurer produced one from nowhere, he added a further ten per cent tip to the *addition*, as well as a completely undecipherable scrawl which the head-waiter was at liberty to read as L. R., since it was quite as likely to be those letters, as the more relevant D. D. of Denis Ducros.

The head-waiter, a large and greasy man whom Denis had detested at first sight, and loathed on second thoughts, bowed from the waist, bowed from the hips, almost bowed from the ankles, as mentally he allotted to his own private pocket, ten per cent of this good bill, as well as commission on the wines.

His thanks were profuse and profound.

"Give that to the Manager," ordered Denis, returning the bill, "and bring me a cigar."

In a minute the obliging man returned, not only with a cigar but with several boxes of cigars, and from the best of these, Denis made a selection.

The head-waiter again admired a man who understood cigars as well as he did wines, and who unerringly selected the best brands.

Personally accompanying the Colonel to the entrance, the head-waiter paid honour where honour was due, by anticipating the hall-porter, and opening the door with his own hand.

Inhaling deeply, as one who appreciates fresh sweet open air after a stuffy interior, or perhaps as one who has just made successful escape from a somewhat dangerous situation, the Colonel strode on, in search of fresh adventure.

CHAPTER IV

THE PATH OF GLORY LEADS BUT TO . . . ?

WHAT an evening he was having!

What a day to look back on, if he lived to be as old as Père Pinard!

Now what? . . .

Leave it to Fate, to Chance, to the whim of *le bon Dieu*; for to-night indeed *le bon Dieu* seemed to be feeling whimsical.

He apparently had no need to go in search of adventure, for adventure appeared to come in search of him.

The Colonel's daughter! . . .

And he had played fairy godfather to that enigmatic and forceful young woman.

And what part had she played?

Had she recognised him?

No; he thought not.

But she had used him . . . Had known him for an impostor and had used him.

Hallo! Here came the man they called Bacchus. A bad man if ever there was one. And not a bad man of the best sort, either. A bad man of the worst sort. A damned rogue in fact. And here was a chance to put a spoke in the wheel of the chariot of Bacchus. At the very least he could give the blackguard as uncomfortable a night as he had ever spent, and at the most he could put the permanent fear of Colonel Louis Rochefort into him. Especially if he were fuddled with assorted wine, absinthe, gin, and *tchum-tchum* spirit, as was more than probable.

Even if Bacchus came to learn to-morrow of the great feats of *le légionnaire* Denis Ducros, in his for-ever-to-be-famous impersonation of the Colonel, he would never believe that it was not Colonel Rochefort who had stopped him in the *Rue de Daya* and given him the dressing-down of a lifetime. It would clip his wings and cramp his style for the rest of his service.

The *légionnaire*, christened Bacchus by some learned wag, suddenly catching sight of the Colonel, transformed himself from a rollicking, rolling, leering, laughing *légionnaire* into a model of military propriety and deportment, drew himself up to his full height, squared his shoulders, and achieved a salute that was positively violent in its speed and smartness.

The Colonel ignored the salute, but not the man.

"*Halt! You!*" he said quietly, his voice cutting in its stern coldness, his eyes like agate.

And Bacchus stood smartly to attention, a model mercenary, a perfect Soldier of Fortune, and of many campaigns . . .

Yes. That's what he's impersonating, thought Denis; he's doing the Bluff Old Soldier . . . the *Vieux Moustache* . . . the Hardy Veteran of Old Wars . . .

The damned, soaking, scrounging, swindling bully and sponge . . .

And, in a voice icy with contempt, he took this Godsent opportunity of saying what he had long thought.

"Name and number?" he demanded.

The man supplied the information promptly.

"*Ah!* . . . *Indeed?* And known to fools who frequent your society, as Bacchus, I understand."

"*Oui, mon Commandant,*" smiled Bacchus, a little fatuously.

"I wonder the god doesn't strike you dead," mused the Colonel. "Such filthy blasphemy.

"As I look at you," he continued, "I see a fat-bellied, fat-faced fraud, with far too much hair on his head, and what would be far too much hair on his face, save that the beastly fungus does serve partly to conceal it.

"Yes, a horrible bush of hair, behind which is a horrible face . . . The face of the most detestable type on earth, the *faux bonhomme.*

"Do you know what you are? . . . Answer me. . . . Do you know what you are?"

"*Mais, oui, mon Colonel,*" stammered the now alarmed Bacchus.

"So do I," continued the Colonel. "You're that God-forgotten—or God-damned—thing, a Character, who is also a humbug. . . . You pose. Yes.

"Great, fat, lousy brute that you are; gross, greedy and vile; you actually *pose*—like a pimping, posturing pansy of the lowest stews—for tourists.

"You grow that filthy mop of hair, and that filthy barrel of lard that is your stomach, and deliberately you play a part:—The Jolly, Jovial, Rollicking Bacchus . . . And you get photographed, living up to the name that some fool gave you, or that you gave yourself.

"In the canteen you roar,

" '*Behold me! I am Bacchus. Pour libations,*' and the wretched recruits, who are your victims, have to pour—or it would be the worse for them.

" '*See how powerful is Bacchus,*' you bawl. And the little herd of swine that surround you, and follow you in the hope of getting the leavings that you yourself cannot quite drink, agree that you are popular, and bid the recruits, or the fool with money, to pour yet more libations, and yet more—enough for them all.

"And what do you do for the recruits in return? Eh, you foul reptile?

"You rob them. And that's only the beginning of it—and the least of it . . . You debauch, deprave and pervert the weaker ones. And what do you do to a strong one who resists and defies you?"

The Colonel lowered his voice to a very audible whisper.

"What did you do to Harald Petersen? Why did he commit suicide?" he asked; and the question was a terrible accusation and indictment, for Bacchus involuntarily stepped back a pace, his mouth opened, and the high colour of his flushed face abated.

He gazed and gaped in horrified amazement.

"And to Grégoire Flammand?" asked the Colonel.

The *légionnaire's* eyes and mouth opened wider for a moment.

"And to Anastasiadi, the Greek? A good sturdy lad that," said the Colonel, cold hate and anger blazing from his eyes. "Shall I tell you what you did? You followed him from the camp; and, walking silently on sand, you came up behind him and clubbed him on the head. . . . As he lay unconscious, you had the courage to kill him with your bayonet. You robbed his corpse and then buried it, an inch-or-two deep in the sand. Next day the Battalion marched on, and poor Anastasiadi was written off as a deserter."

Bacchus appeared to be about to faint. His lips moved, but he was either unable or afraid to say a word in self-defence or exculpation.

"Didn't know that I was so well-informed, did you?"

95

asked the Colonel, in a voice of immeasurable, inexorable doom.

"No. You thought that only a few of the vile clique that are your accomplices knew of your crimes—thefts innumerable, persecutions, bullyings and an occasional murder. Well, you were wrong. . . . I know all about you; and I only wish that I had known sooner.

"*However* . . ."

And to the scoundrelly Bacchus there was a world of terrible threat in the last word. The game was up. And the sooner he quitted the Legion the better.

Privately, Denis Ducros thought that he had not only given a first-class exhibition of acting, but that he had done a really useful piece of work as well.

The ruffian was evidently frightened to the very depths of his soul.

No. Say to the depths of his being, for he had no soul.

And Denis Ducros had enjoyed himself enormously. Not only were there private and peculiar scores of his own to pay off; but as he had shown the brute, he had considerable knowledge of abominable villainies that did not personally concern him. If he did no more than frighten the fellow, he'd have done something; and the probability was that he wouldn't have a comfortable moment for many a long day to come.

Well, he'd give him a bit more of it and let him go—with something to think about.

"Yes," he said, his gaze boring into the flinching eyes of the amazed and terrified man, "and how did you know that Anastasiadi had just received some extra money from his well-to-do father in Athens? . . . Eh? How did you know? . . . Answer me, you dog."

The terror-stricken Bacchus tried to moisten dry lips with a dry tongue.

"I'll tell you," continued the Colonel, "since, for once in your life, you haven't so much to say for yourself. It was that damnable rogue, the *vaguemestre*,[1] your confederate, who put you up to it. . . . Yes. I wonder how many poor devils that unspeakable swine has robbed of

[1] postmaster sergeant-major.

their wretched sous and francs—sent to them from poverty-stricken homes, as often as not. When it is that sort of pickings, of which the intended recipient knows nothing, because the noble *vaguemestre* destroys the covering letter enclosed with the money, the thieving jackal can manage without your help.

"But when a man gets a letter saying that a bigger sum of money is coming under registered cover, he has to hand the draft over. . . . And that's where you come in, eh? On commission.

"And if you can't get the fellow so drunk that you can rob him, you're not above murdering him for his money."

The Colonel eyed the trembling wretch with loathing.

"Yes. I think I've got your complete *dossier*, my good Bacchus," he added. "And if there should be anything missing from it, I shall have that too, pretty soon. *And* the full record of your fellow criminal's filthy breaches of trust as postmaster.

"I'll have you both."

And as he turned to go, leaving the man apparently rooted to the *pavé*, he slowly looked him up and down from head to foot, and murmured apparently to himself,

"Eight years *travaux forcées* with the Penal Battalions? Or shot out of hand? . . . Better dead, I think, on the whole—and that *sale scélérat* of a *vaguemestre* too. I'll send them both before the Oran General Court Martial . . ."

And Denis Ducros went on his way rejoicing, grinning to himself while he contemplated the utter consternation and incredulous dismay of the vile Bacchus, as he attempted to realise and grasp the impossible truth that Colonel Rochefort knew all, knew everything, about him . . . that the Colonel himself, that terrible man, knew of his association with the rascally postmaster in robbing his comrades; knew of the reasons for certain suicides; of a few unexplained disappearances; and of three or four plain murders in barracks, camps, and side-street dives . . .

He'd pass a merry night of it!

And better still, he'd hurry straight to the *vaguemestre*, and tell him that the worst had happened, that the

Colonel had, in some incredible fashion, learnt all about them—literally *all*—and that it was up to him to stand from under . . .

The Colonel almost laughed aloud as he contemplated the scene.

Bon Dieu de Grace! They'd both promptly desert that very night, if they didn't commit suicide. In either event it would be a case of excellent riddance to vile rubbish, and Denis Ducros would be as deserving of thanks and reward as would be any other public benefactor.

How many of his shots-in-the-dark had hit the target? All of them, by the look of Bacchus. Not unnaturally either, for the crimes of which he had accused him were not mere figments of barrack-room imagination, nor begotten of *caserne* gossip.

And lots of them, including himself, had every reason for feeling perfectly certain that remittances from home, financial gifts from friends, or payments due to them and sent by post, had never got past the thieving rogue who held the present office of *vaguemestre*—a post of strong temptations to a dishonest man.

So easy to swindle the poor brow-beaten *légionnaire*, to whom it would never occur to contradict, much less to accuse, a non-commissioned officer. Yes, the *vaguemestre* was going to have a night of it, whatever else he had! . . .

And now what? Another little drink? Music? More of the delightful, feminine companionship? Some dancing? . . . Anything . . . Anything . . . Everything in fact . . . All in due course.

And whatever else he did, he must get the largest possible number of the boys together and give them a good time. . . . Wine unstinted. Good wine too. White and red. Colonel Rochefort didn't do nearly enough of that sort of thing—and it was high time that he improved his ways.

He should start this very night, and earn himself a much more desirable reputation for generosity to his deserving *légionnaires*.

Why, what man on earth had finer opportunities; a more accomplished collection of distinguished drinkers;

an assemblage of united thirsts more worthy of the very
finest efforts of a great and generous Quencher?

Well, this very night, this Night of Nights, the Colonel
in the *rôle* of Quencher, should match himself against his
men in their common *rôle* of Walking Thirsts; and it
would be seen who won, and which out-lasted the other,
the Colonel's generosity or the *légionnaires'* capacity . . .

Meanwhile—to promenade himself in his Uniform of
Glory and await what should befall.

And even as he made this excellent resolution, the
Colonel found himself passing the hospitably open doors
of the wine-shop, well, if unfavourably, known, as *The
Little Dog and Lamp-post*.

Definitely there was a sound of devilry by night, a
sound that plucked at the Colonel's heart-strings. For
while a party of *légionnaires* was beautifully singing *Le
Boudin*, a right rousing chorus, another party was equally
beautifully singing an equally rousing but quite different
chorus.

What a pity! What a great pity—that one's rank pre-
vented one from entering a place where such an aura of
good-fellowship mingled with such an odour of good wine.

A thousand pities that it should prevent . . .

But then . . . after all, why should it?

It was a lonely life, being a *Chef de Bataillon*; but was
it quite necessarily so? Did not the loneliness arise, to
some extent at any rate, from a somewhat overweening
and mistaken sense of exclusiveness and dignity?

And a man who always stands upon his dignity,
generally has little else upon which to stand.

To Hell with such nonsense as exclusiveness, starched
superiority, and cold, stiff, unfriendliness.

The Colonel halted, hesitated, and was lost.

Or found.

Undoubtedly found entering the portals of *The Little
Dog and Lamp-post*—by the eye of an earnest drinker,
industriously endeavouring to empty a full wine-bottle
without once removing it from his lips.

At first, as the pre-occupied and unobserving eye fell
upon this astounding vision, it merely dismissed it for

what it appeared to be—an astounding vision, much of the astonishment arising from the fact that so strange a manifestation should appear so early in the evening.

Why, thought the earnest and industrious soldier, this is only my—what would it be now—second, third, fourth bottle? I can't be very well . . . Seeing the Old Devil walking into the *Dog*, as large as life. Running into the *Lamp-post. Hee, Hee! . . .*

And a sudden rush of hilarity to the head caused the visionary to fail in his brave effort to empty his fourth bottle in one breathless attempt.

With the bubbling cry of some strong drinker in his agony, he banged the bottle down upon the zinc-topped table, pointed accusingly at the phantom which had arisen before his bright young eye, and began, with a hiccup, an impassioned speech.

But beyond the introductory regurgitation, it was not delivered, for suddenly he realised that the astounding spectre of Colonel Rochefort was no spectre at all, but the very self of that terrible man.

Yes. Advancing upon him, Miguel Gonzales, was the Colonel himself, in gold-braided *képi*, gold-braided, five-*galon*-sleeved tunic, treble row of medal and decoration ribbons, riding-breeches and boots, and gloved left hand grasping his other glove and cane, as usual.

There could be no doubt about it, and the first instinct of *le légionnaire* Miguel Gonzales was that of any good soldier, to give prompt warning of the approach of the enemy.

Bereft of speech, and the power to rise, he kicked his *copain*, Cristobal Braganza, and pointed.

This good man was also drinking from a bottle, though not with any foolish and incontinent ambition to empty it at one fell swipe. Rather was he gently lubricating what he termed his works, while washing the day's dust from his throat with a soothing, life-giving trickle.

This silent and beneficent flow suddenly and unexpectedly changed to a shattering, breath-taking gargle.

Glancing at the Colonel, he removed the bottle from his lips and was thereupon delivered of a sound of which the amazing volume was equalled only by its incredible and gross impoliteness.

Using the bottle as a kind of wand wherewith to wave away the approaching apparition, he choked, swallowed, fought for breath, and found words.

"*L-l-look!*" he cried. "Name of the Name of the Name of a Pale Pink Hippo-pippo-pippohotamus . . . Look what's happened to us."

And blinking rapidly, the stricken warrior waved his hand to and fro across his eyes as though to dissipate the horrid and nightmarish figment of a dream, the wine-born monstrosity of delirium.

At his loud and violent cry of "*Look!*" all heads turned in the direction in which the two men stared and pointed, and a sudden and complete silence fell upon the noisy *bistro*, as the amazed revellers stared incredulous.

One after another, as the completely impossible truth dawned upon them, the *légionnaires* sprang to attention, and stood as though petrified. Petrified literally, for like rocks they stood, though one or two suggested, perhaps, those phenomena known as rocking-stones, vast boulders whose unstable equilibrium can be disturbed by the touch of a child's hand.

Each grim face, whether the years of its owner were sixteen or sixty, assumed as innocent a look as was possible; and, to the Colonel's informed eye, some of the achievements went beyond the possible, for on the whole the most blackguardly villains contrived the most lamb-like and endearing expressions.

Old Stenko Schenko there, for example, looked more like a kind of missionary to the other heathen, than what Denis Ducross well knew him to be.

But the thoughts of the blank-faced *légionnaires* as they regarded their Colonel, were neither lamb-like nor loving.

Now what was this, thought they. What new sort of military heresy-hunting and sin-smelling-out was the damned old witch-doctor up to now?

Weren't there enough non-coms and pickets and military police about, that the Old Devil himself must do their dirty work?

Was there no peace on earth? Not even in one's favourite wine-shop? Where could a man take his ease? Or was there a new law in the Military Penal Code that no soldier should have any peace at all, ever? Anywhere? Anyhow?

It was a damned shame.

One fine fellow, the most rigidly upright and motionless of them all, doubtless overcome by such thoughts and emotions rather than by wine, fell back on the bench on which he had been sitting, buried his face in the greasy interior of his *képi*, burst into tears, and sobbed bitterly.

And the Colonel? The infernal back-breaking, heart-breaking, nerve-breaking old devil of a martinet, with whom Satan would almost certainly refuse to share Hell, what would he do about it? Give poor old Georges thirty days cells for a start?

What the Colonel did do, was to make his dignified way to where Georges sat and wept.

"There, there, there, *mon pauvre* Georges!" soothed the Colonel, who greatly admired and dearly loved this old comrade of many a march and bivouac, many an escapade and fight.

"Cheer up, *mon gars*, and have another bottle of wine."

And his comrades, while still refusing to believe the evidence of their senses as to the words they had heard and the scene they were witnessing, moved only auto-matically and as in a dream, in obedience to the Colonel's sharp command which followed.

"Stand at ease."

"Sit down, all of you," was the next order, and obedi-ently they resumed their seats upon chair and bench.

"A litre of white wine for each man, unless he prefers red," called the Colonel brusquely to the fat Spaniard who stood gaping goggle-eyed and open-mouthed at these most amazing proceedings, his big hands resting like a duck's feet on the wine-slopped zinc bar behind which he lurked like a gross spider.

"And send the bill in to me to-morrow," added the Colonel, as bowing frequently and rapidly, the proprietor of the *bistro*. babbling incoherently, began to snatch bottles from the shelves behind him and to plank them down upon the bar.

"There you are, *mes enfants*," beamed the Colonel. "Drink my health, and drink heartily. And if there is any greedy and ungrateful *salaud* here, for whom a litre of wine is not sufficient, why—let him order another, the stout soldier."

And ere the stricken *légionnaires* could collect themselves sufficiently to realise what had actually happened, the Colonel, with a parting wave of the hand, a gesture that was a benediction in itself, turned upon his heel to leave them to it, free to enjoy themselves and to make merry without the embarrassment of his presence.

Automatically, and as one man, the *légionnaires* sprang to their feet. Even if the amazement caused by this incredible event had been so great as to deprive them of their reason and of all knowledge as to who and what and where they were, their sub-conscious military minds knew what soldiers should do when their Colonel turned to go. They arose as one man, and stood at attention.

"Sit down, sit down, *mes enfants*," cried the Colone cheerily, glancing back over his shoulder. "Sit down and drink—till you can't stand up again . . . That's the style."

Georges removed his *képi* from before his tear-stained face, and with it mopped his streaming eyes.

"Was it the Colonel or a blue elephant?" he asked.

"Both," answered his *copain*; an ungrateful remark as he was in the act of drinking the Colonel's wine. "Both, since the one is as likely as the other."

"*Was* it actually the Old Devil?" enquired another, as he removed his bottle from his lips in order to take breath.

"This is actually Old Wine, anyhow," replied a realist, returning his bottle to his lips in order to take drink as well as breath.

"The Old Devil must have gone mad. Heaven is rewarding him at last . . ." suggested another *légionnaire*.

"And us," supplemented his friend.

"Let us pray for him," suggested Miguel Gonzales.

"Let's drink up his wine, and go while we can, more

likely.   There's a catch in it somewhere—naturally," replied Cristobal Braganza.

"There is another *litre* in it somewhere, for each of us—if we're quick," observed Georges.

And the company settled down to what had now become the very serious business of the evening, puzzled, perturbed, yet pleased. For though dreams are dreams, and hallucinations are hallucinations, this was wine.

Eh bien!   Que voulez-vous?   C'est la Légion . . . and in the Legion anything, whether of earth, heaven or hell, can happen—even drinks from a crusty and crapulous Colonel.

CHAPTER V

STILL ON THE PATH OF GLORY

MEANWHILE that gentleman—or rather his admirable counterpart—strolled on, stroked his moustache from time to time, and smiled happily upon all and sundry; for he was feeling magnificent, glorious, positively on top of the world.

That little incident had done him good, and had made him really happy. It had given the boys a very great deal of real pleasure; it would cost Colonel Rochefort such a very little, with wine at three-halfpence a bottle; and look at the tremendous increase it would give his popularity!

One might in fact put it more strongly than that, and say that it would give him the first popularity he had ever had.

And how the story would spread, until there wouldn't be a *légionnaire* between Colomb Bechar and Bizerta, between Oran and Fort Zindernouf, who had not heard of how Colonel Rochefort walked into a wine-shop in Sidi, and treated all the boys to all they could hold, and any amount that they could not . . . Do his reputation a world of good. The generous fellows would be the first to admit that they had misunderstood him, and that he was as noble and as human as themselves.

They'd enjoy their wine in *The Little Dog and Lamp-post*, but even more would they enjoy the thought that their Colonel was, after all, *bon camarade et bon légionnaire*, however exalted his rank.

No. Denis could not feel that there was any load upon his conscience or stain upon his character—so far—in having pledged the Colonel's credit.

Bon Dieu! What a wonderful evening it was turning out! Really worth coming to the Legion for; worth all the sweat and suffering; the gruelling work of marching and road-building; the *cafard*-inducing monotony and misery of desert out-post life.

A perfectly marvellous evening. Incredible. The night of a life-time.

And it had all grown out of his trying on the Colonel's *képi* in front of the Colonel's mirror.

An hour or two ago and he had been a servant in a green baize apron.

And now look at him. And look at what he had done. And even that should be nothing to what he would do before he had finished.

Colonel Rochefort had never had such a night. There was a man who didn't make the most of his opportunities. He ought to come out like this of a night; see a bit of life, and take a hand in it too.

Why, he wouldn't know himself if only he found himself feeling as Denis Ducros did at this moment.

He could hardly put it into words. He felt like . . . he felt like . . . Who was the fellow? Sheikh Somebody, wasn't it? *The Boulevardier of Baghdad*. Devil take it, what was his name? Well, he couldn't remember it, but he felt like him . . . Used to go about of an evening all round the town, in Baghdad, and do just what he liked . . . Have a splendid time, and give other people a splendid time too. Whoop it up for the down-and-outs, and give the pompous officials and oppressors a kick in the pants. Had power, and enjoyed it—just like Denis Ducros was doing this blessed night. Blessed night indeed! . . .

And a passing German *légionnaire*, while saluting with automatic precision and an expressionless face, was astounded to see his Colonel smiling, and to hear him humming beneath his breath,

Stille nacht; heilige nacht . . .

He, Hans Weissmann, must have been drinking, and yet he had come out from barracks without a *sou*, and he had met no comrade who could and would treat him.

Or perhaps it was the Colonel who had been drinking? And yet he knew, everyone knew, that the Colonel never drank. Not even water, it was said, for no-one had ever seen him drink on the march.

Evidently he, Hans Weissmann, had an attack of *le cafard* coming on. . . .

Yes. That had surprised the good Weissmann, smiled Denis to himself, as he passed on, still thinking of the wasted life of Colonel Rochefort.

Well, one thing was certain. To-night was doing the Colonel's reputation a world of good. He would never be the same man again—and a damned good job.

What *was* the name of that lad who used to walk the streets of his capital by night? He'd remember it by-and-bye—when he had just the right quantity of wine aboard. It ought to come easily enough to the tongue, for it was an Arab name, and he should be familiar with them by now. Yes. He'd remember him all right, for he felt just like him . . .

Ah, ha! Who came here?

Why, one of them was the man they called Barberouge, the man with the brightest red beard in the Foreign Legion; and the other would be that wicked *gentilhomme manqué*, known to friend and foe as the Black Snake. In point of fact he was really much more like a lithe and hungry tiger or leopard than a snake. Yes. That pair really did rather suggest a lion and a tiger taking a walk together.

Probably the worst two men in the Regiment, but nevertheless each holding the high rank and title of *bon légionnaire et bon camarade*. Bad men with whom to quarrel; but good men to do and dare, to count their lives as nothing worth, to drink, to fight, to defy authority, and to look for some rule to break.

At three paces from him, the two approaching *légion-*

naires saluted smartly, one a big tall Englishman who had been an officer in a distinguished regiment, the other a black-avised Hungarian, who, not so long ago, had ridden at the head of a cavalry squadron as dashing and smart as any in Europe.

Denis Ducros admired them both, and often wished that he had their devil-may-care swagger, truculence and courage. Privately he regarded them as a pair of Lucifers, Sons of the Morning, fallen from some social paradise and high estate. Certainly they were two most interesting and intriguing men. They seemed to thrive on trouble.

Perhaps the chief of the Englishman's troubles had been whisky, and was now some excellent substitute; and that, for lack of whisky, he had largely to subsist on such imitations of liquor and imitations of mortality as saw-dust-distilled gin; forty-metre methylated spirit (so called because of its capacity to kill an army mule at that distance); bazaar-made brandy which owed nothing to the grape; rice alcohol; and very inferior absinthe.

Failing these assorted aids to health, there was always the admirable Algerian wine, an excellent claret at a penny a pint, but not of course to be regarded by a serious drinker as a serious drink; quite good as a beverage, and for quenching thirst, but then water will do that for you if you have no liquor, and can face it.

The Black Snake, his *fidus Achates*, was in striking contrast to the Briton. Slender, sallow, black-haired, black-moustached and black-eyed, he did indeed, with his cold hard glare, his thin-lipped smile, cruel and tooth-baring, suggest an animal, fierce and treacherous and cruel, a leopard in fact. A Magyar of land-owning family, his bond with the Englishman was that of breeding, education and intelligence on the one hand, and the attraction of contrast on the other. And as Denis knew well, there was nothing and no-one feared by either, and that if the courageous reckless folly of the one, brought him into the direst danger, blackest trouble, or heaviest punishment, the other would inevitably be there to share it.

The Englishman, a very dour, surly and silent man when sober, most expansive, eloquent and violent when drunk, amused and delighted the Hungarian constantly and unfailingly; while the latter with his courtesy and excellent manners, ready wit, devilish courage and daring, well-stored mind and interesting conversation, was the only man of his *escouade* whom the Englishman could bear, and of whom he could make a *copain*.

Barberouge knew the Black Snake for a really Bad Man, who did quite a number of very decent things, while the Hungarian recognised in the Englishman a thoroughly decent man who did some very bad things indeed.

Meeting on a common ground of indomitable courage and unquenchable fighting spirit, a high standard of intelligence and a low one of morality, they just "suited each other down to the ground," as the Englishman was wont to observe when excusing himself for helping his comrade and doing something that the fierce Hungarian might have misconstrued as a friendly, gentle or kindly act. For the hard-faced Briton loathed sentiment and all such foolishness—or professed to do so.

And when he made such a remark, the Hungarian nobleman would agree that they were born to be friends, for they were both born killers, devils, rebels, raiders and rievers, their hand against every man, their arm around every woman—who was good-looking.

"What a man dares, he may do," said Count Johann Czerneski, the Black Snake.

"Aye," agreed ex-Captain Sidney Selworthy, the Barberouge . . .

The *Rue de Mascara* is shaded by fine trees, and, in the semi-darkness, the Colonel, impelled by his great and growing sense of power to mete out an uneven-handed justice, and suitably to reward the good and punish the bad—good or bad according to his own standards as a sinful private soldier—took another risk. It was one that he realised to be considerable, for these two men knew Denis Ducros only too well, and the Black Snake was a difficult man to fool. He had an eye, a perception and a brain that moved like a striking-snake.

"Ah! My fine fellows!" quoth Denis, halting in his stride. "How goes it?"

Selworthy—seeking, as the drill-book orders, a point at which to gaze, a little to the right of the Colonel's left ear, and infinitely distant beyond him—stared with glassy eye, rendered his rufous countenance expressionless, and stood with grimly tight-shut mouth, wondering what new form of *delirium tremens* was now assailing him.

The Hungarian, with the charming smile that showed his perfect teeth, replied as one gentleman to another,

"Oh, but well! But well indeed, *mon Colonel*," successfully contriving to imply that nothing else could possibly be the case when the Colonel himself deigned to notice *un soldat simple* in the street, and actually to address him in pleasant and friendly salutation.

No on-looker could possibly have imagined that the Black Snake was fully prepared, indeed quite expecting, to hear the Colonel's quiet, gentle, and kindly voice change suddenly to a ferocious roar, his deceptively pleasant words to a stream of coldly bitter invective and vituperation.

"Good! Splendid! But when am I going to see the two best men in my Battalion getting their stripes?" asked the Colonel.

The Englishman's firm mouth fell open.

The Hungarian, smiling yet more brilliantly, answered promptly, and in a smart and soldierly manner,

"On our arms, *mon Colonel*? Or on your backsi . . . ?"

"Corporals! Corporals!" interrupted the Colonel. "There must surely be some vacancies in the *peloton* of probationary-corporals. You were both officers in your own armies before you came to this *schweinerei* of a Legion, I believe . . . In point of fact I see no earthly reason why you should not be appointed Corporals at once; both of you, without being probationary-corporals at all."

The two *légionnaires* now stared hard at the well-known if not well-loved face of their Colonel.

What was the Old Devil up to now?

One would have thought he had something better to do than stop soldiers in the street and pull their legs, bait them rather, and try to make fools of them. Not a very gentlemanly game. Nor would one have supposed it to be particularly satisfying to a person of rank and importance. Good enough for a loutish non-commissioned officer no doubt, but . . .

"And Sergeants in the shortest possible time," continued the Colonel. "And *then* you could make some of these rascally Corporals sit up, eh?"

Barberouge almost reeled, but years of drill and discipline stood him in good stead.

The Black Snake's bright smile grew faintly contemptuous.

What poor stuff from an officer who should be a gentleman! Leading them on, that he might the more suddenly trap them. One word of agreement as to Corporals being rascally, and they'd be for the Stone Jug once again.

"And after that, Sergeant-Majors, almost before you'd got accustomed to your 'sardines,' eh? And then, *mon Dieu*, you'd make some of those Sergeants jump to it, eh, what? I must speak to Captain Desboines about it to-morrow."

The *légionnaire* Selworthy silently opened dumb lips that could not pray. He had in his mis-spent life "seen things," full many a time and oft, varying from phantom rats in pink to fiery serpents in violent motion.

Was he now hearing things? Hearing his Colonel address him in a kindly speech, and promising him promotion. . . . His Colonel whose voice had hitherto never been uplifted in his direction save to curse, to threaten, and to bestow harsh punishment, all in the coldest, quietest, and most deadly menacing tones that military defaulter ever heard.

And now hark at the old bastard! Cooing like a damned sucking dove. Selworthy almost broke into a favourite dirge anent a mavis singing its love-song to the morn. Instead, he laughed, checked himself, received a dig in the side from his *copain*, hiccuped, excused himself, and to his further amazement found his apology well received by his kindly-smiling superior.

"Not at all! Not at all, my dear fellow," smiled the Colonel, graciously excusing this breach of social and military good manners.

"Yes. I must speak to your Captain about it to-morrow," he continued.

The face of the Black Snake hardened. He didn't like this sort of humour at all.

"M'sieur le Colonel is too kind," he murmured, half-way between a sneer and a jeer; for when his temper was roused, he feared neither God nor man, including that very redoubtable man, Colonel Louis Rochefort.

Yes, altogether a damn sight too kind, he decided. What was the Old Devil up to now? And thinking rapidly, the Black Snake's quick mind searched about among his more recent crimes, trying to decide which particular one, having come to the Colonel's knowledge, would more especially have enraged him.

"Not at all, *mon enfant*. Not at all," said the Colonel once again. "No kindness; merely justice . . . And where are you two fine fellows off to now?"

"Barracks, *mon Colonel*. Tattoo," replied the Black Snake. Did the old swine know that they were confined to Barracks and were at the moment wilful-missing, absent-without-leave; and that it particularly behoved them to be present and correct when the bugle for defaulters-parade went at . . .

"Nonsense! Nonsense!" ejaculated the Colonel. "Go along to *Le petit Chien et Lampadaire* and enjoy your-selves. You'll find some more of my rascals there, drinking at my expense. Tell that fat knave Ramon to give you all you want. Yes. Just as much as you can drink—and to put it down to me. Enjoy yourselves well, *mes enfants*, and when you return to Barracks, tell the Sergeant of the Guard that those were my orders to you.

"Go along now," concluded the Colonel, striking the Black Snake playfully with his cane. "Make the most of your opportunity. You may not find me in this mood again," and with a sort of dry laugh, with which Colonel Rochefort was wont to punctuate his allegedly humorous remarks, the Colonel turned on his heel and went on his way rejoicing.

Good fellows! He hoped they'd make a merry night of it—and that their excuse to the effect that they had been misled would be accepted. Anyway, they'd have had their happy hour, their wine and song and laughter.

And as the Colonel strode off, the taciturn Selworthy found his tongue.

"Now would that anointed peacock be drunk, or am I?" he asked.

The Hungarian, licking thin dry lips with the tip of a darting tongue which did indeed remind one of that of a snake, carefully considered the point.

"*Hombre*," he said at length. "Everyone's drunk except you and me, and we're going straight to the *Dog and Lamp-post* to remedy the defect."

"Aye," assented Selworthy sententiously. "I have never disobeyed my Colonel's orders yet, and I'm not going to start doing so to-night."

"There's a catch in it somewhere though," opined the Black Snake. "And we'll go to *The Little Dog and Lamp-post* and find out what it is."

Glancing back as he spoke, the Count saw the Colonel languidly raise a finger to the peak of his *képi*, as he received a smile and bow from a tall and angular woman, bony, grim and horse-faced, the well-known and widely detested sister and housekeeper of an officer of high rank; but the Black Snake did not hear him murmur with the utmost distinctness as he passed by,

"Now who *is* that dreadful person?"

Had he not turned his head away, the Black Snake might, however, have observed that Madame lost some of her high colour, and then more than regained it all.

"There, my sweet young thing," thought Denis Ducros to himself, as he passed the lady by, "wouldn't it interest you to know that only yesterday evening you observed that I was a clumsy creature, because you nearly knocked an entrée dish out of my hand with your bony elbow."

But the Colonel's sweet smile quickly changed to a heavy frown as his eye fell upon three elegant models of military perfection, and recognised three ambitious young Corporals, newly promoted and keen beyond measure, who, while excellent friends, vied each with the others in a smartness and sartorial perfection approaching dandyism.

To young ambition, rightly directed, Denis Ducros had no particular objection. But he had a very strong dislike for that particular form of successful climbing that uses the well-being of others as its stepping-stone.

Only too well he knew that a successful non-commissioned officer must be known as a firm disciplinarian, a man who unerringly detects military crime and unhesitatingly punishes it with all the severity in his power. And that again was all very well, but there were ambitious young corporals, who, not content with discovering crime, imagined it, manufactured it, reported it; and reported it before it was committed.

And of such were these three specimens, Prussians to a man, and determined to rise in the minimum time from Corporal to *Adjudant* on a reputation for severity, harsh discipline, and the ability to prevent wicked *légionnaires* in all their doings.

Raising his gloved hand and cane, the Colonel peremptorily signalled to the three musketeers to halt; the which, with mechanical precision, and as one man, they did in mid-stride and mid-salute.

"And pray where might you think you're going?" the Colonel enquired contemptuously, as his icy glance swept the three stolid heavy faces and met the gaze of three pairs of piggish little eyes.

"We promenade ourselves. We take the air, *mon Colonel*," faltered the senior of the three Corporals, stammering not only in great surprise, but in some consternation and alarm, as he viewed the angry and contemptuous face before him.

"*Ah! . . . Indeed?*" sneered the Colonel. "You take the air, do you? Well, take eight days *de consigne* as well. All three of you. Get you back to Barracks as quickly as you can march, and I'll see you in the morning . . . Reduced to the ranks . . . *And* eight days cells . . . Do you hear me? . . . For having dirty boots, dirty belts and dirty buttons."

The faces of the three brilliant and impeccable Corporals fell, almost audibly.

"Yes. And for having dirty hands, dirty habits, dirty

tongues and dirty minds," added the Colonel as he turned away and passed on, leaving behind him three of the most crestfallen men in Sidi-bel-Abbès, if not in all Algeria.

"And that'll do Michel Aubraine a bit of real good when I tell him about it," he smiled to himself. "Those swine have made a dead set at him.

"Ambitious Corporals!" he growled. "*Sales cochons* . . . Show me an ambitious Corporal, and I'll show you *un vrai batard d'une truie*," and he twirled his moustache fiercely.

This action caught the roving eye of a saucy little *midinette*, who thereupon gave the Colonel *en passant* an entirely approving glance from a most obviously glad eye.

It was a challenge, and one that no true descendant of a d'Artagnan and a du Geusclin could possibly decline.

"*Mais ma chère fille!*" cried the delighted Colonel, halting, throwing a *galoned* right arm about her waist, drawing her to him and kissing her warmly upon her ripe, smiling and undeniably up-raised lips.

"*Oh! La, la! Fie l'horreur, mon Commandant!* . . . *Quelle méchanceté!* . . . *Finissez-vous donc!*" cried the laughing girl, scarcely able to believe her good fortune . . . A lovely officer of high rank in full war-paint.

And since the lips remained upturned and the smile undiminished, the Colonel finished, as requested—but in his own good time.

Yes. Undoubtedly an elevated position in the military hierarchy and the social scale has it compensations as well as its cares.

Chaque age a ses plaisirs'—et chaque dignité aussi sans doute.

Very nice . . .

As he released the laughing *grisette*, he was aware that a group of *légionnaires* had halted, almost unconsciously it seemed, as they came upon the unusual, nay, unique sight of their grimly austere Colonel embracing and kissing a giggling woman in the street.

"*Salutations, mes enfants!*" cried the Colonel unabashed, as the men saluted.

"Well, how goes it?" he enquired affably . . . "Now what was your dinner like this evening?"

"Oh, but very good, *Monsieur le Colonel* . . . Our *soupe* was most excellent," stammered the *légionnaire* whom the Colonel was tapping encouragingly on the chest with his cane.

And similarly murmured in agreement all those whom incredulous surprise and amazement had not completely deprived of the power of speech.

"Oh, it was, was it? Then all I can say is that you're a set of poor fish who are damned easily satisfied," commented the Colonel brusquely. And with a snort of contempt, the great man passed on.

He did not hear, nor would I repeat, the comments of the simple soldiery . . .

And so it went, that crowded hour of glorious life. Truly and deeply satisfying, but heady.

Thirsty work though; and, as he passed an invisible house embowered in a thickly over-grown garden, whence came the appealing and disturbing strains of *Donna è Mobile*, he suddenly halted in his triumphant march.

Ah! He knew what establishment this was, and felt sorely tempted to inspect its mysteries. More so because it was sacred to officers, and strictly forbidden to *les soldats simples*. Never had its polished floors or thick-piled carpets been defiled by the hob-nailed *brodequins* of *légionnaire*, Spahi or any other lowly representative of what are known as "other ranks."

Not even a *sous-officier*, a sergeant-major or an *adjudant*, had set foot in those gilded halls.

For not only was Madame de Beuglant a rigidly scrupulous upholder of her iron rule that none but officers should pay a call upon any pupil in her School for Young Ladies, but curiously enough, the Law itself—Military Law, that is to say, was equally arrogant. It was as much a canon of Military Law that no-one below the rank of Lieutenant should ring the bell at Madame de Beuglant's door, as that soldiers should salute their superior officers, or that they should wear a uniform prescribed for, and issued to, the Regiment which they adorned.

And, moreover, had there been no such rule made by Madame de Beuglant, and no such law promulgated by

115

Military Authority, the officers who visited the School for Young Ladies would themselves have instituted such a regulation and have seen that it was most scrupulously observed and kept.

It was perhaps the realisation that the prohibition was of this three-fold and ineluctable order, which determined Denis Ducros to defy it.

It would be the most splendid achievement of the marvellous evening. Not only would he have been, for however brief a space, an officer, but he would have entered a forbidden place where none but officers might go.

What a tale to tell Michel Aubraine and the rest of his more especial friends! They probably wouldn't believe it, but he himself would have the satisfaction of knowing that it was true.

Perhaps he would be able to bring out with him something which would be in the nature of a piece of evidence. Something he could show them in support of his incredible story.

Perhaps a scented, lace-edged handkerchief, with initials worked on it?

Perhaps not.

He did not know whether the pupils at Madame de Beuglant's Establishment for Young Ladies used handkerchiefs like that, or gave them away as *gages d'amour*, if they did.

Anyway, go in he would; and if no-one on the morrow believed his account of what happened to him beneath Madame de Beuglant's hospitable roof, it would not alter the fact that he had actually penetrated the thrice-guarded and forbidden portals of this sacred *bouzbèr*.

CHAPTER VI

THE POWER AS WELL AS THE GLORY

DENIS, with a most Colonel-like air of determination and assurance, pushed open the gate. From it a narrow drive led into a pillared portico over which profusely rioted a fine bougainvillæa. Beside the front door of the house, which probably looked more imposing and attractive by moon-lit night than by garish day, hung an iron bell-pull supported by a chain. Seizing this he tugged it hard, and, somewhat to his surprise, heard one or two deep notes from a heavy bell that evidently hung round the corner, somewhere outside the house.

A moment later, a very big white-clad Arab materialised beside him, somewhat in the manner of Aladdin's *genie* evoked by the rubbing of the Lamp.

But it was the *genie* who bore the lamp, and who raised it, brightly burning, that he might be quite certain as to what manner of person it was who had summoned him from the outer darkness.

Seeing that it was no less a visitant than a gold-braided Colonel, he salaamed deeply, his dark impassive countenance hiding any surprise he might have felt. And as the Colonel acknowledged the obeisance by sketchily raising one finger in the direction of the peak of his *képi*, there followed in the semi-darkness of the porch a piece of jugglery which he could not exactly follow.

He was under the impression, however, that the Arab pulled the end of a small piece of stout wire that protruded through the door-post, thereby setting in motion machinery both mechanical and human. For the stout front door promptly and silently opened, apparently of its own volition, and the dark interior behind it was instantly flooded with light, revealing a carpeted and curtain-hung hall. To the right of this, a door opened, and a young and beautiful girl, smiling bright welcome, emerged.

At the same moment a much less young and much less beautiful girl pushed through a bead-curtain which obscured a staircase immediately opposite the front door.

The general effect was suggestive of that consequent upon putting into the slot of a machine a penny that set in sudden motion the apparently immobile figures which stand eternally awaiting such propulsion.

It was the less young and less beautiful figure which was set in continued motion by the pulling of the wire, and, as it advanced from the jangling and tinkling bead-curtain of which the strings were still swinging, Denis decided that, in the first place, this must be Madame herself; and, in the second, that unless appearances grievously belied her, she was a most evil and horrible hag.

Madame de Beuglant was obviously a *maîtresse femme*, a woman who would terrify and dominate anyone who was not strong enough to dominate and terrify her.

Denis however felt that the man or woman was yet to be born who could terrify and dominate Colonel Louis Rochefort; while, on the other hand, Denis well knew the Colonel's capacity for terrorising and dominating those against whom he chose to exercise his remarkable gifts in this direction.

And it was up to the Colonel's high level of arrogance and autocracy that Denis proposed to live, while within the shelter of the seminary presided over by this sinister and dangerous-looking woman.

Denis Ducros was a man of sensibility as well as sentiment, and if not remarkably sensible was unusually sensitive; and Madame affected him in much the same way as did a tarantula or a snake.

He was conscious of an emanated aura that was wholly maleficent, and he recognised in her a woman of evil power who used that power to the utmost, and to wholly evil ends.

The extremely low estimate that Denis formed of Madame was wholly intuitive, as never to his knowledge had he seen her before; while toward him her attitude and manner were more than friendly.

That Madame was surprised beyond measure, was evident.

Also that she was delighted beyond belief.

That it was a Colonel with sleeves five times *galoned* she saw at a glance, and could not doubt the evidence of her eyes; but that it should be that model of propriety and austerity, Colonel Louis Rochefort, was more than she could have thought possible, though, in her long life of the widest experience, she had learnt that all things are possible—where men are concerned.

With regard to women of course she knew that little was improbable and nothing impossible.

And yet the grim face in the shadow of the peak of the *képi* certainly appeared to be that of the famous Colonel.

The famous Colonel removed the *képi*, and with it, any doubts that may have lingered in Madame's mind. Instantly she fawned upon him with a gushing, excessive and unnatural sweetness which suggested to the simple-minded man the idea of a hard-cased hornet endeavouring to produce honey as doth the soft, velvety and industrious bee.

"My dear Colonel! What a pleasure! What an honour!" gushed Madame . . . "Charmed and delighted. Had I only known earlier . . ."

What Madame would have done had she only known earlier, was left to the imagination, but was obviously something that only a brightly vivid, not to say riotous, imagination could envisage.

"*Ah!* . . . *Indeed?*" murmured the Colonel non-committally; for though, on this great night when he wholly held the stage, he could have acted the part of beguiled admiring fly to Madame's enchanting and designing spider, he did not feel in the slightest degree disposed to impersonate that character. Greatly he preferred to enact the *rôle* of *blasé roué*, for whom Madame's establishment was provincial to a degree, Madame herself something of a *type infecte*, and the *jeunes filles* whom she chaperoned, probably a dull and unattractive litter.

And so indeed they must be, he reflected. What else could be the pupils in a school of which this was the head-mistress?

"*M'sieur le Colonel* wants a little cheering up," suggested Madame. "A little music, a little wine . . . a little amusing conversation with . . ."

"Yes," agreed the Colonel, still without enthusiasm. "By all means a little amusing conversation . . . with an intelligent person."

Madame's elastic smile stiffened.

What a difficult creature the man was. What did he think the place was? What did he come for? . . . Conversation? One would have thought he could get plenty of that at home. Possibly too much.

Could it be that this was a visit of inspection? Was he deeply interested in the morals as well as the manners of his officers? Sour old gooseberry . . . Well, what of it? Wasn't it Madame's admirable and beneficent aim, her delightful task in this vale of woe, to cheer the bored and down-hearted, and to brighten the days—no, the nights— of those o'er whom Life cast a shadow.

Yes; a noble duty and a rewarding, to brighten the lives of one's fellow-men.

That the lives of certain of her fellow-women might not only be dulled, but permanently blackened, in the brightening process, was not worthy of consideration. She knew how ungrateful women are. None better.

How many of the girls whom she had taken into her School for Young Ladies, and to whom she had given a thorough and comprehensive education, had ever shown the slightest gratitude, not to mention ordinary affection? One or two had indeed tried to thank her "as she deserved," to use their own ambiguous expression; but she had her own way of coping with people of that sort.

It was rather discouraging, for Madame pined to be loved, and only asked people to be reasonable, and to act in the manner that she considered right. After all, though kindness is kindness and philanthropy is philanthropy, Madame had her living to earn; and didn't she maintain them in luxury? . . .

Now which of her young charges would be likeliest to provide this glum creature with what he appeared to want . . . What was it? "Polite conversation"? No. "Intelligent conversation"? . . .

There was Annette . . . But Annette was not what most people would call polite. A merry and a hearty girl. But polite? No.

Justine? A model of politeness, but definitely not intelligent. Justine thought with her stomach, and thought hard. But as Captain Montpierre was wont to remark, Justine had a complexion of soft ivory and a brain of hard ivory . . . solid right through.

No. Neither Annette nor Justine seemed indicated. Who else was sitting around, eating her head off and wasting her time?

Odette? No. A crude and common girl. Intelligent as the devil. But common and vulgar. She could not imagine Odette sustaining a profitable conversation with Colonel Louis Rochefort. Not profitable from the Colonel's point of view, *c'est à dire.* He would quickly dismiss her as a nasty gold-digging little shark from the sewers of Paris.

With a conscious effort Madame pulled herself together. This would not do at all. This self-satisfied, self-righteous old stick was cramping her style, disturbing her calm and even mind. There are no sharks in the sewers of Paris, and sharks don't dig gold anyway.

There are rats, however, and Odette was a fair specimen. She had had a few words with her only that day—sharp words from Madame, and loud words from Odette, and Madame had been under the unpleasant necessity of showing her little Odette exactly how noisy people are rendered quiet. If there were any more trouble from that quarter she'd have to hint to Mademoiselle Odette that, though a sufficiently foolish person might try to make a habit of noisiness, a sufficiently competent one might make complete quietude both sudden and final.

No, not Annette, Justine or Odette. Bother the man. Did he think her School for the Daughters of Gentlemen was the Sorbonne, or what?

The Colonel gazed severely around the intriguing entrance-hall to this mysterious institution, which he had heard referred to both as a Young Ladies' Seminary, and as the Gilded Halls of Vice. So far he had seen only a very personable young lady, and a hag who was undoubtedly the headmistress—the Head and the Mistress—of the place; but no other signs of gilt or vice.

"Nicolette!" ejaculated Madame, as with her own white hands, soft and fat, she took the Colonel's *képi*, cane and gloves. Of course! The very girl—if she were in the right mood. Quiet as a mouse and modest as a nun. Probably very appealing to a man of the Colonel's type. Undeniably a polite girl, and reasonably intelligent . . . And as to moods, Madame herself would turn on a mood that the girl would remember—if that should be necessary. And there was one thing quite certain. The longer a girl stayed in this finishing school, the better she knew that Madame never made a promise she did not keep. And if one liked to call the promise a threat, it was all the same—to Madame at any rate.

"I beg your pardon," observed the Colonel, bringing his gaze back from dusty potted palms, brass pots, Moorish hanging lamps, fretted screens and Arab rugs, to Madame's enamelled face.

"Nicolette!" she repeated. "The very girl to interest *M'sieur le Colonel*. Oh, but of a discretion and *très serieuse*, *très gentil*. So truly modest and well conducted. Really *bien élévée* and *comme il faut*. But yes, *au bout des ongles*. A girl in a million."

"Must be," grunted the Colonel. "How does she come to be here?"

"But naturally—to add to her accomplishments," replied Madame promptly; and though the smile did not leave Madame's face, it seemed to stiffen, as though her face froze suddenly. Certainly it radiated no warmth.

St. Louis smite the stiff-necked old poker-back. What the hell did he come for? This wasn't a cemetery, even if he were a walking corpse looking for somewhere to lie down.

"Perhaps *M'sieur le Colonel* might like to meet all my young ladies and select the one that most appeals to him as likely to provide him with—what was it—polite and intelligent conversation?" suggested Madame.

Doubtless *M'sieu' le Colonel* liked parades. He had but to say the word and she would order one forthwith.

On the spur of the moment, at first, she had been delighted to see him; but if he was going to be heavy in hand and difficult, he'd be far more bother than he was worth, especially as he perhaps would not wish to meet any of his gentlemen who might happen to be calling on any of her young ladies. In fact, even now, the sooner she got him out of this hall the better.

That young Ybarronne, for example, was a very wild lad, and apt to grow wilder as the hours went by and the bottles went down.

"Come, *M'sieu' le Colonel*," she said. "I prescribe a glass of my champagne."

That would warm the old mummy up, when Hassan had doctored it a little, in accordance with his own private and remarkable prescription.

"Thank you," replied the Colonel, still without enthusiasm. "I only drink claret."

Madame tittered.

"I thought you were going to say 'water,' " she said.

"No. Not always," replied the Colonel, following Madame toward a curtained door in the far left-hand corner of the hall.

"But doubtless *M'sieu' le Colonel* would like to offer a glass of something a little more festive than water to these young ladies, if he is feeling . . . er . . . kind," suggested Madame, as she threw open the door of a room which appeared to be a curious combination of bar and *salon*.

The drawing-room suggestion was furnished by the presence of some two or three fashionably dressed young ladies, some two or three ladies who if fashionably dressed were not young; and, strangely enough, two or three young ladies who were neither fashionably nor unfashionably dressed, as it would appear that they had abandoned the effort of dressing when they had arrived at the moment to struggle into a gown.

It was a hot night of course.

"Young ladies," called Madame, as all eyes turned to the opening door. "I have the great pleasure to present *M'sieu' le Colonel* Fait-en-fer, who has done us the immeasurable honour of visiting us this evening."

The girls rose and bowed, silently, with the utmost correctness, altogether in a manner which to the eye of this particular beholder, suggested *discipline, discipline, et toujours la discipline.* And although the Colonel's face remained austere, as politely he acknowledged their bows, his heart warmed to them.

Poor girls! Poor dears!

"Filles de joie."

At a generous estimate, and at a considerable distance, they might be classed as *"filles,"* but where was any sign of *joie*? Their faces as he first caught sight of them, far from being joyous, seemed rather the personification of sadness.

Before they had time to turn on their mechanical smiles, display their teeth, force a gleam of brightness to their eyes, the composite face of which he had caught a glimpse was expressive of hopelessness, profound unhappiness, boredom and gloom; and though, with all his soul he loathed, hated and detested Madame, he already felt that with all his heart he could love these wronged and wretched girls. Wretched, he could see they were.

Wronged, he felt sure they were.

Anyhow, they were pitiable, for they were held in as tight a grip, and as iron a system of discipline as any *légionnaire* who, did he hate his servitude, need bear it but five years. Moreover, he was a man, a soldier, a member of a noble and honourable profession, whereas these were women, camp followers, and members of a profession ignoble and dishonourable that was only the oldest in the world.

It was damnable. Infamous. Devilish . . .

It was slavery. Sheer unmitigated slavery, and more degraded and degrading than the black slavery that certain of the Great Powers were trying to stamp out. This upholstered cage was as abominable and disgraceful a place as the foul hold of a slave *dhow*; and if, as any right-minded civilised man would agree, the enslavement of black man by white man was one of the vilest criminal customs that had ever disgraced the world, what was the enslavement of white women by white men? Surely *the* most unutterably horrible of them all.

Thus, Denis Ducros, who had hitherto given the subject little or no consideration whatsoever.

But to-night he was acting a part. Nay, living a part, the part of a man of rank and power; and surely power was given to a man that he might do good with it? It was not the *rôle* of a well-intentioned Man of Power, to walk into a place like this and add the weight of his authority, the force of his influence and example, to the recognition and support of a human institution so abominable and so inhuman.

The inhumanity of man to man.

And worse, the inhumanity of man to woman.

And worst of all, as exemplified by this Madame, the inhumanity of woman to woman.

Madame . . .

The gimlet-eyed, trap-mouthed, steel-faced creature whose voice was so false, whose smile so hypocritical, who, behind a mask of hospitality, jollity and good cheer, was as coldly evil as a snake, as rapacious as a shark. If he were any judge of character, the woman was greed personified; and next to greed, her most distinguishing trait was cruelty. Or perhaps one should say—he reflected, as he glanced again at the repellently smiling face and then at the faces of the girls—that no-one, not the woman herself, knew whether she were a living and walking Rapacious Cruelty, or an unmitigated Cruel Rapacity. Well, he'd see whether he could give the girls an hour's pleasure.

Pleasure . . .

Joy . . .

How they must loathe the very word.

"Filles de joie."

What they wanted was happiness, not joy.

What could one do for them?

Were they well-fed? Or would a good supper be appreciated?

They didn't look starved, and doubtless Madame was too good a business woman to let them grow skinny, since their beauty was their stock-in-trade.

Probably their idea of a good time, or a stroke of luck, would be peace and quite . . . oblivion . . .

He had known what it was to ache for it himself when, so weary at the end of a long forced march that, had he collapsed and fallen down, he could not have risen to his feet again.

Yes, a glass of really good wine, and a little tranquillity. An early evening for once in a way. Late hours, night after night, were the devil. He knew something about that too, when Madame Rochefort had a series of parties at the festive season, and he had to start a day's hard work in the middle of the night.

Well, he had been standing smiling at the girls long enough, and that didn't help them much.

"Charmed," he said. "Delighted . . . And now what about a glass of wine . . ."

"Champagne," specified Madame.

". . . and a little music, I was going to say," continued the Colonel in his coldest voice. "As to the wine, we will have precisely what we prefer; and if Madame will be so good as to consult the tastes of the young ladies, and indicate her own, I personally should like a little claret."

"But *M'sieu' le Colonel*!" expostulated Madame. "I am indeed desolated; but I am afraid I cannot offer you sticky Algerian claret. I fear there is nothing of that sort in my cellar; nor should I know where to send for it."

"*Ah! . . . Indeed?*" observed the Colonel, characteristically giving his moustache an upward brush. "Remind me to tell you, before I go. Everyone who appreciates good wine should know where to send for that admirable product of our local grape. Admirable and excellent. I drink it daily."

This was profound truth. With almost a start Denis realised it. He recognised it, smiled upon it, almost shook hands with it, so to speak. It seemed to him delightful that Truth could penetrate into this place. Delightful also, that Truth should bolster up, countenance and support his play-acting, his rendering of a leading *rôle* on the fine large stage that was Sidi-bel-Abbès.

Good, kindly truth. He patted it on the head.

"Yes. I drink it daily. Twice. Have done so for years." But he did not embellish the truth. He did not add "With morning *soupe* at ten-thirty, regulation quarter-litre, with evening *soupe* at four-thirty, regulation quarter-litre."

"But, in point of fact, I don't think I mentioned 'sticky Algerian claret,'" continued the Colonel, fixing Madame's eye with a glassy and somewhat embarrassing stare from his monocle.

"Doubtless Madame's cellars contain plenty of the best French wine; and if Claret is not readily accessible, I have no objection to a vintage Burgundy. Anything . . . Anything . . . *Mouton Rothschild, Nuit St. Georges, Clos Vouguet*. Anything . . ." and the Colonel reeled off quite a little list of the best years of the best vineyards of the best districts of France.

A girl tittered.

Both Madame and the Colonel glanced at her, but there was a difference in their regard.

Madame smiled bitterly.

"Odette is pleased to be amused?" she said in a voice that contained a message.

The girl, red-haired, with high cheek-bones, tip-tilted nose and prominent chin, faced Madame squarely.

"Very pleased. Very amused," she said. "*Ha! . . . Ha! . . .* and then *Ha!*, making three."

Madame eyed her for a few seconds before replying with a remarkably acid sweetness,

"It must give *anyone* pleasure to amuse you, dear child."

"Even *M'sieu' le Colonel* Louis Rochefort Fait-en-fer?" grinned the girl impudently.

Madame made a significant motion with her hand.

But the austere-seeming Colonel Fait-en-fer laughed.

"I am sure it would," he observed pleasantly. "I must remember to advise him to come and give himself that pleasure."

"Merci, *Monsieur le Colonel*," grinned Odette. "Tell him I'll amuse him all right . . . Do him a world of good . . ."

Madame's thin lips tightened a little. These Parisian gutter-snipes took more breaking-in than some. What little Odette needed was a holiday—in Port Said.

She again made a significant and more imperious motion with her hand, a gesture which Odette again ignored. Whatever virtues Odette might lack, she possessed the greatest of all, courage; and in great measure.

Odette laughed again. Some of the other girls glanced at her in awed admiration and approval.

"And what is it that amuses Mademoiselle Odette?" smiled the Colonel.

"Oh . . . wine, *M'sieu' le Colonel*. Wine . . . and *M'sieu' le Colonel*."

"Now I am a very inquisitive man, Mademoiselle Odette," smiled the visitor, "and should very much like to know why wine should amuse M'selle."

"It shouldn't. But it does," answered the girl. "It'll amuse *M'sieu' le Colonel* if he goes so far as to try to drink it," and Mademoiselle Odette laughed a little shrilly.

"Well," said the Colonel, "let's all be amused. Call a servant, Madame, and let us give our orders. What kind of wine do you think you will find most amusing, M'selle Odette?"

"Well, since you ask, *M'sieu' le Colonel*, it would be to find myself sharing with you a bottle of such wine as you suggested Madame should produce for you. A bottle of Madame's own private wine."

"You shall share with me a bottle of Madame's best," promised the Colonel.

"And you, my dear?" he asked a dark, stupid-looking girl of considerable beauty of a somehwat course and obvious kind.

"Oh, *merci beaucoup*, *M'sieu' le Colonel*," replied the girl, glancing quickly from him to Madame. "*Champagne, s'il vous plaît*."

"Don't you believe her, *M'sieu' le Général* Fait-en-fer," interrupted Odette with her *gamin* grin. "She has the distinction of resembling *M'sieu' le Général* himself in one respect. She prefers wine to champagne. Good red wine such as Madame knows so well how to select from her own corner of the 'cellar.' "

The dark girl glanced apprehensively at Madame, finding as she expected, a smile on the face of the tigress.

"*Non, non, Monsieur le Colonel*," she said quickly. "Champagne for me, since you are so kind."

Odette's exclamation, though it delighted the Colonel, seemed to shock the delicate ears of Madame.

Perhaps to cover this distressing sound, Madame clapped her hands loudly. An Arab servant entered, and firmly she gave her order for champagne for the young ladies, and a bottle of Madame's own invalid wine for Monsieur and herself.

"A bottle, did Madame say?" enquired the Colonel, raising an eyebrow.

"Two bottles," amended Madame.

"And four more," yet further amended the Colonel, "and of the same kind."

"*Monsieur le Colonel* is too generous," observed Madame.

"One cannot be too generous," corrected the Colonel. "Very few try; and none succeed."

"We'll try to-night," he murmured pensively, as Madame and the young ladies eyed him with varying degrees of interest.

"A little music while we wait?" suggested the Colonel, looking round.

"Fifine! The gramophone," said Madame, and a somewhat negroid-looking girl, whose magnificent flashing eyes and teeth atoned for her somewhat pronounced nostrils, and slightly kinky, not to say woolly, hair, sprang up and crossed the room. She wound the handle of the gramophone, and loosed upon the heavy air, certain brassy and strident notes that soon resolved themselves into the tune of an allegedly comic song, popular at the Moulin Rouge some three years earlier.

"But I said music," expostulated the Colonel, coldly. Madame raised a hand sharply, and the girl stopped the infernal machine, and changed the record.

A minute later the well-known and, in some places, well-liked strains of "*Funiculi, Funicula*," succeeded those of "*Monsieur, mon oncle, le bon Edouard.*"

Abruptly the Colonel rose from the armchair, where at Madame's suggestion he had seated himself.

"*Really!*" he expostulated quietly; and again Madame raised a restraining hand, and again the music ceased. For all his air of annoyance and distaste, Denis Ducros—but for the presence of Madame and his respect for the sacredness of his Thespian art—would have loved to sing to the girls a novel (Legionised) version of the well-known words of that justly famous song. He knew they would enjoy and appreciate it.

"*Monsieur le Colonel* does not like the little tune?"

"No, Madame, he does not. He has listened too long and too often to the serenade of the jackals."

"Has Monsieur any special favourite?"

"None, Madame, none. I ask but that the noise be music."

Music! Madame would have liked to give him some music of her own. Give him real cause to enquire "*Qu'est-ce que c'est que vous me chantez là?*"

What the Devil did the man want? There was a pile of good records there. No-one else had ever found any fault with them. They had been a real bargain, and Fifine had not put on any of the cracked ones; nor had the thingummy got stuck and run round and round in the same circle. That, as a just woman, she fully admitted, became boring after a time, if one noticed it. And in point of fact, it was extremely humorous when the machine, instead of singing Madame Butterfly's beautiful song in the usual way, stammered and stuttered like an aged drunk trying to tell his wife where he had spent to-morrow evening.

She wondered if one of those would amuse the Colonel. Quickly she decided that it would not.

Devil take the finnicking old dodderer. What did he think her place was? The Opera?

If he wanted music, let him go there . . . And have a bellyful.

"Perhaps some of the young ladies sing," suggested the Colonel, smiling round the circle of now definitely interested and animated faces, his eye coming to rest on one that fascinated him in its sudden, frequent, and apparently automatic, change from a mask of misery and hopeless despair, to one of politely smiling, but obviously false gaiety.

"Sing? . . ." said Madame dubiously. "Sing? . . ." What did the man think she was? A sacred canary-fancier, or what? . . . Sing? . . . Perhaps he'd like to hear that stupid lump Nicolette caterwaul to that guitar of hers. She was fond enough of doing it when she was by herself, as Madame had had cause to complain. She'd had to remind her that she wasn't on the slum music-halls of Marseilles and Barcelona now.

Yes. There she sat, mum and glum as usual, looking as though her coffin didn't fit and the vault wasn't warm enough.

"Nicolette," she said sharply. "Go and get your strum-box and give the Colonel a hot rousing chorus about *The Little Cross Where Lilies Grow* or something."

CHAPTER VII

REST-HOUSE ON THE PATH OF GLORY

THE girl addressed flushed in spite of her rouge, and the Colonel noted how nervously she twisted her fingers together.

"*Segnour Diéu*," whispered the girl to herself, as her eyes fell before Madame's stare—and the Colonel's interest was instantly awakened.

It was many a long year since he had heard that varia-tion of "*Mon Dieu.*" Why, this girl was more than a fellow country-woman.

She was a Provençal, and not very long from Provence either!

She was more than a Provençal, for Provence has many corners. She was a neighbour. Why, he might know the very village from which she came.

He must know it.

"*Segnour Diéu.*"

He savoured it to himself.

"*Segnour Diéu.*"

"Indeed, yes," he said softly. "Please sing for me, *mon enfantounet.*"

It was the girl's turn to start. And her quick glance at the Colonel disclosed what Denis Ducros considered a very lovely pair of eyes.

"Bono Maire die Diéu," she whispered. *"M'sieu' le Colonel parle le Langue d'Oc!"*

"Oui! Santouno! Mais oui," replied the Colonel. *"Mademoiselle est d'Arles?"* he enquired kindly.

"Oui, M'sieu' le Colonel, je suis Arlesienne," replied the girl, and her smile so lit up her face, that for the moment it was bright and animated.

"Positively she looks almost happy," thought Denis Ducros.

"Sarnipabiéune!" he exclaimed, treating her to an exclamation she must have heard a thousand times on the lips of her father, her brother, her lover, and any of the men of her native countryside.

For though she called herself Arlesienne, he very much doubted whether she had been born and bred in that ancient Roman town, so famous for the beauty of its women.

Probably born and bred in one of the near-by hill villages. Quite probably attended Arles market with her mother, until she was old enough to go there to earn her living . . . How? . . .

In good domestic service?

Shop?

A stall of her own in the market-place?

Arles. He knew every stone of it.

La place. He knew every inch of it. He could see it now. The Arena. He knew every stone of it . . .

Arles, Nimes, Avignon. *Aïlas!* Would he ever see Provence again? *Malau de Diéu.* Why had he ever left the loveliest countryside in the world, for this dusty graveyard?

As he was about to repeat his request that Nicolette-from-Arles should sing, the Arab waiter, followed by a negro boy, again appeared, each burdened with a large brass tray on which stood a number of bottles of the shape dedicated to champagne, and two or three which appeared to contain claret or burgundy. The bottles looked not so much old, as weary; not as though they had lain long in dark wine-cellars, but as though they had seen considerable service in beer-gardens.

The Colonel eyed them with cold contempt.

"Just filled them?" he asked the Arab in his own tongue, and in the true Rochefort manner, with the result that the Arab was surprised, nay stampeded, into the commission of an unwonted act. He spoke the truth.

"*Ah! . . . Indeed?* Well, now go and empty them again."

"Where, *Sidi Général*?" asked the servant, doubtless glad to be taking his orders from a man again.

"Down the sink, or . . ."

Mademoiselle Odette obliged with a suggestion.

". . . over the rose-beds, I was about to say," concluded the Colonel amid the nervous tittering of the girls, among whom, encouraged or led by Odette, a mild spirit of rebellious courage seemed to be abroad.

"But before you do it," said the Colonel, eyeing the man with a steady piercing stare which seemed to fascinate and almost paralyse him, "suppose you bring half a dozen of the best champagne that Madame has, and another half-dozen of the best *vin rouge* of France—not Algeria. Madame's own, you understand.

"That is what Madame meant, is it not?" he smiled, turning to that stricken lady, who for the first time in the girls' experience of her, seemed bereft of speech.

"So much better if one can talk to these people in their own language, which Madame naturally would not understand," he added.

Yet, to those who knew Madame's history, it would not have seemed wholly unnatural that she should both understand and speak the gutter Arabic of the town-bred Arab mongrel, who had never so much as seen the black tents of the Bedouin.

Although Madame repeatedly informed the young ladies of her Seminary that she herself had gone to "school" in Paris; and had spent happy, happy years under a kind and generous Mother-Superior, who reminded her so much of herself, in a delightful School for Young Ladies, not far from the Bois de Boulogne, this was not strictly true.

In fact it was not true at all, for Madame had been born

quite near the Kasbah in Algiers city; had spent her childhood in ancient and narrow alleys, speaking a language unknown in Paris; had gone to "school" at the age of fourteen, in a seminary kept by a lady who was not a Mother, and who surely was not the Superior of any woman on earth.

From this school she had gone on to a higher educational establishment, a finishing school in Pera, where she had almost learnt Greek while not forgetting the guttural accents of the old home.

In Pera, by adopting a lofty standard of conduct and pursuing most conscientiously the exact path of duty, she had risen from the humble rank of Mademoiselle to the exalted status of Madame.

So there was no *nuance* of the Colonel's Arabic that she did not understand; and for a moment she thought of spirited and piquant stories that she had heard in Pera of Constantinople, concerning gentlemen whose wine had disagreed with them—after they had disagreed with the lady who dispensed it.

"Monsieur le Colonel will ask for everything he wants, will he not?" suggested Madame; and the accompanying contortion of her lips could hardly be described as a smile.

"Yes," replied the Colonel simply, and again Odette laughed. The Colonel, who admired courage, smiled encouragingly at her.

Odette winked at the Colonel and hummed an air.

"That will be enough, thank you," interrupted Madame.

"But not nearly enough," contradicted the Colonel. "Let's have it all, Mademoiselle. Words and music."

"Oh, la! la!" commented Mademoiselle Odette; and, endeavouring to look coy, she rose to her feet and bounded into the middle of the room. There she not only sang her song, she danced it, she acted it, she embroidered and embellished it. By the time she had finished, there was but one person in the room who was not genuinely amused and laughing heartily.

Madame was not amused.

"I don't think one quite follows some of the allusions

in that vulgar caterwaul, but it is not the sort of song I care to hear in my *salon*," she said.

"Mademoiselle must warn us next time, in order that Madame may depart in time," suggested the Colonel, who had appeared to thaw more rapidly with every verse, and had now shed his austerity completely.

"And now, Mademoiselle Nicolette," he said, turning to the Provençal girl, "sing for me, *enfantounet*."

"*Monsieur le Colonel*," deprecated Nicolette, "*Anasvous-en au Tron de Diéu*," and the private smile that she flashed to him, said quite plainly, "There, *that's* a saying from home if you like; and you'll understand that it is a quotation, a message, and not a piece of impudence."

At that moment the door again opened, and the Arab with his black satellite appeared, and the Colonel used the incident, glancing from the wine to the girl, to reply with an idiomatic proverb which he knew she must have heard a thousand times.

"*Lou vin es' fa' pèr bèure*," he said in the Langue d'Oc, and as he glanced at her, he fancied that her eyes grew brighter while he spoke. Not with tears, of course. How could the sound of her childhood's tongue cause unshed tears to rise to the eyes of a girl of this kind, in a place of this description, run by such a woman as this Madame? Surely such a girl could be but a brazen symbol of womanhood?

"And if so," cried Denis Ducros angrily to himself, "was a brazen vessel to blame that it had been fashioned in brass?"

This girl had not been brazen when she ran barefooted about some village of Provence. If she were brazen now, she had been made so by the hand of her fellow-man . . . her fellow-woman . . .

The Colonel rose to his feet.

"Now let's see," he said, picking up a bottle of champagne and studying the label and the foil that covered the wired cork.

"Ah! Not manufactured on the premises. Not a drop of Madame's own home-brew, just like Mother used to make in the stone bottles . . . Yes, this should be drinkable by those who care to drink it.

"And the red wine of France? . . . Positively imported. Actually bottled at the Château. *Premier cru* and whatnot. Madame, I congratulate you . . . and ourselves," he bowed.

"It is expensive wine," observed Madame dryly, and mentally began the making out of a bill that should pay not only for the wine, but show such a dividend as would make even this awful evening worth while.

"Open them," he said to the Arab, brusquely.

"How many, Sidi?" enquired Hassan.

The Colonel's look was a sufficient rebuke, as again he growled,

"Open them."

"Madame," he said a minute later, taking up a glass of what purported to be a *Nuit St. Georges*, "I drink to the happiness of the young ladies of this seminary. Mesdemoiselles, your health, happiness and prosperity . . . May each of you have the wish of your heart."

CHAPTER VIII

GENTLE USE OF GLORIOUS POWER

AND he looked as splendid as he felt. He was simultaneously overwhelmed and uplifted by a wave of pity, sympathy, affection and admiration.

Poor brave girls.

They were not good girls of course, but neither were the people through whose fault they were there.

No, they were not saints.

Nor were *légionnaires*. What was wrong with the holier-than-thou hypocrites and humbugs was the fact that they got hold of the wrong end of the stick. It was not because these girls were sinners that men were vicious; it was because men were vicious that these girls were sinners.

Anyway let him—or her—who was without sin, come and chuck a brick through Madame's *salon* window. Why couldn't some of the righteous ones do something *for* them for a change, instead of always trying to do something against them?

Something for them? What would most of them answer if one said to them now,

"If you could have a wish granted, what would you wish for?"

Money presumably.

Well, and if they did, so would most people if the wish were to be secret.

"Mademoiselle," he said, touching Odette's glass with his own. "Wish!"

"For what?" asked Odette, surprised by the sudden suggestion.

"For what you would like most in the world."

The girl answered almost without a pause.

"I? For what I'd like better than anything else? Most of all things? . . . Why, I should like to go for a drive," she said. "A long, long drive in the beautiful, cool night . . . The glorious fresh, sweet air. The moonlight . . . The stars . . . The cleanness . . .

"Oh these walls! These walls!" she cried.

"Odette," snarled Madame, in the voice that had the effect of the crack of a whip.

"I will arrange it," said the Colonel. "If not to-night, then another night."

And he meant it—when he spoke. He was the man of power and patronage. The girl should have her wish, and the drive should be for fifty kilometres, or a hunred.

He emptied his glass to Odette.

"And you, Mademoiselle?" he asked Fifine, having re-filled it.

"I? Oh . . . It's a big question, *M'sieu' le Général* Fait-en-fer. Just one wish, and that for what one would most like in all the world? I think I would wish for . . . What? Oh, I don't know. I think I would wish for . . . For a lovely long drive by moonlight, right away from here. Far, far away to where it is . . . quiet and cool. And one could be quite alone. Where there are no . . ."

"No francs," sneered Madame. "No food, no roof, no bed. *Hein?*"

"Ah, well," sighed the girl. "Then I'd like a pile of fresh gramophone records, and none of them cracked."

"It can be arranged, Mam'selle," said the Colonel gravely. "And you, *chèrie?*" he asked, clinking glasses with Annette.

"I? *I* should like," she began with assurance and gusto, but catching Madame's basilisk eye, faltered. "I think, too, that I should love a drive . . . With someone nice . . ." She sighed deeply.

"Someone like you," she added with an impudent grin.

"That too can be arranged," smiled the Colonel.

"And you, *ma petite?*" he asked of the beautiful but bovine-looking Justine.

"I?" yawned Justine. "Oh, I don't know . . . Don't think I want anything much. Perhaps *un amant de cœur* who adored me. Young and handsome, and very rich. And . . ."

The girl Odette gave a whoop of laughter. "Nothing much," she jeered. "Only a rich young lover who adores her."

"Yes," agreed Justine. "That's all I want . . . I think . . ."

"That arranges itself, Mademoiselle," the Colonel assured her.

"And you, Mademoiselle Nicolette? Supposing I could grant you your dearest wish, what would it be?"

The girl smiled shyly at him.

(How could a girl, a pupil of Madame's, living here in Madame's house, smile as sweetly and diffidently as that? Almost he had thought, as innocently as that, which was patently ridiculous. It was absurd. It was sentimental. That's what it was. He was a sloppily sentimental fool. 'Innocent'! . . . 'Diffident'! . . . The kitten of a cat-house! *Pfui!*)

Without hesitating, she replied,

"*M'sieu le Colonel est très gentil.* What would I like most in all the world? . . . A glimpse of my village. That is all."

And, as he met the gaze of her large eyes, still young and clear, he found himself, for some reason, unable to assure her that it should be arranged.

But he realised that if, by giving everything he possessed, and was ever likely to possess, he could truthfully have so replied, he would have assured the girl that she should see Provence again.

"And this young lady?" he asked, turning to a thin, hard-faced woman, who for some reason reminded him of a burnt-out stove.

The girl uttered a coarse and vulgar exclamation, and a sneering laugh.

"What would I like? *Zut!* I'd like some more wine."

"That is now being arranged," smiled the Colonel, as he presented her with a full bottle.

"But I expect there to be something else in life that Mademoiselle would wish for," he said kindly, as he filled her glass.

"Hell!" sneered the girl. "Yes. I'd like to go to bed."

"That is also arranged," was the reply "Go now . . . And sleep well."

The girl angry, confused and puzzled, rose to her feet. Who was this fool that he should come here and mock her. She'd take him at his word. She'd go to bed. She'd lock her door, and he could deal with Madame. She'd take the bottle of wine he'd given her too, and he could settle with Madame for that as well.

She wasn't a slave, was she, that . . .

But she knew she was a slave.

She knew she was getting older and plainer.

She knew she was losing what looks and what attraction she had ever had.

She knew that when Madame eyed her speculatively, as with increasing frequency she did, she was considering whether the time was not approaching to start her off on the next stage of the road to Port Said.

How could she be such a fool as to dream, for one second, of defying Madame?

No-one ever defied Madame twice. She had done it once, and . . . it was hopeless. Life was hopeless . . .

Hopeless . . . Suddenly she put her face in her hands and burst into tears.

The Colonel put his glass down and crossed to where the girl sat.

"Yes. Tired. I thought so. Mam'selle was quite right when she wished for sleep. Come along, my dear," and putting his hand beneath her elbow, he helped her to rise.

"Now you come along with me," he ordered, and led her from the room.

Madame said nothing, although she appeared to try to say much. Although she got up from her chair with alacrity, she sat down again with resignation.

"The sacred arranger!" she sneered, recovering speech. "Well, he has arranged for himself apparently. *Chacun à son gout!*" she shrugged; and directed Hassan to re-cork the open bottles.

"Let me see you to your room," said the Colonel politely, as he closed the door of the *salon*; and the girl mechanically led her weary way up the stairs. As she paused at a door on the landing, the Colonel opened it and said,

"Good-night, Mademoiselle. Pleasant dreams. I'll send the boy up with your wine . . . *Dormez bien.*"

Quietly he closed the door.

Well, she had her wish, anyway. Had it only been as easy to give the others what they wished for!

Within the room, the girl stood staring at the closed door.

When the Colonel opened the door of the *salon*, within a couple of minutes of leaving it, he interrupted what appeared to be an impassioned harangue addressed by Madame to her young ladies.

"Now!" he said brightly. "What about a little more music?"

At a nod from Madame, Odette rose obediently, to go to the gramophone.

"No, no," expostulated the Colonel. "No more cracked records.

"Even if cracking them does improve them," he added in the tone of a dissatisfied connoisseur.

Two more girls had come into the room in the Colonel's absence.

"Does either of these young ladies sing?" he asked, smiling upon them kindly.

"Not to friends," replied one of them perkily; while the other admitted freely that she had never sung twice to the same audience. By special request.

"But nobody's drinking. Come girls, come Madame, a glass of wine with you. Order your man to open some more bottles."

Promptly Hassan removed the corks he had inserted at Madame's behest. Being Burgundy corks that he kept for just such emergencies, this was a simple matter, but the explosions were those of damp squibs, and the Colonel was not deceived.

"Stop those damned tricks! Open fresh bottles!" he growled in Arabic—to Hassan's approval.

Though a domestic servant, and the servant of a woman, he was still sufficiently some sort of a kind of a Son of the Prophet to resent and to dislike the sight of a man, and a good man at that, being swindled by a woman, and especially such a daughter of the Devil as Madame.

Now, between men, swindling was a different matter . . . Let all men swindle, and the best man win.

"Sing again, Odette," bade Madame, the wineglasses having been replenished.

Odette sang again, and the Colonel was amused, for the song was daring, and the Colonel admired courage. To what lengths and heights—or depths—Odette's daring would carry her in this direction was a subject of interesting speculation.

But it was not the extent of Odette's repertoire which interested the Colonel at the moment.

"Very good," he nodded. "I think Odette must have her drive now," and, turning to Madame, he bade her send her servant for the best carriage he could procure.

Madame almost achieved the feat of lifting her own face, so high did she raise her eyebrows.

Was the man mad?

What on earth did he think he had come for?

To send girls off to their rooms; to send girls out for drives; to give girls real wine, and see that they drank it!

Well, if that was his idea of fun he could have it; and *pardieu*, he should pay for it.

No fool like an old fool, but this man was a fool *par excellence*, on which ever side of forty he might be, to spend his money like this . . .

To come to *her* house and start sending the girls out of it! But money's a good plaster, and a wad of hundred-franc notes can be spread over quite a big bruise. He should pay for his fun. Nevertheless, who was master here? This *blagueur* or Madame?

The point soon became quite clear.

"*Mais, Monsieur*," said Madame, her eyebrows having slowly come again to earth, so to speak. "We don't go out for drives at this time in the evening."

"Pity!" replied the Colonel. "You should. Best time of the day."

And again turning to Hassan, he curtly ordered him to get a carriage—and no bazaar rattle-trap but one of the sort used by Officers.

Madame sprang up from her chair with an alacrity almost surprising, and with an involuntary exclamation which was quite surprising.

"But, *Monsieur le Colonel*, this is impossible!"

"Not a bit. Perfectly simple. Let Madame watch," and with a look before which Hassan quailed, he pointed that noble Arab to the door.

Hassan went. It was a pleasure to receive orders from a man like the Colonel. And a joy to see him so firmly humiliating Madame. He sped forth into the night, and quickly returned with an excellent carriage, the property of a gentleman who was not too contemptibly mean in the matter of *bakshish* to a profitable messenger.

The returning Hassan, having signified in the usual and somewhat mysterious manner that the front door should be opened, Madame arose, begged that she might be excused for deserting her honoured guest, and departed from the room. But the Colonel, quite well-endowed with his own forms of wiliness, got up and followed her, beckoning as he did so to Odette.

"Come along, Mam'selle Odette. I think I heard wheels," he said.

The Colonel was right. He had heard wheels; and he would have heard them again, departing, had he not been the quickly-acting *légionnaire* that he was. As he and Odette reached the front door, Madame was in the act of telling both Hassan and the driver of the carriage what she thought of them. Apparently she thought little, but needed many words in which to express it.

"Ah! So. Good. Not really worthy of Mademoiselle Odette, but quite passable," said the Colonel, and cast an eye over the two horses in just that all-seeing and know-ledgable manner which Denis Ducros had so often seen Colonel Louis Rochefort use when regarding his charger, before mounting it.

The driver sprang from his seat with great agility, and salaamed humbly as the rays of the lamp fell upon the Colonel's sleeve, gold-braided to the elbow.

"Look you!" grated the Colonel. "Take this Mademoiselle for a drive. Take her in whatever direction she wishes to go, and do not turn back until she tells you to do so. One word of complaint from Mademoiselle, and you'll get no *bakshish* . . . Something else instead . . . You understand me?"

The driver assured the Colonel that he understood perfectly, and that the *Sidi's* orders would be obeyed to the letter.

The Colonel opened the carriage door and handed Mademoiselle in, with the same courtesy that he would have shown to Madame Rochefort or her daughter.

"What about a wrap, or a shawl, or something?" he said. "Madame, I wonder if you would be so good as to send for—er—something suitable. Coat . . . Rug . . . What-not."

"*Merci! Merci beaucoup, Monsieur,*" replied Odette, wondering whether this were a dream blessed by St. Louis himself. But catching Madame's eye as she spoke, she realised that this was not a dream, and that however

143

much of a Prince Charming, *ce beau Monsieur* might be, Madame was no Fairy God-mother.

"*Mille remerciments, Monsieur*," she continued, "*mais il fait chaud ce soir*. Pff! Much too hot. I really want nothing."

But the Colonel perhaps knew more about night temperatures than did Odette, and had too often lain down on baking hot sand to awaken later frozen stiff with the cold of a bitter wind.

"Well, we'll have a rug anyway, and then you can use it if you want it. Madame, a rug, if you please, I said."

"Perhaps the little one would like the eider-down from my own bed?" cooed Madame, and the number of the teeth that adorned her smile was, in the Colonel's estimation, thirty-two if not more.

"Perhaps so," he said, "but I think a light woollen rug would be better. Hurry up, Madame. The night is but young, but—like you and me—it's growing older."

Silently Madame entered the house, and a minute or two later a mysterious-looking female, who incongruously enough, looked like a figure from a biblical picture, appeared, bearing in one hand a striped woven rug, while with the other she held across her entire front, with the exception of one half of one eye, the border of a comprehensive and all-concealing garment.

As he took the rug, the Colonel wondered if this excessive modesty were due to modesty, or to a regrettable ugliness of feature.

"There we are, *chèrie*," he said, putting the rug across Odette's knees. "Now go for your drive. Enjoy yourself . . . Be happy . . . And don't come back until you want to . . .

"Dawn is very lovely . . . Sometimes . . ." he added. "It is a pity you cannot get out to the real desert, and see the sun rise above the palms of an oasis . . . *Au 'voir*, Odette."

"*Mais, Monsieur le Colonel; cette Madame!* . . . She will . . ."

"Leave Madame to me. Forget Madame, and enjoy yourself," replied the Colonel.

And Odette, with feelings of deep and unadulterated gratitude such as she had almost forgotten, tried, wholly in vain, to tell this kind and courteous man what it meant to her to be treated with kindness and courtesy. Just as though she were really a woman with a woman's feelings.

"Drive on," he said sharply to the man, and turned back to enter the house.

He was feeling splendid; enjoying himself as he had never done before; savouring his power, importance and pride of place, as the sweetest draught that in a hitherto thwarted life had ever been presented to his lips.

He was like a Prince.

He was like that fellow whose name he could not remember; like one of those Kings who went about in disguise among common men, doing good secretly. Doing it for their own satisfaction, but with the gloriously satisfying knowledge that they had the power to carry out any benevolent scheme that, at the moment should appeal to them.

Well, for the moment, he had power, the undoubtedly considerable local power of Colonel Louis Rochefort.

CHAPTER IX

DIVERSIONS ON THE PATH OF GLORY

AS he turned from the front door and the salaaming Hassan to go back to the *salon*, he was aware that someone was descending the principal staircase, across the entrance to which hung the jingling bead curtain.

At any rate a pair of highly-polished and spurred black riding-boots was doing so.

And Spahi riding-breeches above them. Yes. A Spahi! Now who would it . . . ?

Name of a name . . . It was the Spahis' Major . . . It was. Yes, it was Major de Beauchamp!

As that distinguished officer stepped through the bead

curtain, he hummed a merry little tune, swung his great cloak gracefully about him—and saw within a few feet of him the grim and stern-faced figure of his enemy, the man with whom he had had bitter words, and had waged bitter official warfare. Almost he could have shot himself, with mortification, for he had frequently and publicly spoken evil of the morals of the Foreign Legion, and had condemned them as men incontinent and carnal. Men wholly unlike those mounted paladins, those centaur heroes, those models of discipline and virtue, his own Spahis.

And doubtless this wooden-headed foot-slogger was here as Senior Officer of the garrison, on some official visit.

Sort of Cantonment Magistrate, or something, wasn't he?

Peste! What a devilish piece of bad luck.

What line should he take? The gay insouciant . . . Both men of the world . . . Boys will be boys, and all that. Or pretend that he had taken it into his head to pay a visit in his official capacity and see that Madame's little restaurant was conducted in a quiet and orderly manner, since he had reason to think his own officers looked in here occasionally—for a coffee-and-cognac and a little music . . .

Too thin . . . Rochefort wasn't a fool. He could see those hard eyes glitter and the thin lips curl with contempt, if he tried any nonsense of that sort.

Nor was Rochefort the sort of man with whom one could take the line of:

"Well, well, Colonel! Here we are again . . . What? Official? Periodical visits of inspection?" and then roar with laughter.

No . . . Rochefort was what he looked. What everyone knew him to be—a man of strictest life and most rigid principle.

But, damn it all, the fellow wasn't his Father Confessor, was he? To Hell with him.

Curse it all, he'd take no line at all, except a straight line to the front door. He'd cut him dead.

146

Thus thinking, and without pause, the magnificent Spahi officer, as fine a figure of a *beau sabreur* as could be found in all Africa or Europe either, strode haughtily past Denis, who, *planté là*, stood with hand on hip in the Rochefort manner and eyed him with coldest severity.

Just as Major de Beauchamp reached the front door he heard the voice of the man whom he detested and, for some reason, feared a little.

"Will not *Monsieur le Majeur* take his *képi*?" asked the cold suave voice, with more than a suspicion of mockery.

"Damn the fellow!" cursed de Beauchamp, thus halted in his stride, his gallant exit ruined.

Savagely he swung about and nearly knocked Hassan head over heels, for that ubiquitous and soft-treading minion had appeared at the right moment, bearing the Major's cap, gloves and riding-whip.

The beautiful gold-embroidered *képi* was thus knocked from Hassan's hand, and in the act of stepping forward, Major de Beauchamp trod heavily upon it.

Flustered by anger and annoyance, he did what, in his normal condition, he would never have dreamt of doing.

He actually stooped for his own *képi*.

So did Hassan, just as swiftly and suddenly.

Their heads collided with resounding impact.

Denis Ducros laughed aloud.

Major de Beauchamp sprang erect, and with a violent shove that was hardly a blow, sent Hassan reeling backward till he fell over a chair and knocked a large brass vase, containing a potted palm, from a marble-topped blackwood table that stood against the wall.

It fell upon the tiled floor of the hall with a crash that seemed to shake the house, and which shook the soul of Madame to its depths.

The *salon* door flew open and she rushed forth, a tigress in defence of her own.

Rough-housing! She knew how to cope with that if anyone did.

"*Messieurs! Messieurs!* But what is this?" she screamed, looking like an enraged macaw.

"Major de Beauchamp fighting Hassan," replied Denis. "First round is the Major's."

Hassan, thinking doubtless that discretion is the better part and that there is something in the "happy low lie down" theory of life, remained where he had fallen, his body artistically draped about the palm, which now indeed appeared to grow from him, his head reposing in reasonable comfort upon a little pile of earth.

He felt fine, and that he looked fine—lying there prostrate, wounded, bleeding he hoped, possibly dying, doing his duty. (There'd certainly be *bakshish* in this.) A simple man, humble, obscure, but faithful to the last . . . defending . . . Oh, Allah! What was this? He was going to sneeze. The earth just beneath his nose was but dust.

Violently he sneezed and abandoned the pose of the Dying Servant.

"Good! I thought *Monsieur le Majeur* had killed him in the first round," observed Denis, regarding the body.

Madame said something that she certainly had not learned in her Passy boarding-school.

De Beauchamp said something that he certainly had learned from the rude soldiery; and marched from the house, loudly banging the heavy door behind him.

Madame and Denis eyed each other, the former with emotions which she strove to conceal, the latter with undisguised amusement.

"Evening's waking up, Madame," he smiled. "Getting quite gay, aren't we?"

"A matter of opinion and a matter of taste, *Monsieur le Colonel*," replied Madame somewhat shortly. "I do not like anything unseemly in my house. And I won't have it. We live very quietly here, and . . ."

"Quite right, Madame. I fully agree. If I were you I should remove the name of Major de Beauchamp from my visiting-list. Disgraceful . . . Coming here throwing potted palm trees at the servants . . . And then marching off without saying good-bye . . . Not *comme il faut* at all . . ."

The Colonel's reference to servants and potted palms turned Madame's attention to the still prostrate Hassan, who had decided to hope that there was still a sound chance of *bakshish* for any man who, in the proper pursuit of his lawful tasks, should be wantonly and violently assaulted and felled to the ground. A pity about the blood. A spot or two would have been worth a lot.

But there was one thing he could do, if he couldn't bleed. He could limp—and limp he would until . . .

The current of his thoughts was suddenly broken . . . An assault in the rear . . . Madame's toe.

"Are you going to sleep there all night, you lazy dog?" asked the well-known voice of the faithful servant's understanding mistress. "Get this mess cleared up, and re-pot that plant."

Turning away, she added with complete finality, and, as Hassan realised, complete truth,

"You're fined a week's pay."

Hassan watered the earth with his tears, as he re-potted the palm. . . . *Bakshish!* . . . By Allah, it was too much; and Hassan wept afresh.

On returning to the *salon*, the Colonel found it apparent that a certain unrest, not to say discontent, was manifest. The centre of the mildly cyclonic disturbance appeared to be Fifine, who seemed to feel that, though neither she nor Odette had the slightest claim or right to an evening drive, she had at least as much a right and claim as Odette.

And Odette had gone.

Then why should not Fifine go? For an hour or two Odette was as free as a bird. She had escaped from her cage. Then why not Fifine? Surely Fifine was at least as deserving as Odette.

Like Hassan, Fifine wept.

The other girls comforted her; the Colonel enquired as to the cause of her tears, and promptly bade her dry them. Of course she should have her wish, exactly as Odette had. She should go for a drive, and go at once. Turning to Madame, he begged her to be so good as to send Hassan for another carriage.

So good? Madame replied, in effect, that though undoubtedly good, she did not propose to be as good as all that.

Whereupon the Colonel, though he did not remove the velvet glove from the hand of steel, did seem to loosen it.

"*Ah!* . . . *Indeed?*" he said, a Rochefort to the life. "I can only doubt that Madame failed to hear exactly what I said."

"But not at all, *Monsieur le Colonel*," replied Madame. "My hearing is perfect, and *Monsieur le Colonel* spoke with moderate distinctness."

"*Ah!* . . . *Indeed?*" said the Colonel once again, and yet more sarcastically. "Madame positively declines to send Hassan to get another carriage?"

Madame indicated that the Colonel had grasped the idea quite accurately.

"So Madame is thinking of retiring!" observed the Colonel conversationally, and as though changing the subject.

Madame's narrowed eyes opened a little.

"Retiring, Monsieur? Does *Monsieur le Colonel* think then that I look tired, or that my evenings end thus early?"

The Colonel yawned and poured wine.

"Retiring from business, Madame," explained the Colonel patiently. "Closing your school and sending your pupils home."

It was an absurd supposition that Madame's face seemed to him to pale a little. But its expression undoubtedly changed—for she had understood the hint.

The Colonel had given a slight nod of his handsome head, and a nod was quite as good as a wink to Madame, who was so very far from blind. This man had powers in Sidi-bel-Abbès; tremendous powers, legal powers, as well as command of the absolute and blind obedience of hundreds of men who would—remove her house, stone by stone, if he told them to do so.

And of course he had come to spy upon her.

What a fool she'd been!

Could it be that she was getting old, losing grip? Never. No.

Not if she lived to be eighty, ninety, a hundred even. But she'd have to go carefully with this Menace.

It was a shame that women should be put upon as she was.

Always the way! The same old story. Men were the enemy, the loathsome creatures. They hated to see a woman successful.

It was a cruel shame. Just when everything was going so nicely. No trouble anywhere. Everybody happy. And such nice girls, with plenty of kind friends.

And now this . . .

What was his object? Just sheer trouble-seeking for the sake of seeking trouble? And one of the sort that makes it if he cannot find it?

Well, there it was, and no help for it. What he said, went—and anyone whom he told to go, went; "also ran," in fact.

Ah, well! she had handled men before—and got the best of them.

"Why, no, *mon cher Colonel!* Not, at least, while I have the pleasure of visits from so distinguished a gentleman as *Monsieur le Colonel* Rochefort," she said.

And let the interfering, tricky, trouble-maker take note of *that*. For, when all was said and done, he *was* visiting her house—and although undoubtedly he could ruin her, she might sing a little song about him, herself.

And was not Madame Rochefort said to be *très sérieuse*, and as genuinely strict and proper as this sacred animal pretended to be?

"Good," responded the Colonel blandly. "I somehow got the impression . . . just a foolish idea . . . that we might be losing Madame . . . But no, of course not," and with a slight change of voice and apparent inconsequence added,

"But we are forgetting about that carriage."

And steadily the Colonel looked Madame in the eye.

Madame hesitated but for the fraction of a second, and then rose to obey what was evidently a command.

As the door closed behind her, the girl Fifine rushed at the Colonel, flung her arms about his neck and kissed him rapturously, and with abandon.

Ere the Colonel had time to acknowledge and return

this demonstration of affection, it appeared that the example of Fifine was inspiring and irresistibly infectious.

Justine, the beautiful, showed that, though she might think but slowly, she could act quickly—and headed the swarm. Almost simultaneously the Colonel was seized, embraced, kissed, patted, hugged, and richly endowed with every term of endearment, by the spontaneously enthusiastic group of laughing grateful girls.

Only one stood smilingly watching the scene—the Provençal girl, Nicolette.

The door opened, and Madame entered.

"Mon Dieu!" she whispered, at the sight. Was she wrong after all? Had she misjudged the man? . . . In every way? . . . Unless her eyes deceived her, he was now over-doing it. Kissing the whole bunch at once, and enjoying himself hugely.

Well! Well! She thought she knew something about men, but this one was a puzzler.

At the return of Madame, the bright enthusiasm of the girls waned a little, or its expression became more restrained. Nevertheless they looked happier than they had done for a long time.

The sound of approaching wheels was heard, and Madame addressed Fifine, first with a snake-like stare and then in acid mockery.

"The carriage waits, *miladi*," she snarled.

But Fifine was not to be daunted or deterred by Madame's venomous manner and address. She sprang up, clapping her hands, and ran to enjoy her little breath of freedom.

"Ah, good!" said the Colonel, following her. "Let's see what the carriage is like."

Bowing and smiling, Hassan assured him that it was of the best; and the Colonel assured Hassan that, for his sake, he hoped it was.

All was satisfactory. Hassan had done as well for Fifine as he had for Odette; and to the driver the Colonel gave the same orders and the same cold quiet threat that carried deep conviction.

The driver was the third Arab, that night, who, while

freely admitting that all things are possible to Allah, realised that he was beholding wonders.

As Fifine swept gaily away, waving her hand, kissing her finger-tips to the Colonel, and crying like an excited child, *"Merci! Merci! Merci!"* Madame's feelings completely overcame her.

She was driven to speech.

She spoke to Hassan, to his detriment and sorrow.

Once again the Colonel returned to the *salon*, lingering, ere he closed the door, to lend an appreciative ear to Madame's plaint. And this time it was quite clear that that discontent which has been termed divine, was rife and rampant. . . .

Obviously the girls had decided that Odette and Fifine had chosen the better part and they wanted a part of that part. Woman like, they wanted to do as others did. They wanted to go out and escape from this stuffy hole of a house. As Justine said, they wanted to *brrrreathe.*

The Colonel assured them promptly that, by the laws of Madame la République, which in their military manifestations it was his privilege to administer in that garrison city, they had a perfect right to breathe; and breathe they should.

Springing up, laughing, singing, and with little exclamations of happiness that did almost lend them the air of being what they were called, *filles de joie*, the girls again surrounded the Colonel and signified in what they considered the appropriate manner, their gratitude and appreciation of his amazingly disinterested kindness.

Were there really men, pondered Nicolette, who could do something for a woman and expect nothing in return? Men who were kind for the sake of kindness, and in the true spirit of kindness; who gave pleasure for the sake of giving pleasure?

And was this one of them?

If so, he was the first she had ever met. She had known very little of men, scarcely anything of boys, indeed; until, as a gaping country fool, she had listened to the lies of the abominable half-mad poseur and liar who had made her believe she had something more than a

153

pretty face; that he was desperately in love with her; and that she was in love with him . . .

Yes, this Colonel was *kind*.

"A drive! A drive! A drive!" chorused the girls, dancing round the Colonel.

"Well now," asked that hero, "would you like to go in pairs or all in a party, or what?"

Quickly it was decided that Marie and Greta would go together; that Tatiana, the tall, temperamental Russian girl, who was now crying for joy or for some other reason, would go alone; and that Dolores, Concepcion and Maddalena would like to share a carriage.

"What a din! What a din!" protested the laughing Colonel, as the girls made their arrangements.

So thought Madame as she entered the *salon* with her sharp and menacing cry of,

"Girls!" only to be swept through the doorway and back into the hall by the rush of her excited flock, now undisciplined to the point of mutiny. Indeed, to Madame, it was mutiny most complete; most appalling and villainous, that these slaves of hers should treat her with this utter disregard.

Better insolence, insult, defiance, anything rather than this complete ignoring of herself and her authority.

"Girls!" she screamed, again both looking and sounding like an angry parrot. "Stop! Stop! Come back at once. Come here, all of you!"

But she might as well have addressed a flight of chattering starlings, swift upon the wing, for all the response vouchsafed to her cries and orders.

Nothing remained but a vision of long silk-stockinged legs and twinkling heels vanishing up the stairs as the girls rushed to their rooms to find what they could in the way of scraps of chiffon, scarves and wraps.

Madame eyed the Colonel in doubt, fear and seething rage.

"It would appear *en effet* then, that *Monsieur le Colonel* proposes to take charge of my poor establishment."

"Just like that," smiled the Colonel.

"Please send Hassan for—let's see—three, four, oh,

154

better say half-a-dozen more carriages; and tell him to see that each is better than the last."

"Better than the next, too," he added. "Far better. Tell him I'll have a look at them—and at him as well, if they are not to my liking."

Madame, suppressing sentiments that were better suppressed, left the *salon*, to see what could be done to induce the girls to take a more serious view of life; and the Colonel, as he poured himself a glass of wine, realised that he was not alone.

CHAPTER X

THE WOMAN ON THE PATH

IT was the girl Nicolette who had remained behind.

He poured two glasses.

"Mademoiselle is not going for a moon-light drive with the others?" he asked, as he gave her the wine.

"No, *Monsieur le Colonel*," smiled the girl.

"But why? It would do you good, I'm sure . . . Don't you worry about anything Madame might say. *I*'ll do the 'saying' to-night, for a change."

"Monsieur is too kind. But it was not that," replied the girl.

"Oh, well!" thought the Colonel, "probably expecting somebody"; and then found himself most inexplicably and unexpectedly wishing that she had not been expecting somebody, and that she had accepted his offer of a drive, and been as pleased and grateful about it as all the others had been.

"And what would Mademoiselle like to do instead?" he asked with the air of a *grand seigneur* whose protégés had but to ask and their wishes were inevitably granted— provided he felt like granting them.

"*Monsieur le Colonel* was good enough to say that he would like to hear a Provençal song," replied the girl. "If so I should like to get my guitar and sing him one or two—that he has probably heard before."

155

"There is nothing that would give me greater pleasure, Mademoiselle," replied the Colonel, quite truthfully—for at the moment he could think of nothing nicer than listening to a song from home, sung by a very pretty girl in the patois that had once been the real language of a great country, the patois that was his mother tongue.

And 'pretty' girl did he call her? She was more than that, and only wanted a month on a sea-beach with sunshine, pure air and plenty of sleep, to be a very beautiful girl.

She was a real type; the sort of lovely that had made Arles, Nimes, Tarascon and Avignon famous for the beauty of their women; and it was weariness, late hours, wretchedness and general illness and misery that spoilt and obscured the loveliness of the perfect features. Thin-faced, pale, hollow-cheeked, with dull eyes set in dark rings, or rather saucers, she was but a caricature of what she would be under healthy and happy conditions, and leading the sort of life for which God had meant her.

"Do you often give them the pleasure of hearing you?" he asked.

"What, here in the *salon, Monsieur le Colonel*? Oh, no. They aren't the sort of songs that would interest the girls. Nor would Madame be entirely—er—sympathetic. But I could sing our little folk-songs to *Monsieur le Colonel* if we could be alone."

The Colonel was conscious of a slight sense of disappointment. Wanted him alone, eh? Natural enough, wasn't it? What else should he expect?

"I'll get my guitar," said Nicolette. "If it would really give Monsieur pleasure to hear some songs."

"It really would," smiled the Colonel, and opened the door.

How long was it since a man had opened a door for her; shown her a little politeness for politeness sake?

There was the sound of an avalanche descending the stairs, enriched by that of a wild tornado, the shrill high shrieks of which were provided by the voices of the girls, the ominous undertones by that of Madame, who completely failed to ride this whirlwind or to direct the storm.

Avalanche and tornado swept through and out of the house, leaving behind it a great peace. This, however, was soon broken by the never still small voice of Madame, valiant in defeat; still brave, if broken in spirit.

Catching sight of Nicolette, who was going up to her room for her guitar, Madame nodded her head in confirmation of her suspicions. So that was the idea.

But, Name of St. Louis! Did he have to empty the whole house that he might talk in private with this Nicolette creature. Would he like Madame, and Hassan and the rest of the domestics to clear out too? The whole house to himself?

What this man wanted was a town to himself. Why didn't he take a few marquees and half a dozen tents and a caravan, and have an oasis in the Sahara all to himself?

Or was she wrong, and had he bidden this one also go for a drive? Perhaps in a State Coach and four.

There were things called hearses, weren't there, in which some people took drives?

"And would one be over-inquisitive in enquiring whether *Monsieur le Colonel* intends completely to empty my poor house of all its occupants?" she asked sweetly. "Would *Monsieur le Colonel* prefer that I too went for . . . a drive?"

"Do you a lot of good, Madame," said the Colonel, showing his teeth in what may have been a smile. "But there is one girl who, I hope, is sound asleep in her bed, since she chose a little rest as what she wanted more than anything. And Nicolette is going to sing to me."

"*A-a-a-h-h-h!*" breathed Madame, on a note of deep and wide comprehension. "But that arranges itself, one sees. But *Monsieur le Colonel* could have enjoyed his music without all the unnecessary expense to which he has put himself, surely?"

"For me that is nothing . . . Nothing," replied the Colonel truthfully.

Nicolette returned with her guitar.

"Oh, you're going to strum on that thing too, are you?" said Madame, and Madame sniffed.

"One can hear them at any time," he agreed graciously.

"What one cannot hear every day," he added, "are the songs of one's childhood, sung in the language in which one talked as a child."

"I am not a great player or singer," said the girl deprecatingly, as she smiled and glanced towards the Colonel.

"*Monsieur le Colonel* will excuse me," said Madame, turning to depart.

"With genuine pleasure, Madame," said the Colonel. "But if I may first so far trouble Madame, I should like her to show us to a clean and quiet room where the air is fresh, and . . ."

"All my rooms are clean and quiet—and fresh," answered Madame, as indignantly as she dared.

"Doubtless," said the Colonel. "But this one, for example, has some faint suggestion of a bar-room, hasn't it? Just a *soupçon* of a smell of tobacco, alcohol, scent, and—other odours. All very nice indeed, at the right time."

"What's wrong with the girl's own room?" snapped Madame, whose politeness, under the wear and tear of this trying evening, was growing thin.

"I don't know," replied the Colonel. "Nothing, I imagine. Unless it be the size and ventilation. What I want, as I just endeavoured to indicate to you, Madame, is a cool, quiet and clean sitting-room; one reasonably comfortable, in which I can hear Mademoiselle's songs without being suffocated, annoyed, or reminded of where we are."

"One quite understands, *Monsieur le Colonel*. It leaps to the eye. A setting suitable for Mam'selle and her world-famous performance. . . . One's only regret—and it will be with one while life remains—is that *Monsieur le Colonel* did not give one a little notice of his coming. . . .

"One could have had something suitable built," added Madame.

"Well, failing that," replied the Colonel, with the Rochefort rasp invading his voice, "show me another room."

"If *Monsieur le Colonel* and her Ladyship would graciously follow me," said Madame, and led the way across the hall to the room from the door of which the

Colonel had seen a girl watch his first entrance into the house.

Although it probably would look different in sunlight, it had, at any rate, the appearance of being the kind of room for which the Colonel had asked; and was at any rate free from tobacco-smoke, the fumes of alcohol, or evidences of recent occupation.

"Would this be a reasonably suitable setting for the distinguished performance of . . ."

"It will do," answered the Colonel shortly. "Kindly note that we do not wish to be disturbed."

"But naturally, Monsieur. *Cela va sans dire,*" said Madame, with an edged smile. "Would not Monsieur like a little wine?" she enquired perfunctorily, as she turned to go.

"Mademoiselle?" asked the Colonel, turning to the girl, with an enquiring lift of his eyebrow.

"No, thank you, *M'sieu',*" smiled Nicolette, pleased at a deferential courtesy to which she had long been unaccustomed.

Madame, on the other hand, did not look pleased. Had not the fool yet learned that one of her few uses in life was to further the sale of Madame's wine?

"No wine," replied the Colonel. "But I am sure Mademoiselle would like coffee and a sandwich later. So should I. I will ring."

Madame departed.

Coffee! There were people in Constantinople and one or two other places who had found coffee an unwholesome form of refreshment! However, she promised herself a word, several words indeed, with that Nicolette. The girl had quite a lot to learn even yet.

Well, she was in a good school.

"Where would Mademoiselle like to sit?" asked the Colonel.

"This will do beautifully, thank you," and Nicolette seated herself on a *pouffe* of Moroccan leather. The Colonel settled himself comfortably on the deep wide divan, and relaxed.

Real comfort! Luxury! This play-acting, strutting

159

and striding, was apt to grow tiring if the play went on too long. Three hours was long enough for any performance. Now he'd rest for a while. Just rest and sit back and look at himself—and at this delightful girl whom he felt he had known all his life.

What a night it had been!

And in what an amazing situation it had landed him. Lying on an infinitely comfortable divan, with a most charming and acquiescent companion anxious to entertain him and give him pleasure.

Really he was like that fellow, What's-his-name— Sheikh or King or Caliph Somebody—sitting there in lordly ease, with a *houri* in attendance to make music for his sole delight.

He was dreaming, of course, probably on the plank "bed" of the guard-room.

"What shall I sing first, Monsieur?" asked Nicolette, as she strummed the air of *Sur le pont d'Avignon*. "Why, as much of all that as you can remember. I never heard more than the one verse."

"Nor I," replied Nicolette, "though I believe some of the old people know a whole song, of which we now know only the chorus. Grandmère used to say that her grand-père knew dozens of verses."

"Quite likely," said the Colonel, "and very probably he knew a lot of old *jongleur* songs in the Langue d'Oc, and very much as the minstrels and troubadours used to sing them in the days of King René."

"I know some that are said to be quite old," said the girl. "I tried to make a collection of them when I was going on the stage."

"Oh, have you been on the stage? Actress? Professional singer?" asked the Colonel. "That accounts . . ."

"'Going,' I said," interrupted Nicolette. "Still going for that matter."

"Didn't it come off then?" he asked.

"No," replied the girl shortly, as she struck a chord on her guitar.

"I was a complete failure," she added, as the plangent wail died away.

"Do you know the song of *The Cat who went a-fishing*?"

"*Pardieu*, yes! I haven't heard that song for a quarter of a century," laughed the Colonel. "And there was a time when I used to hear it almost every day of my life."

The girl broke into a lively air which to a stranger, or even to a Frenchman who knew neither the place where the Cat went fishing, nor the patois in which his adventures are told, would have been merely a lively air. Just a primrose by a musical river's brim.

But to Denis Ducros and Nicolette, it was something more, a whole garden of memories.

There was a little silence after she had finished.

"Do you know what I would like next?" asked Denis.

"What, Monsieur?" The girl smiled happily.

"The same song again, please," was the reply, and the delighted Nicolette sang again the song that she had first heard in her cradle.

"And now what about *In the Vineyard of Monsieur Dulac*."

Nicolette laughed.

"Yes. He was a queer old gentleman, *ce bon papa Bompard Dulac*," nodded Denis, in answer to the girl's laugh.

Silence again followed the singing of the *chanson* which enshrined the epic story of the notorious love affair of the respectable Monsieur Bompard Dulac, who owned the famous vineyard of Valcœur.

Song followed song, each bringing back memories, happy, painful and poignant.

A long silence fell, and Nicolette sat gazing into the past.

The Colonel stood up.

"I will not try to tell you how much I enjoyed that, Nicolette," he said. "It is a pleasure I never expected to have again. I don't profess to be a judge of music nor of singing, but I should hardly have thought you could have been a failure. For my part I found the performance . . . entrancing."

"Monsieur is too kind; and of course Monsieur is biased," replied the girl.

"In favour of Nicolette?" smiled the Colonel.

"In favour of Provence, Monsieur."

The Colonel studied the girl's face.

How in the name of God did she come to be here, a slave in the chain-gang owned by Madame. Literally a slave, bought and sold and owned for life, body and soul. And different from the other girls as though she were of some other race and breed, some other natural order of a different world.

And yet she was not. She was of the same world; the half-world.

Yet that face bore no sign of vice, depravity, nor even that feeble weakness which is so often the cause and origin of both.

It was a calm face, kind, and sweet; the mouth was generous, the eyes gentle; there was nothing hard, or predatory in its expression; nor was it a sensual face.

No, he was not idealising it. Not seeing it through a vinous haze of silly sentimentality. Nor through the golden dust-haze of a Provençal evening.

It was a good face.

And yet here she was, in Madame's house, earning her living—like this.

It must have been a long and weary road and full of strange turnings, by which she had travelled from the village near Arles, to this house in Sidi-bel-Abbès.

Poor little pilgrim!

What could her story be? Probably quite common and sordid. No. Not with that face. Not common; but no doubt the element of sordid villainy was not lacking somewhere in the tale.

The girl looked up at him and smiled.

He liked that smile.

He loved it.

Not professional. Not intentionally alluring. Not the provocative invitation.

It was just friendly, spontaneous. Kindly.

God bless his soul, he had almost called it *innocent* again.

He must be careful. He must remember that he was tough; that he was a *légionnaire*; that he neither feared, nor believed in, God nor man, much less in woman. There was a lad named Samson once, wasn't there, who had been a useful scrapper in his day. Doubtless he thought that his Delilah's smile was just friendly, spontaneous, and kindly.

Conceivably the fool had almost called it innocent; and, so far as one knew, the good soldier Samson had not met the young woman in quite such a dubious place as this.

Perhaps Samson the Soldier had . . . To Hell with Samson the Soldier and his Philistine tart.

This was a Provençal girl, with a friendly face; a good face; an *innocent* face . . .

"Come and sit by me," he said abruptly. "I want to talk to you."

And the two lost children of Provence seated themselves, side by side, on the divan.

"Tell me," said Denis Ducros, "if you care to . . . Everything . . . Or tell me nothing at all, if you'd rather."

Nicolette sat silent beside the man whose kindness was almost unbearable.

What a fool she was, to be unable to speak when she so longed to tell him of her gratitude that he should be so *gentil* to a girl like her.

It was the unexpectedness, the incredible difference. She had not known that there were men like this. Probably there were no others. And yet he was a great man; a distinguished and powerful man. To think that such a one should have time to be courteous and kind to Nicolette, the . . . the girl in Madame's House! No doubt he was kind and courteous to everybody, but he had been, or he had seemed to be, so genuinely interested, understanding. But then he had been like that to all the girls.

It was only because she came from Provence that he had taken special notice of her.

And he had treated her as though she had been of his own world.

Suddenly she found her voice.

CHAPTER XI

A STORY BY THE WAYSIDE

"I SHOULD love to tell you . . . everything, *Monsieur le Colonel*," she said. "If it would really interest you."

"It would really and deeply interest me," was the reply.

"I suppose Monsieur does not know Domeuil, near Arles."

The Colonel gave a short laugh.

"Know it! I know every house in it! Almost the name of every occupant of every house—and of his dog too. I can see the *brioches* and the long crusty loaves in the window of the shop of old Pierre Boulanger."

"Why, yes!" said Nicolette. "I used to go to that shop every morning, to fetch his little grand-daughter to take her to school; and he always used to give us one of those *brioches* between us, and tell us not to swallow it whole. . . . He was a dear old man."

"And got drunk every night of his life at Benoit's wine-shop, after three games of dominoes with Jean Tousseau; and was fetched home by his wife . . . *Ma foi!* But that one was something of a Sergeant-Major."

Nicolette laughed delightedly.

"I went in terror of her," she said, "though she was never unkind to me, and I had no reason to fear her. But I always imagined myself mislaying the little Hélène on the way home from school, and having to go to Madame Boulanger and confess that I had lost her. I think I should have run away from home rather than face her."

"I certainly should never have faced her," said the Colonel. "I was more afraid of her than I was of any man."

"I don't think Monsieur was ever afraid of anybody."

"I was of that one, I assure you! I used to think she was a witch and in league with the Devil. Probably was . . ."

"And poor old crippled Gautier, the cobbler?" asked the girl. "Do you remember him?"

"Rather. Twisted and lame, and blind in one eye, and

as good a workman as ever stitched leather. A humorist too, in spite of everything. Always amused, and amusing."

"And kind, too," said Nicolette. "One gets the idea that deformed people are always bitter and malicious. But he wasn't."

"No," agreed the Colonel. "He had a great heart, and real courage. Do you remember how one went inside his little cave of a shop, to take him a pair of shoes to mend, and there was always a clean duster or towel on the little seat opposite to where he worked—all ready for you to sit down and have a chat? He loved to talk. The tales he used to tell of 1870. I am not sure that it wasn't he who made me a soldier."

"Yes, yes," said Nicolette eagerly. "Why, he'd even tell us girls about 1870. Not about his own doings or the fighting, but about how hard it was for the women to keep their homes going; to feed the children; and to carry on while the men were away, fighting for our France; how the women tried to do the men's work in the vineyards, in the fields; and in the forests, getting wood in the winter ... I've sat for hours on that seat, listening to Père Gautier."

"So have I," said the Colonel. "But it must have been long before your time. I am nearly old enough to be your father."

Nicolette turned and studied his face again ... What a nice face it was, with its steady eyes, and kindly mocking smile—the face of a *giver* among all the millions of takers.

"No, *Monsieur le Colonel*," she said. "My father is a very much older man than you."

"Anyway, I can hardly imagine that I ever saw you when I visited Domeuil," said the Colonel. "Though it would be pleasant to think that we had actually met before—in Provence."

"That would be wonderful indeed," said Nicolette. "But it is already wonderful that *Monsieur le Colonel* should know the place at all. And the very people among whom I grew up."

"Some wise man has already discovered that the world is a very small place, Mademoiselle."

"I suppose Monsieur must have visited Domeuil quite often," said Nicolette.

"Yes ... Yes ... I used to spend my holidays there. Staying near some people named—er—de Cassignac."

"*Oh!*" said the girl; and there was something in the exclamation that caught the Colonel's attention.

"Now that de Cassignac was another queer one," he said. "There was madness in that family. Been in that tiny corner of the world too long, and thought there was no one good enough to marry them, except their own cousins. A thoroughly bad man," he mused. "One of the sort they did well in clearing out, during the Revolution ... Always a marvel to me that he kept clear of the Law ... A wonder no one ever shot him from behind a hedge, one moonlight night. There were brothers, and husbands and fathers enough, who had reason to ... Just as well that he was the last of his line."

He yawned and apologised.

Silence.

"Had no children at all, had he?" he asked casually.

"One," replied the girl.

"Really? ... After I left those parts, perhaps ... Don't say it was a son to carry on that noble line ..."

"It was a son," said Nicolette.

"And he is following in father's footsteps no doubt," hazarded the Colonel.

"No ... He's not," she said shortly. "I killed him."

It took a great deal to surprise Denis Ducros nowadays, but here was something quite out of the ordinary. He had heard of fiends in human form; women with lovely faces, who were devils; but he had not the faintest belief in such phenomena. In his humble opinion and wide experience, evil people had evil faces, and good people had good faces.

This girl had a good face, and on that fact he built his faith in her.

"You did what?" he said lightly, as though she must be joking.

"I killed Raoul de Cassignac."

"Good! I am quite sure he must have deserved it."

166

Still he asked no questions, though he drew quick and obvious conclusions.

So that was it! That was how this unusual girl was started on that dreadful road which led from Domeuil in Provence to Madame's house in Sidi-bel-Abbès.

The old, old story. The petty Seigneur's dissipated son, and the village beauty. Following in his father's footsteps.

Pity the old man's footsteps hadn't led him to an earlier grave.

Same sad old sordid story. But, for once, a damned scoundrel had got what he deserved. A marvel she had got away with it. As a rule the police haven't far to look for motives when a young blackguard of that sort gets what is coming to him. It can't be often that a village girl shoots or stabs the son of the big man of the neighbourhood, and lives to tell the tale.

"And so you killed him, eh?" mused Denis in some wonderment.

Well, this weird old World can still provide its little surprises. This dove-like girl a, well, what they call a murderess.

"Yes. Yet for some reason I don't feel like a murderess. Perhaps because it was an accident, in a way," she said, as though following his unspoken thought.

"Oh-h-h! An accident, was it?"

"Well—yes and no. It was both an accident and a murder, you see. It was an accident, because I never dreamt of causing his death in that way. It never entered my head."

"Well, if it was an accident, and you never thought of doing such a thing, why call it murder?"

"Because I had murder in my heart. Because I wanted to kill him. Because, if I had known that what I did would kill him, I would have done it intentionally."

"Well, then it looks more like the finger of Providence, or what they call the hand of God, or something of that sort. Since, as you say, you hadn't set out to kill him."

"Set out to kill him!" said the girl. "That evening . . . I set out to meet him because I loved him. Loved him . . . there are no words . . .

"I was in love for the first time in my life, and it was the full of the moon, and the most perfect night the world has ever seen. And I thought he was the noblest, truest, kindest ...

"Little *fool*! I thought he loved me as I did him. Truly and for ever ... And that he ... I thought he ... Oh, what does it matter what I thought?

"Well, my Fairy Prince begged his village Cinderella to come up through the vineyards and meet him in the Château rose-garden by an ancient marble seat that was supposed to have come from Rome in the old days. I slipped out and went to our meeting as though I were walking straight to Heaven. He was there, sitting on the seat, waiting for me—which was something, I suppose.

"Probably he had no better sport for that evening.

"When I sat beside him he put his arms about me and kissed me. So sweetly, so kindly, and oh, had I but known it, so expertly. Such knowledge and experience of women and fools of village girls!

"I thought I should die of happiness and joy and love.

"Ah, well! I was a girl of Provence, and in love for the first time. And oh, how deep in love! And then, in his laughing whisper, he said that Roman seats were hard and uncomfortable and never made for love, and begged me to creep with him into the house, which by now was all dark and silent.

"Just up that little outside staircase and through that door we could see in the moonlight, and we should be in his room, which he'd love to show me. We should be so much more at our ease. We had to be so cautious in the garden. Servants. Watchmen. And his father often walked in the garden after dinner. He pretended to be afraid of his father, and that he had so nasty a mind that he would think ill of me if he caught us there.

"Would you believe it, Monsieur, that a girl could be such a fool? Even a village girl, ignorant and innocent as I was then; though that may seem impossible to you. Can you believe that I went into that house with him without a thought of harm or wrong or danger?"

"In point of fact, I believe anything you tell me,
168

Nicolette, and I am perfectly certain that you were a sweet fool, innocent and ignorant," said Denis Ducros.

"What with excitement, and a little fright, and immeasurable love, I was trembling. My heart was beating so fast and so loudly that I thought people might hear it. And as he closed the door behind us, I turned and put my arms about Raoul's neck, overcome, overwhelmed with love for him . . ."

Silence.

"That was the last kiss—of love—that I ever gave a man."

Silence again.

"It was like one of those folk-tales about bewitched and transformed beasts and men. The Princess kisses the Beast and he turns into the beautiful Prince. That sort of thing. Only this was just the opposite. I kissed the Prince and he turned into—the Beast.

"It *was* a beast. A savage and horrible beast. I don't think I ever quite recovered from the shock I got that night. It seemed to me that he had gone completely mad, and that I was in most horrible danger.

"He *was* mad, and I had to fight for my life."

"He was mad, Nicolette," agreed the Colonel. "There was a *terrible* form of madness in that family. Terrible . . . vile . . . and historical. Had you heard no tales in the village?"

"No, but I knew there were tales about the old man. I never knew quite what it was, because people always stopped talking . . . And Raoul was only just back from Paris . . . And he had been gentleness and sweetness itself until he locked that door and I kissed him.

"It really was like our were-wolf stories. It really was just as if one saw a man turn into a wolf or some other dreadful beast, before one's eyes.

"And how strong he was! But so was I; and I knew I was fighting for my life. Time after time he got me down, but we struggled and fought and fell, and when he had to pause to recover breath, he still held me by the throat until I felt I should suffocate.

"After a time—how long I do not know, but it seemed
169

a very long time indeed—I tore myself free and got away from him. I dodged behind a sofa as he rushed after me, and, as he jumped over it, he fell. As he got up, he stood for a moment between the open french windows that gave on to a little balcony. He snatched at me and with my hands against his chest, I thrust him off with all my might. To my utter surprise he fell right over backwards, crashed against the wooden railing of the balcony and went right through it and down into the garden below."

Silence again.

"I suppose he caught his heels against the ledge of the door and it tripped him."

"Broke his neck, eh?" said Denis.

"I rushed across the room, unlocked the door, ran down the stairs by which I had come up so happily, and ran all the way home. I met no one, and I got safely into my room without waking my parents.

"The next day there was a terrible to do . . . Young Monsieur Raoul de Cassignac had been found lying dead on the stones of the terrace immediately below the balcony of his room. They could see that he had fallen, or been flung against the frail wood-work of the railing, which had given way. At first they thought that he had met with an accident, but then decided that the room was in what they called a 'state of disorder'. The police were not satisfied, and were convinced that there were 'signs of a struggle'. However, they received very little help from the inmates of the Château, for these were only three in number—an ancient house-keeper, a young servant-girl, and an old man who had once been butler. These said they knew nothing at all about Monsieur Raoul's movements that evening or at any other time.

"Old Monsieur de Cassignac himself was really at Monte Carlo, and the house was practically shut up.

"Can you imagine the state of terror in which I lived? Everyone was talking about it. It was a nine days' wonder. Everyone had a theory, and hardly anyone was content with the suicide story.

"He *must* have been murdered.

"I was positively grateful to old Père Gautier who

pooh-poohed the wild murder stories, and, with a shrug of his shoulders, said,

" '*Qu'est-ce que c'est que vous me chantez là?* Murder? Why? Like father, like son. He got drunk, staggered about the room catching a moth or a pink rat, staggered out on to the balcony and fell through it. *Voilà tout.*' "

"And of course nobody would have anything as simple as that," observed the Colonel. "Not while there was a chance of making a juicy murder of it."

"It was dreadful. I couldn't sleep. Every time I saw a gendarme coming towards me, I thought he was going to arrest me. I wonder I did not have a nervous break-down. The shock I had had that night was quite enough, without the prolonged strain.

"I used to dream about the guillotine."

"Poor child!" said Denis, and put his hand protectingly over hers.

"And in the end I did the silliest thing that, in the circumstances, I could have done. Can *Monsieur le Colonel* guess what that was?"

"Yes," replied the Colonel. "I did it myself once. You ran away."

"One does not imagine *Monsieur le Colonel* running away!" smiled Nicolette.

"I had saved just about enough money to take me to Marseilles. I made my way, cleverly, as I thought, to Avignon; and there I caught the Paris-Lyons train, with a change of clothes, my guitar and barely a hundred francs."

"So that was it," thought Denis Ducros. "The simple country mouse among the rats of Marseilles. Loneliness. Poverty. Hunger. Stark starvation. And a girl, like everybody else, has the need to eat.

"And you had a very terrible time at Marseilles?"

"No," replied Nicolette unexpectedly. "Not at all a bad time, really. Of course, at first, I was very lonely and very frightened and terribly anxious about what would happen to me when my hundred francs were gone. But Providence watches over babes, and innocents and fools . . .

"For a time," she added bitterly. "In the queer cheap *pension* where I stayed, there was a girl from Nimes who told me the best way to go about getting employment. I had idiotic ideas about 'going on the stage', as I called it. She had more sensible and experienced ones about getting a job in a cabaret-show. She thought really well of my singing and guitar playing, and offered to take me to see a man who was a kind of music-hall and theatrical agent."

Enter the villain, thought Denis Ducros. This is where the old, old story does start. Low-class scoundrelly theatrical agent and ignorant country girl at the end of her resources.

"I was so stupid that, at first, it seemed to me quite wrong that I should have to give ten per cent. of my earnings to a person who did nothing at all but tell me where there was a vacancy.

"However, Nanette laughed me out of that *sottise*, and told me the first thing was to 'find a vacancy' as I called it— before a hundred other girls had discovered it. Anyway, I went with her to see the man of whom she spoke, and found that he lived in a tiny little dirty office up the longest and steepest staircase I have ever seen. It was quite a rabbit-warren of a place, above a little café; and I didn't at all like the look of the men and women that went in and out, and up to the rooms above.

"The man turned out to be a Jew, small and fat, and very friendly. Too friendly, I thought, when he told me in the first five minutes that I was a lovely girl."

"Stock villain," thought Denis.

"He turned out to be one of the kindest men I have ever met.

"Not that I have met many kind men," she added. "But he really did have a kind heart, and proved to be a true friend. And quite disinterested beyond his ten per cent. He wasn't over-familiar, and when I went to see him, from time to time, I had no feeling that I must take someone else with me.

"He too thought well of my singing and playing; but only up to a point. He told me quite frankly that I hadn't the ghost of a chance of ever getting on to the big halls, as my voice was not powerful enough, nor my songs of the kind to appeal to the taste of the sort of people that formed the bulk of their audiences. But he said he thought he could always find me something in the *café-chantant* line, though not in the Cannabière.

"Well, believe it or not, *Monsieur le Colonel*, I actually maintained myself almost comfortably, and quite respectably, for several months, in Marseilles of all places in the world.

"Then one day I got a message from my agent, as I liked to call him, asking me to go and see him at his office the next day. I went, and found the good little man quite excited. He had got a job for me, he said, a good job. One much worthier of me than this hand-to-mouth *café-chantant* scramble.

"A real part in a real play on the real stage ... Actually a part ... I should be an actress.

"But I couldn't act. I knew nothing whatever about acting.

"Beyfus reassured me, however, and said that that simply did not matter.

"All I had to do was what I was now doing, only under very different conditions. What the producer wanted was a girl who could play a guitar and sing some Provençal songs. She must be pretty and have a figure for doublet and hose, as it was a period costume play.

"'And now I ask myself,' said Beyfus, rubbing his hands together and seeming to twinkle all over, 'whether this part was especially written for you, or whether you were especially born to play this part.'

"Poor Beyfus! He was so genuinely delighted to have got me this wonderful chance, although he knew that it would soon take me away from Marseilles, and the thought of that brought tears into his eyes.

"Poor Beyfus! He thought he was doing such a good thing for me—and he was sending me to Hell.

"I couldn't thank him enough, of course; and I was in the seventh heaven of delight, for the company had come from Paris, was opening at Marseilles, and was then going to make a complete tour of the Mediterranean.

"It seemed to me that Providence was indeed watching over me, taking me right away from France and all danger of arrest; for even here in Marseilles, I was still terrified at the approach of a gendarme, and I knew that if I were arrested and questioned, I should blurt out that I had killed Raoul de Cassignac and was glad that I had killed him.

"Do I bore *Monsieur le Colonel*?"

By way of reply, Denis Ducros put his arm about the girl.

"Well, I was a success. All I had to do was to put on the costume of one of King René's pages, sing two or three songs beneath the casement of a lady, and two or three more, in a garden-setting, to the King, as a wandering *jongleur*.

"It was all so easy. It was wonderful; and I walked on air. Almost everyone in the company was extremely nice to me, and nobody tried to be too nice.

"Then we moved on. Eventually we went across to Algiers, and life was even more interesting and exciting than in France, and I was beginning to lose my fear. I felt safe in fact; quite safe, as one of this large and happy family. Of course we didn't live in luxury or anything like it, but we did very well, and I for one had nothing whatever of which to complain.

"And what a traveller I considered myself! Nicolette from Domeuil writing letters home from Algeria. I thought I was being very artful and rather witty, when I headed a letter to my mother, '*From Africa*'. By-and-bye, I changed this to Egypt, for we went to Alexandria and Cairo—still quite successful and prosperous.

"Then our manager made the mistake of going to Constantinople where neither the Turks nor the Greeks were in the slightest degree interested in us, and the French community was either not big enough to make a theatre audience, or preferred other forms of entertainment.

"The Manager tried a Great Special Week with a change of programme every night; but, judging by the dwindling box-office returns, the public liked each play less than the last. I think the Provençal one bored them most of all. Certainly I was quite unable to feel that my Provençal songs and tunes were their idea of entertainment at all.

"In fact, we who'd had quite an appeal in French places were just dull to the Constantinople public.

"At the end of the Special Week the Manager called us all together and announced quite frankly that to-morrow the treasury would be just about empty; and that when he had paid everything, including our salaries for this and the following week, there'd be no money at all.

"This was bad, but not as bad as it would have been if he had just bolted with what money there was, and left us stranded with nothing at all. As a matter of fact, he was a completely honest man; and when he left Constantinople he owed nobody anything, and, before he went, he did his best to find jobs for us.

"It was easy enough for those of us who could dance. It seemed essential that one must dance. However well one could sing and play, one must still dance.

"My poor little stock-in-trade seemed to be of no value at all in Constantinople. And I found a different type of agent there. Not at all like my dear little Beyfus.

"I remember one fat gentleman who heard me sing and play, and almost before I'd finished, simply made a vulgar noise with his mouth and pointed with his thumb over his shoulder, at the door.

"I got a job through another girl, before my savings were quite gone, at a big café in Pera, the Greek quarter of Constantinople.

"Because I was a French girl from Provence, and knew the old Provençal airs and folk-songs, I was dressed up as a Hungarian and had to sing the latest and silliest and vulgarest music-hall songs from Paris.

"What I hated, at first, was having to go round the tables and talk to the men, between my songs. It was my first experience of selling wine on commission; urging people who had already had quite enough wine, to drink more, for the benefit of the management; and the hours were terrible. I had to stay in that beastly place until the last patron had gone, even if that were not until day-light.

"The cabaret manager was a horrible man, just a fat beast who fawned on the patrons and treated all his employees abominably; just as though they were slaves whom he had bought.

"And besides behaving like a savage to girls who were not willing to do everything he demanded, he persecuted us with a system of fines which took nearly all our earnings, and left us with scarcely enough to starve on . . . You were either one of his 'dear little girls', or you were constantly harassed and persecuted until you felt you'd be better dead.

"But does not all this bore *Monsieur le Colonel*?"

"No," replied the Colonel. "What does bore me is the thought that this gentleman is not in Sidi-bel-Abbès.

"Yes. A pity," he mused. "We might almost do something with the good slave-owner if he were here."

Nicolette laughed.

"*Monsieur le Colonel* sounds quite dangerous!

"Slave-owner!" she said. "It describes him, for he bought us, body and soul, through our need to eat. He owned us completely, through our fear of being out of work in a foreign land; and I honestly and truly believe that he sold us like slaves.

"I'll tell you . . .

"There was a woman who used to come to the café quite frequently. Besides watching the cabaret turns, she took an interest in the girls, especially the new-comers. She was very quiet, and *très correct* and *comme il faut*.

"What my friend found curious about her was that she always came alone. That did not seem at all strange to me, for she was not young, and it seemed to me that it was just because she was alone that she wanted to chat with us girls. I liked to talk to her because she was French, and knew Marseilles. She actually professed to know my dear little Beyfus.

"She seemed to like talking to me, and before long she would make a point of calling me over to her table. She was very friendly and interested, and asked me all about myself and what she called my career. I was just a little bit wary, and simply said I was a stage-struck Marseilles girl who had joined a touring-company and been stranded here in Constantinople.

"She was quite frank about herself too. Apparently she was a business woman who loved a little excitement and company in the evening."

"Business woman!" said the Colonel. "What kind of business?"

"She said she had a dress-making establishment. She spoke of her work-girls as though she were fond of them. I thought how nice and kind she must be as an employer. I compared the lot of anyone who worked for her with that of the employees of the *Café de Pera*. How safe her girls must feel in their jobs!

"She told me how happy they all were, singing at their work, and what gay meals they had in the big work-room when work was done. I asked her where the girls came from, and she said from one place and another, mostly brought to her by their mothers—for training.

"They all lived in the house, for she would have no one whose only thought was to get away quickly from work to outside amusements; but she provided ample leisure, and let them have friends to see them. It was just a big happy family living in a comfortable home.

"How I envied those girls!

"Then, one hot thundery night, I defied our cabaret-manager. I just could not and would not give in to him; and after an angry and ugly scene, he told me my job was finished.

"I was finished too. It was the end. I could go. I was to go at once. That night . . . as soon as the café should close.

"Well, my new friend saw that I was in trouble, and asked me, so kindly, what was wrong. I told her."

"And what will you do now?" she asked.

"*Do?* What *can* I do? Where can I go? I have no money," I said frantically.

"She considered the situation.

" 'My child,' she said, 'are you determined to lead this café life? This uncertain, worthless way of life? . . . Why not give it up?'

"'Give it up?' I said. 'I would do so, only too gladly. But what else can I do? Where can I go?'

"And then it seemed as if the good St. Louis himself must have led me to her, for she said,

"'Would you care to give up all this, and join my girls in their work-room? I could not pay you much. *Au contraire*, most of them pay me to teach them their business. But you would be learning how to make a career for yourself, and you would have food, a home, and a little something to save . . . I think you would be happy with them and with me. I will see that you are well looked after.'

"I looked at her in wonder.

"'But why? Why should you do this for me?' I asked.

"'It so happens that I have just one vacancy,' she said. 'Our little Julie has left us to be married, and I have been looking for someone suitable to take her place. I have talked with you, and I like you . . . And you like me, *hein*? Well, come and try for a little while. You can always return to the cafés of Constantinople, if you prefer that way of life.'

"I shuddered . . . The cafés of Constantinople! . . . Each one worse than the last.

"'Oh! Is it really true? May I really come?' I asked.

"'We will try you,' said Madame. 'And, what is better, you shall come home with me this night. I will wait for you.'

"And so I went away with my kind friend—that night—to her establishment, where all the girls were so gay and happy in their work.

"It was quite a nice house in a turning off the hill that leads up from Galata Bridge, the *Grande Rue de Pera* I think it is; and, as we got out from the *fiacre*, my benefactress mentioned that this was her private house, not her place of business.

"I was a little puzzled, very upset by the fright I had had when I was dismissed, very relieved and grateful for this unexpected help, and so tired I could hardly keep my eyes open.

"However, she insisted on my having some little sweet

178

cakes and thick bitter Turkish coffee, in a room she called her boudoir, before she took me up to the room in which I was to sleep that night."

A brief silence again, which Denis forbore to break. He saw it all now, and he felt savagely angry.

The poor, poor, foolish innocent little simpleton.

"I slept all night and the next day," continued Nicolette. "It was evening when I woke up. I was puzzled and a little alarmed, and yet, at the same time, stupidly content, if you know what I mean. All I wanted was to sleep and to sleep, and there seemed no reason why I should not do so."

"Drugged, in fact," growled the Colonel. "Opium, morphia, hashish, or some other filth."

"I woke again towards evening, and I suppose I had been asleep then for at least two days and nights. While I was lying awake, feeling extraordinarily stupid and drowsy, the maid, who had waited on us when we arrived the first night, came in with a tray of food. *Soupe*, a roll and some *pilaf* stuff.

"I didn't like the maid. She was a great strong horse of a woman with a cruel face and a surly manner. She dumped the tray on a chair by my bed and went out of the room without a word. I suppose she resented having to wait on me, and then I wondered if perhaps she spoke only Turkish. I was not feeling at all well, and was not hungry. I was very thirsty however, and the *soupe* was strong and good, and so was the coffee.

"'I will get up now,' I thought to myself, and looked round for my clothes.

"'*Why, they've gone!*' I said to myself stupidly. '*My clothes have gone!*' and almost in the act of getting up to see if they had been tidied away, I fell asleep again . . .

"Now it's a curious thing," said Nicolette. "I remember every detail of what I've told you, as though it happened yesterday, but my memory is quite blurred about what happened from that moment.

"For days and weeks, perhaps for months, I must have been about a quarter awake and three-quarters asleep, when I wasn't asleep altogether.

"Just a few memories here and there stick up, like the rocks do out of black water at twilight.

"I remember realising that my clothes really had gone, including my shoes; that my 'benefactress' came into the room, now and again, and talked quite differently from the way in which she had done at the café.

"I told her that I felt terrible, and I could only tell her that I was ill. That I felt so weak that I wondered if I might be dying . . . That I felt I must get out . . . That I must have my clothes . . . That I must go away . . .

"I was very ill of course. I was three parts poisoned, and I was frightened to death.

"The woman agreed that I was ill, and said that what I needed was a doctor. She would bring her own, for she could not have me lying ill there in her house for the rest of my life. I had come to work. Why had I not told her I was so delicate, and suffered so much from this sort of *malaise*?"

Again Nicolette fell silent.

"She brought the 'doctor'," she said at length.

"He was not a doctor," she added.

The Colonel said nothing, but the girl felt the muscles of his arm tighten across her shoulders.

"By God!" he whispered. "If I . . ."

Nicolette suddenly began to cry, and turning up her face to his, Denis Ducros kissed her on the lips.

"Don't!" he said. "Don't!"

With an effort the girl regained her self-control and dried her eyes.

"That's my little story, *Monsieur le Colonel*," she said. "I have no excuses to offer for myself. I was a stupid, simple, silly fool, who got what she deserved for allowing herself to be so easily caught by our dear Madame."

"*Madame!*" cried Denis. "*This* 'Madame'?"

"Yes," answered Nicolette. "This Madame. Our dear Madame who loves all her girls, and takes such care of them."

"By God!" swore Denis. "I'll break . . ."

"Too late, *Monsieur le Colonel*. You can do nothing. Nothing for any of us."

"I can do something for her, though. And I . . ."

"You have given us all a happy evening, *Monsieur le Colonel*. You have given me the happiest evening that I have had since I killed Raoul de Cassignac. Truly you can do nothing more. Be content."

"It's abominable! It's monstrous! It's almost unbelievable," he stormed. "Couldn't you have escaped from that house in Pera?"

"Not without clothes," was the brief reply.

"Couldn't you have opened the windows in your room and screamed and *screamed*?"

"It did not open."

"Could you not have broken the window?"

"I tried, with my bare hands. The little panes of glass, set in iron, must have been an inch thick."

"Couldn't you have opened the door of your room, and . . .?"

"It was locked on the outside."

"Couldn't you have fought and fought and *fought*? . . ."

"That maid, the Turkish woman, was as strong as a strong man; and, do you know, the whole of the time I was there, I never stood on my feet without feeling so sick and giddy that I must either sit down or fall down . . .

"Please . . . Please don't think I am making excuses," she continued. "A better and a stronger character than I would have found some way out *sans doute*, or would never have got into such a position . . .

"Yes, I fully admit I was defeated. I gave in. Madame won. She broke me, mind and body, so that I cringed when she came into the room with that dreadful Turkish woman."

"How do you come to be here, Nicolette; here in Sidi-bel-Abbès?"

"I scarcely know," replied the girl. "I lived in a kind of dream, a nightmare of horrors, until I was completely obedient and docile and had given up everything— including courage and hope—and was altogether finished as a self-respecting human being.

"Madame must have used her opium or chloral or hashish or whatever it was, quite regularly. Every day I

181

must have had the poison in my food or coffee. Of course, if I'd been a person of any strength of character, I should have starved myself to death or deliberately died of thirst, rather than take any food or drink, knowing that some of it was drugged."

"Yes. That's what it comes to," agreed the Colonel, with a restraint that gave no indication of his fierce anger and indignation. "You were poisoned, mind and body as you say, and you were not responsible for your actions. Of course you could not commit suicide in such a horrible way as to refuse food and drink. No young girl could face such a lingering death as that. It is unthinkable."

"Well, anyhow . . . I didn't do it; and after I'd once been thoroughly drugged and stupefied, I could not think and plan and *do* anything, to help myself. I just drifted."

"Or say rather that you were drowned and your lifeless corpse drifted," said the Colonel.

"And really I remember very little after the first days in that house in Pera. As I say, it was a drugged sleep with appalling nightmares; and I had an almost unbearable headache the whole time.

"But I do remember that there was some sudden and serious trouble with the police, and Madame was in a great state of fear and anxiety. It was evidently something quite out of the ordinary, for she was then, as always, on excellent terms with the authorities.

"I never knew the facts of the matter, but a very rich and important Turk, a *pasha* and high official of some kind, died in that quiet house in the Beyoglu quarter, and naturally there were searching enquiries.

"Apparently that always means bad trouble in Constantinople.

"The police have to make good, which means making or finding something bad; and Madame complained bitterly, for long afterwards, that the girls were not loyal, not faithful, not grateful to her, and told the police the most wicked lies. And apparently, from what I've heard her say, one trouble led to another. As if the death of a *pasha* were not bad enough, it was discovered that one of the girls was a spy—a Russian girl.

"So Madame had not only ordinary criminal-police trouble, but political-police trouble, which is far worse. However, she had friends among both, and was able to do the wisest thing—escape. She left Constantinople in a hurry and very quietly.

"I think she simply abandoned all the other girls. But she took me with her. Me and the Turkish servant woman. We went by boat to Alexandria."

"Wasn't that your chance," asked the Colonel, gently. Nicolette shook her head.

"I was so ill that, even now, I've only the vaguest memory of being dressed, taken in a carriage down to the water-side, and on to a ship. I was Madame's sick daughter, and the Turkish woman was my nurse!

"She was so strong that when I could not put one foot before another, she carried me as though I was a child.

"It was the same when we got to Alexandria. The Mother, the nurse, and the half-sick half-idiot daughter.

"Curiously enough, one thing I can remember to this day, about that journey, with the utmost distinctness, is the terrible feeling that there was something I *must* do. I must *do* somthing. But I could not realise what it was. Dimly, I knew that, as you just said, this was my chance. But my chance to do what? And how was I to set about doing what I had to do? It was almost one of the worst parts of the nightmare, that indescribably awful feeling that I could save myself if only I knew what to do and how to do it.

"I know that, once or twice, I cried out, and that if anyone else was present Madame would say,

"'Oh, the poor child! *Pauvre petite!* How she suffers! When shall we reach home, and the good doctor? . . . Give her her medicine quickly, Nurse. An injection, I think, and she will sleep.'

"But almost all the time we were in a wretched little cabin; I was never left alone; and I scarcely saw anybody when we left the ship.

"But when in the cabin I had that impulse to help myself, it was a different story. It was not 'Poor child' then. That Turkish woman was truly skilful in inflicting horrible agonising pain without causing the slightest bruise or any mark whatever . . .

"I daresay *Monsieur le Colonel* knows the pain of a twisted wrist."

"And you did not scream?" he asked.

"Only once or twice, at first. After that it was a whimper rather than a scream.

"No, believe me, Monsieur, one did not scream, or disobey those two women. Nor, for the greater part of the time, did I know where I was, where I was going, or what I was doing. The horrible little Turkish coasting-ship rolled like a tub, and I was deathly sea-sick in addition to being poisoned with the drug.

"Another thing I remember out of all the far more important things I have forgotten, was a hideous delusion that I was drowned under some terribly heavy, sticky mess that was neither liquid nor solid; and that I could only save my life by getting to my feet and raising my head above it. But the effort to stand up was terrible, as though one were lifting tons of huge chains; and when at last, with a tremendous effort, one got to one's feet, one was completely coated, a foot thick, with this awful sticky horror, and the weight of it bore one down again . . . still suffocating . . . down into it to drown and die like . . . like . . . a fly in treacle."

"That was how the opium, or hashish, or whatever the filthy poison was, affected your brain," said the Colonel. "I wonder you did not go out of your mind, or die."

"I went out of my mind, all right," said the girl, "and I wish I had died. But I was too ill, too stupid, too drugged to put an end to it, and I shouldn't have had the courage, anyhow."

"My poor Nicolette," murmured Denis. "I should like to take our Madame and . . .

"And you came here from Alexandria?" he interrupted himself. "More trouble there for Madame?"

"I don't know. I never heard of any special catastrophe. I think it was just that Madame did not flourish. The English are a queer people. Madame does not like them."

"It is conceivable that they did not like Madame," observed the Colonel. "She may have been invited to travel further."

"Yes. She was always muttering '*Ces Anglais! Mon Dieu, ces Anglais!*' and I remember being very ill again, and being taken by train to Cairo, where Madame thought a pleasanter atmosphere might be found."

"And how long were you in Cairo?" asked the Colonel.

"There again, I really don't know. It can't have been very long; but as in the other places, I lived in a sort of dream. I was never quite awake and I slept a great deal of the time. I scarcely remember anything at all about Cairo; and I doubt if I ever once went out of the house, the whole time I was there."

"And why did Madame leave Cairo?" asked the Colonel. "I feel one cannot know too much about Madame's interesting history. Was there more trouble?"

"I am sorry to keep on saying 'I don't know'," replied Nicolette, "but I think there must have been. I think it was due to her doing something that, in Constantinople, would have been quite in order. For here again she kept on saying what imbeciles the English were, and that she'd like to see every English official pushed into the Nile, with a brick tied round his neck. Anyway, Madame began declaring that she'd go where there was less British hypocrisy and more civilisation.

"I don't think she was actually turned out of Cairo but I know we went to Algiers, for I have vague recollections of another ship's cabin, and, later, of seeing from a window a view that was familiar.

"Here again I remember something that, although it is only a memory of thoughts, is stronger and clearer than any memory of people or events. I distinctly remember coming to myself, so to speak, one day, and realising the awful difference between my life during my former visit there as an actress, with real friends, in a happy hard-working company, and my position, my life, on this second visit.

"I think it was only then that I really awoke, though only for a brief space, to the knowledge and understanding of what had happened to me. But I soon lapsed back into stupidity; a dreadful drugged drowsiness; apathy."

"And why did Madame leave the flourishing town of Algiers? I should have thought the Kasbah would have been her spiritual home," said the Colonel.

"Once again, I don't really know. But I think it was a man."

"Another dead one, or a live one this time?" enquired the Colonel.

"Very much alive. I believe he had some hold on Madame."

"Very likely, I should think."

"She talked a great deal about blackmail. . . . Oh, I remember. Yes. . . . It was the manager of the Pera café. He had come to Algiers and set himself up there in the *Café de Stamboul*, with real Turkish coffee and odalisques to serve it. Madame started going there, as she had done in Constantinople. Yes, that was it. Odette knew all about it and told me.

"Apparently, in the end, Madame simply ran away from this man. The police had nothing to do with it at all."

"I begin to think better of him," observed the Colonel. "Pity he could not have come on here."

"He was a terrible man," said Nicolette.

"And so you came here from Algiers?"

"Yes, *Monsieur le Colonel*, we came here."

The Colonel sat silent for a moment.

"It's incredible," he said. "Wouldn't one have thought it utterly impossible that a grown girl, who was neither insane nor dumb; neither blind nor bed-ridden; could be carted around the world like a piece of luggage?"

"One would, Monsieur. But, believe me, one would be wrong. Far from being impossible, such a thing is perfectly easy. . . . . However unwilling or combative the victim may be . . . I would have given anything in the world, *everything in the world*, to have escaped, the moment I realised what Madame was.

"But as I have tried to show you, I had no chance. As I have said, she broke me, mind and body and soul,

186

until I cringed at the sight of her and at the sound of her voice."

Denis Ducros rose to his feet.

"She . . . broke . . . you . . . and . . . you . . . cringed before her," he said slowly.

"Look you, Nicolette, I, Denis . . . I mean Louis Rochefort, solemnly swear that *I* will break *her*, and that *she* shall cringe before *me*—in your presence."

The girl stared at him wide-eyed.

"No! No! No!" she protested. "It is too late. We are what we are, and Madame is our . . ."

"*Stop!*" he said angrily. "You are what you are, and I am what I am. We are what Fate has made us. Tell me. Would you like to go away from here? *Would you like to go back to Provence?*"

CHAPTER XII

REAL POWER AND GREAT GLORY

"OH!" cried Nicolette. "Oh! If only that were possible! I'd give my soul . . . anything . . . anything—if I had anything to give."

Never did Colonel Louis Rochefort speak more convincingly, with more certain assurance and more moral grandeur, than did Denis Ducros at this moment.

"My child," he said. "You shall leave here. *You shall go back to Provence*. And you shall go *to-night*."

Nicolette leapt to her feet, and he took her in his arms.

They kissed and clung spontaneously like young lovers, and with uncontrollable emotion, devotion—and no trace of passion.

Denis Ducros felt that he loved this girl. Loved her, and would save her.

Not only would he be the great Caliph who amused himself incognito, pulling strings here and there; he would be the real Fairy Prince, of a real and living Fairy Tale which was a real tale of real life.

He would save her and set her free.

And if he never did another decent thing, he would not have lived in vain.

"Sit down," he said, "and *I* will talk."

They sat down together, his arm about her.

"Listen, my Nicolette," he began. "Is there any real reason why you should not go home? To your people, I mean."

"No," replied Nicolette, "except that I cannot leave here. How can I, without money for fares, without clothes?"

"They would be glad for you to go back to them, your parents?" he asked.

"Yes. They have always loved me very dearly, and I have always reproached myself for running away as I did . . . but I was so frightened."

"You were never suspected—in the matter of Raoul de Cassignac? That's all forgotten long ago, and . . ."

"No, I couldn't go back there," said Nicolette decisively. "Not to Domeuil. I couldn't bear it; apart from any fear. It's still my worst nightmare, even after all I've been through since. And my parents have moved to Avignon."

"Then you could go to them there?"

"Yes. If I could get away from here. But I haven't the necessary money—or anything."

"Does Madame give you no money?"

"No. *Au contraire!* We are all in Madame's debt. And the longer we are here, the bigger the debt."

"*Ah! . . . Indeed?* One begins to wonder how the poor woman lives!" said the voice of Colonel Louis Rochefort.

"However, we'll go into that with her later. Now then. There's a train leaves Sidi-bel-Abbès Station in about an hour's time, for Oran. You'll catch that train; and it'll ramble along the eighty miles to the coast in such a leisurely manner, stopping for half an hour at every station, that it won't get you to Oran much before breakfast-time.

"You will go straight to the *Hôtel de la République* for *petit déjeuner*. They'll tell you when the next boat is

188

leaving for Marseilles, and book a berth for you. You'll get to Marseilles in about thirty-six hours; and then it won't be long before there is a train to Avignon. If you have to stay a night in Marseilles . . ."

Nicolette laughed.

What a wonderful dream!

But really rather too painful.

Of course, he meant only to be kind and agreeable, this charming and adorable Monsieur.

The station . . . The train . . . Oran . . . A ship . . . Passing the Château d'If . . . the harbour . . . Marseilles . . . France . . . Then *home*!

Monsieur le Colonel did not wish to be unkind. Furtively she wiped her eyes.

"Is that understood?" demanded Denis the Colonel.

"Oh, but yes, Monsieur. Quite understood. I go straight from this house to that of my parents—without clothes or money or Madame's permission."

The Colonel permitted himself his most superior smile.

"Not quite like that," he contradicted. "With clothes, with money, and with Madame's permission.

"And we'll arrange it now," he added, rising and opening the door.

Hassan appeared from nowhere, bowing low.

"Madame!" said the Colonel.

Hassan disappeared, and a minute later Madame sailed majestic into the hall.

"*Monsieur le Colonel* desires . . . ?"

"An outfit of clothing for Mademoiselle Nicolette, including a travelling suit, a cape, and . . . what-not.

"Also a small sum of money. Let us say ten thousand francs, in fifty- and a hundred-franc notes."

Madame stared in complete bewilderment.

"The good Nicolette would also go for a drive, and *Monsieur le Colonel* would borrow . . . ?"

"No, Madame. *Monsieur le Colonel* is not going to borrow. But Madame is going to repay. Not in full, of course, for Madame could never do that in this life— though she surely will in the next.

"No. Madame is merely going to pay ten thousand francs of what she owes, to one of her girls."

"But, *Monsieur le Colonel*," protested Madame on a rising note, in which incredulity struggled with indignation and alarm.

"I? Pay Nicolette ten thousand francs? *I* pay *her*, did *Monsieur le Colonel* suggest? Why, *she* owes *me* more than that. . . . Far, far more than that."

"They all do, I expect," agreed the Colonel. "You stagger along under a crushing and increasing load of unpaid credits. That's how you live!

"Now then," he continued with an abrupt change of voice, "go and get me ten thousand francs, Madame."

"*Monsieur le Colonel* is joking! Even if I had ten thousand francs in the world, does *Monsieur le Colonel* suppose I should have it in this house?"

"Yes."

"And would it be in a little drawer in a table in the *salon*? Or on the mantelpiece, or under the front-door mat? Or perhaps in an old stocking hanging . . . ?"

"Or in an old tea-pot, perhaps. I don't know and I don't care. But I suggest a perfectly good safe in Madame's bedroom. Anyway—*get* it."

"The safe, Monsieur?"

"Look you, Madame. Wit and humour are excellent things at the right time. This is not the time. And speaking of that, my time is rather short. Mademoiselle Nicolette has a train to catch."

"Mademoiselle Nicolette has a . . . ?" gasped Madame.

"Yes. I said a train. She is leaving Sidi-bel-Abbès."

Madame's face seemed to turn into granite, her eyes into cold steel.

"And," continued the Colonel imperturbably, "so is Madame—unless she is very careful."

"I? *I* leaving Sidi-bel-Abbès, *Monsieur le Colonel*?"

"Yes."

And the Colonel's face was as hard as Madame's.

"Don't forget I can have you out of here, lock, stock and barrel, and in short order. Give me any trouble; tell me any more lies; or attempt to disobey any order I may

190

give you—*and I'll do it*. And I'll only give you twenty-four hours' notice."

"*Monsieur le Colonel.* . . . I . . ."

Was it possible that the redoubtable Madame quailed? Quailed and shrank before a man—a mere man, which is the most contemptible object in all creation.

"And I'll tell you one thing more, Madame, for your information—that unless Mademoiselle Nicolette is swiftly and suitably fitted out, and ten thousand francs paid to her, I'll send for a *péloton* of my men who'll remove the entire contents of this house—including the wall-paper and the nails, before you can scream, and they'll . . ."

Madame did cringe, as he had promised. Visibly she cringed, shrank, blenched.

The Foreign Legion!

Name of Satan! Those fearful foreign devils! Why at the order of this arch-fiend they'd do anything. Anything.

And—apart from that—at a word; at a stroke of his pen, he could ruin her. She had forgotten. She had not realised the power of this terrible man. The danger . . .

But—*ten thousand francs*! *Ten* thousand francs of her hard-earned money. . . . And she had been going to send it to the Bank to-morrow, as she did every month. Well, then let her imagine it had gone. He couldn't prove she had that amount of money in the house.

She plucked up spirit.

"*Monsieur le Colonel!* Once and for all, I have not . . ."

"Then, for a start, Madame, your house is out of bounds for officers of this garrison; and to-morrow you'll be out of Sidi-bel-Abbès. I will send Hassan for the picket."

Madame capitulated. Almost she collapsed. With the police she had always been able to deal satisfactorily—the police of several nations; but this was no case of a police underling anxious to improve his bank balance. This was the military; and an officer of high rank, stern, harsh, incorruptible.

And suddenly Madame had a dreadful thought, one which caused her swiftly to change her manner and her attitude. *God alone knew what the girl had told him!* And if she only told him the truth of what she knew—or half the truth, or a little part of the truth—it would be enough.

"*Monsieur le Colonel*, one can only do one's best. Doubtless I can find some odds and ends of clothes for the girl, if *Monsieur le Colonel* wishes to take her for a trip to Algiers. And I will scrape together what money I have in the house. I fear it won't be ten thousand francs, or . . ."

"It will be ten thousand francs, Madame," the Colonel reassured her, "and the clothing will be entirely adequate and suitable. I give you ten minutes," and the Colonel turned towards the room in which the girl sat nervously biting at her handkerchief.

"If *Monsieur le Colonel* will permit Nicolette to come upstairs with me," suggested Madame, following him anxiously, "I will . . ."

"Get the clothes and the money, and bring them here," interrupted the Colonel. "You now have nine minutes."

"Hassan," he added, turning to where that acquiescent individual stood at the post of duty, "yet one more carriage. The last and the best."

"Nicolette, Madame will bring you your clothes, your money, and her permission to depart—if not her blessing on your journey."

Nicolette sprang up.

"*Monsieur le Colonel*, you do not mean . . ."

"I mean, my child, that you are going home; and you are going now," interrupted Denis grandly. "I have arranged it."

Unbelieving, half-believing, yearning to believe, the girl, in a transport of madness, put her arms about her benefactor's neck.

"*How I love you!*" she whispered.

"And I love you, my sweet, my Nicolette!" answered Denis fervently, as they clung together—a poor Daughter of Joy whom Fate had treated with the utmost brutality, and a poor Soldier of Fortune, badly wounded in the Battle of Life.

Nicolette drew back and looked into his eyes.

"You *mean* that?" she whispered. "You mean you really *do* love me a little?"

"Yes. I do mean it . . . I find I have fallen in love with you, my Nicolette. If only I had met you—there in Domeuil before you ever saw that *scélérat* of a de Cassignac."

"And, oh, if you were only an ordinary man!" sighed Nicolette. "Just a *soldat simple*, and not a Colonel."

Denis Ducros' laugh was brief and enigmatic.

"Listen, my dear," he said. "I shall retire from this high rank of Colonel that I now adorn. Retire very soon indeed, in fact. Much sooner than you would suppose. And, as soon as I can, after I have retired, I shall return to France; and from Marseilles I shall come to—Avignon."

"Oh!" breathed Nicolette. *"Monsieur le Colonel!* If I could see you there, just for a minute! To try to thank you. To tell you I was safe . . . and free . . . And to try to express what I shall be feeling . . . I would meet every train that came to Avignon by day or night. I would live at the railway-station, if only in the hope of seeing you pass by."

"Tell me where to write to," said Denis, "and I will tell you the time of the train by which I shall come to Avignon . . . to see you, Nicolette."

The girl's face was transfigured, and it was as though a light shone from her eyes, a light of hope and of love.

And the face of Denis Ducros softened, and seemed to lose certain lines. His lips lost bitterness and his eyes gained brightness and warmth.

Again they kissed and clung, the girl forgetting the past, the man ignoring the future.

"You will go straight to your parents?" he said. "You will let no other devil in human form delude you. It's a hellish world, Nicolette, for a lovely girl alone and . . ."

"Have no fear. I shall go straight to my mother and father, without the loss of a minute. And there I shall wait and wait and wait—for the rest of my life, hoping that you may come. . . .

"Am I dreaming? Do you really mean this, *Monsieur le Colonel?*" she asked.

"I mean it, Nicolette. If I do not come, it will mean that I am in . . . I am in . . . Well, in my grave; a grave of some kind."

(The living death in the grave of prison. Might he not get eight years' *travaux forcées*?)

"Please do not talk of graves . . . to-night. I think I should die now if I ceased to believe that . . ."

"Listen, Nicolette. Would you wait eight years, if I did not come?"

"Eighteen, *Monsieur le Colonel*. Or twenty-eight.

"And then I should not be an old woman," she smiled.

"So you'd wait twenty-eight years, my dear?"

"I shall wait all my life. What is twenty-eight years if I am waiting for you."

Denis kissed her again.

"Well, it won't be as long as that," he said. "Nor eighteen. But possibly it might be eight. . . . On the other hand, it might be only a little more than eight months."

"Look you, *Monsieur le Colonel*. Waiting will be happiness. Thanks to you, my life is being turned from hell to heaven. From blackest misery to pure golden happiness. Waiting, waiting to see you, will be the great part of that happiness. On my knees I could ask nothing better of the Blessed Virgin than to be allowed to live, waiting—for you. Only one thing better, and that I should scarcely dare to ask—that you might really come."

"I shall come, Nicolette. I shall come."

Followed by Hassan, Madame entered, carrying a collection of clothing over one arm, and a roll of notes clutched in one hand.

The clothes she flung upon the divan, with a gesture of angry contempt. The money she offered to the Colonel.

"Before witnesses, I *lend* this money to *Monsieur le Colonel* Louis Rochefort," she said. "I do not ask for interest, but I should like prompt repayment."

"Before witnesses," smiled the Colonel. "I remark that you do nothing of the kind. You give it freely and unconditionally to Mademoiselle Nicolette, because you owe it to her. Take notice also, that you do moreover owe her about another forty thousand francs, of which we will say nothing at the moment . . .

"Unless," he added, "Madame would like to make full admission of the fact, and payment of the remainder of the sum owed? . . . Put the ten thousand francs on the table there."

One is never too old to learn, and Madame, to her profound surprise, discovered that she was learning restraint and self-control, even thus late in life. She felt she was also learning wisdom. She contrived to hold her peace, though peace was not within her.

"Dress quickly, Nicolette," he said, "and count the money. . . . Come, Madame, let us have a chat, shall we?"

"There is indeed a little I should like to say to *Monsieur le Colonel*," responded Madame grimly.

"There is a lot I should like to say to Madame," replied the Colonel, even more grimly.

And in the *salon*, to which Madame led the way, he said quite a lot; said it with point and eloquence; and said it to such purpose that Madame was almost convinced that she was not a public benefactress; was not even a real friend to unfortunate girls who had, for various reasons, left their homes and been rescued by her from the dangers notoriously resultant upon homelessness.

"Yes, my dear Madame," concluded the Colonel, just before Nicolette entered the room, "speaking judicially and impartially, without rancour, wrath or resentment, I should say that you and your kind are the most poisonous reptiles in Creation. You and your sort are the most vile, depraved and abominable bestialities that disfigure and pollute the world that God made for humanity to be happy in. You are a malignant microbe, Madame. Beside you, cancer is a mild misfortune, almost a beneficence; leprosy a trifling nuisance.

"It is not so much that you are a living Crime as that it is a terrible crime to let you live.

"We guillotine murderers for killing the body; what then should we do to you who kill souls; kill happiness; hope; self-respect; kill the life that is in the living body, leaving that body alive to suffer utter degradation?

"There is no fate bad enough for you; this world has no punishment adequate; and that, I think, is why your fate and punishment are reserved for you in the next world—a punishment quite beyond our present poor human comprehension.

"Madame, you are a foul sub-human incarnation of Evil, and a disgrace even to that section of humanity that is so much lower than the animals. When, in Hell, you encounter Monsieur Judas Iscariot, he will doubtless feel ashamed that . . .

"Ah! Here is Mademoiselle Nicolette . . .

"Have you everything you'll want for the journey? . . . Come along then."

Hassan entered to announce proudly that he had produced an absolutely super carriage.

The Colonel and Nicolette left Madame standing speechless, themselves refraining from speech as they went from her house.

It gave the Colonel a sense of pleasure and approval that, unlike himself, Nicolette, triumphant, uttered no reproaches or abuse of Madame. Could there be such a contempt as she deserved, Madame was treated with that contempt by the girl almost young enough to be her grand-daughter.

As the Colonel followed Nicolette into the carriage, Madame rushed forth, having recovered her powers of movement and of speech.

"And the bill! And the bill!" she screamed. "The wine! The carriages! Entertainment! My time. The time of all my girls! Is it desired that I send my little bill direct to the house of *Monsieur le Colonel*? Or does he prefer to settle with me now?"

"Now," replied the Colonel. "I never leave debts unpaid. Madame may take it out of the forty thousand francs still owing to Mademoiselle Nicolette."

"*Monsieur le Colonel!*" screamed Madame. "This is monstrous! This is . . ."

"Devilish," supplied the Colonel.

"And one more word out of *you*, Madame, and I'll return and have a talk with the other girls. You probably

196

owe each of them a great deal more than fifty thousand francs. . . . Still, they'll doubtless be glad of ten thousand francs apiece, on account."

Madame did say one more word, but the Colonel behaved like a gentleman, and affected not to hear it.

"Drive to the station, *cocher*," he ordered, and as Hassan salaamed low, he delighted that admiring man by his last words to Madame.

"Give the good Hassan ten francs *bakshish*, please, Madame, and put it on the bill."

The delight of Hassan was unbounded. Idiot's delight.

"There's the Law! There's the Law, *Monsieur le Colonel*," screamed Madame, as the carriage started on its way.

"Beware of it, Madame! Beware of it!" replied the Colonel and shut the near-side door with a slam of complete finality.

As they turned into the darkness of the tree-shaded road, the Colonel took Nicolette's hand in his own, and they sat silent, the girl utterly unable to believe in this sudden amazing miracle of Love, and of release from the House of Bondage, of dreadful slavery and dark despair.

Denis, for once, was dumb; and dumb with the overwhelming need for speech.

He had fallen in love as suddenly as a man, walking in darkness, may fall in water.

Thus suddenly. Thus completely immersed in a new element . . . *Coup de foudre!*

What had he done? What had he not done, this night? This marvellous night of freedom.

In his brief and beautiful freedom he had walked into this long and beautiful bondage. Bound for ever with the golden chain of love.

He was in love. He was in love. He was in love. His heart sang.

And suddenly his soaring spirit stooped, drooped, and fell to earth.

He had plumed himself on being a mighty actor, a marvel of lost and wasted histrionic genius. He had played the Colonel!

He had also played the fool, the liar, the swindler and blackguardly cad. He had won Nicolette's love under false pretences!

Fine feathers make fine birds; and as a fine bird with golden feathers he had deluded this poor girl sitting beside him.

The Fairy Prince!

What would she say if she knew that her fairy prince was a greasy batman, serving tables, cleaning boots, brushing clothes, doing menial jobs at the behest of a fat Natalie; bowing and scraping, "No, *Monsieur le Colonel;* Yes, *Monsieur le Colonel.*"

A serving man.

Free?

A free Frenchman?

He was a slave. The slave of the Legion. The slave of Colonel Louis Rochefort.

And now the slave of a lie.

He loved Nicolette, and he could not make the foolish attempt to base their life together on a lie.

A cold sense of failure, of loss, of cruel and bitter disappointment settled upon him; and for the first time in his life he experienced that oft-imagined but sometimes very real pain, a physical aching of the heart.

He must lose Nicolette by letting her go now, out of his life, to-night. Letting her go, in the happy belief that she had been befriended by, had indeed been loved by, a distinguished man, a great man, a Colonel famous throughout a crack Army Corps.

Or, even more painfully, he must lose her by telling her the truth; by endeavouring to make her see him as he should be, a servant in a green baize apron.

He could never go to Avignon to find Nicolette in the *rôle* of Colonel Louis Rochefort, retired—whether he got heavy or light, long or short, punishment for to-night's doings.

To-night's escapade had started merely as a joke, though Colonel Rochefort might think it a joke in bad taste. To carry the joke to France would be carrying it too far.

From every point of view it was unthinkable.

What a fool he had been!

Clever Denis Ducros!

Once more he had landed himself on the horns of a dilemma; and was also firmly caught in a cleft stick of his own making.

Well, which would be the less cruel course—for her? To let her wait and wait at Avignon for the man who never came?

That would be a wicked thing to do.

To tell her suddenly, as they parted, that the man with whom she had fallen in love, the man she trusted, the first man in whom she had believed since the terrible lesson taught her by Raoul de Cassignac,—to tell her suddenly that that man was a play-acting rascal, a fraud, an impostor?

That would be a cruel thing to do—and cruelty was worse than wickedness.

Denis Ducros was not wicked, and he was not cruel.

But oh, what a fool! What a ten thousand times despicable damnable fool!

"Nicolette," he said.

"*Monsieur le Colonel . . .*"

"That's just what I was going to say, '*Don't say*,' " he smiled ruefully.

"Say '*don't say*'?" smiled the girl.

"Yes. Don't say '*Monsieur le Colonel.*' "

Nicolette pressed closer to his side.

"I feel somehow, I could never call you Louis, *Monsieur le . . .*"

"No. Don't say that either. Do you think you could call me Denis?"

"Denis? Is that Monsieur's second name?"

"No. It's his only name, Nicolette. My first name is Denis . . .

"And my second name is Ducros," he added sullenly, as one who makes unwilling confession.

"*Denis Ducros?*" repeated Nicolette, in some bewilderment. "But you are *Monsieur le Colonel* Louis Rochefort."

This was difficult. This was painful. This was terrible. And beads of cold perspiration gathered on his forehead.

"Listen, Nicolette," he said heavily.

"I am *le légionnaire* Denis Ducros. I am also an impostor, a humbug, a play-acting fraud, and a fool."

"You are a private soldier?" exclaimed the girl.

"I am."

To the shocked amazement of Denis Ducros, Nicolette burst into tears.

This was what came of play-acting!

This was the real punishment for that folly. What *they* could do to him would be nothing.

"Really and truly an ordinary, common *légionnaire*?" she sobbed.

"Yes."

"Truly?"

"Yes."

Nicolette sobbed more bitterly. Her tears flowed yet more freely.

The remorseful heart of Denis sank more heavily within his gentle breast.

He must try to comfort her. Risking indignant rebuff, he put his gold-braided arm about her.

"Don't cry, Nicolette," he said. "Don't cry. At least you are *free*. There is no deception about that. And you are going home to Avignon. Don't cry."

"But I must ... I am so happy," sobbed Nicolette. "So very ... *very* happy."

"To be free and going home to Avignon?" he said, a little sadly.

"No. That is nothing ... I am in a heaven of happiness —to know that '*Monsieur le Colonel*' is Denis Ducros, *le légionnaire*. ... I thank God!" she said.

"Denis Ducros!" she whispered.

And with tears in his own eyes, and a lump in his throat, Denis kissed her.

"My Nicolette!"

This was true. This was real.

There was no play-acting about this.

He was in love with this girl, and toward her he felt as

he had never felt toward any other woman. He wanted to give, and to *give*, without the slightest desire to take and to demand. And he was also aware of a feeling of pity, unfathomably deep; and Pity is the wonderful and beautiful sister of Love.

And without any amazement he found that with his new and fine love, his great and profound pity, he felt a real and true respect for her. And of that he was subconsciously but greatly glad, because he knew that without real respect, there could be no real lasting love.

Sympathy, yes; pity, yes; passion, yes—but not the love that lasts as long as life.

"My Nicolette!" he said again, and drew her yet closer to him.

"My Denis!" she whispered, returning his kiss with a warmth and strength equal to his own. "I am *too* happy. I am bewildered. I have known you for hours, and I seem to have known you for years and years. It really does seem years since you walked into Madame's *salon*, and I thought,

" 'What a handsome man! What a fine face he has! How can he bring a face like that into a place like this? He looks so restrained, so disciplined; so controlled, austere and cold.'

"I was so glad to see you, Denis; and I was so sorry.

"And then almost immediately I understood that you had merely come to see the place, to inspect it; and that while you loathed the place, and detested Madame, you were sorry for us.

"But how has it come about? How could you have done all the wonderful things you have done to-night, defeated Madame, given the girls what most they wanted, and set me free—if you are Denis Ducros, *le légionnaire*? . . . Of course they all think you are really the . . .

"You aren't making fun of me, *Monsieur le Colonel*?" she implored, gazing with love and anxiety into his eyes.

"Would you be really sorry to learn that I was?"

"That you are the Colonel Louis Rochefort after all, and not Denis Ducros? . . . It would be a dreadful disappointment. It would almost break my heart."

Again he kissed her.

"I am Denis Ducros all right," he said. "I am no Colonel; nor anything but a private soldier."

"But, Denis . . . Denis . . . Why are you dressed like this? Why are you in the Colonel's uniform? Why did you come and make them think you were Colonel Rochefort?"

"Fate . . . Chance . . . God, Himself, I think. . . .

"Or if it is presumptuous of me to think *le bon Dieu* takes any interest in my affairs, let us say the little blind god who sees so much, the god of Love."

"I prefer to think it was the good God Himself," replied Nicolette. "Is it not true that God *is* Love? Is not *le bon Dieu* good and kind? I prefer to think it was He, and I shall thank Him all my life, every day; every morning, every night. God and the Blessed Virgin."

"We'll both thank God, then, Nicolette . . . Well . . . *le bon Dieu* saw me brushing the Colonel's uniform.

" '*Ah!*' thought *le bon Dieu*, 'there's that rascal Denis Ducros; a great actor* manqué*; a wonderful impersonator; also a romantic, a dreamer, a submerged soul, drowned in the dreadful commonplace of routine and servitude . . .*

" '*Poor devil! He has made a mess of his life as so many of them do; and, being the All-Just Fountain of Justice, I'll admit he has never had much of a chance in life! I'll give him his chance now; his opportunity to do something for Me; something really worth while and useful. Also the chance to live for an hour the sort of life he would have loved and would have lived well, had it fitted in with my schemes for mice and men.*

" '*Yes, I'll give him the Stage to himself, and while he struts his little hour, he shall have a chance to realise the courage and spirit of the girl Nicolette from Domeuil. She has kept her soul alive, and in the midst of evil is untouched by evil.*

" '*That shall be his moment. If he has eyes to see, let him see. Let him act to some purpose.*'

"Thus, perhaps, *le bon Dieu* thought to Himself, and a mad idea entered my mind. Now whence do thoughts come into our minds? Obviously this one came from God, and you are right, Nicolette. What seemed a mad, wild and idiotic notion, has resulted in—your being here beside me, our being in love.

"*Of course* it came from God—although it was no better an idea than that I should try the Colonel's *képi* on, and then his tunic . . . And the rest followed."

"But where was the real Colonel?" asked Nicolette.

"In his bed."

"And where should you suppose he is now?" Nicolette said.

"Still in his bed—I hope. He has got fever," replied Denis, "and I pray *le bon Dieu* may remember to keep him in bed until I get back and return the clothes he doesn't know I've borrowed."

"But, Denis, won't you get into most terrible trouble?" asked the girl.

"Oh, I'm not caught yet," replied Denis evasively.

"But if they do catch you?"

"My darling little Nicolette, what can they do to me that will be more than a grain of desert sand in the scales against what *you* have done for me?"

"But, Denis, what will the punishment be, if you are caught?"

"I don't know. It depends on how the Colonel takes it," said Denis, and began to laugh.

"Do tell me what is the worst, the utmost . . ." begged Nicolette urgently.

"I should say Madame de Beauchamp," replied Denis, and laughed afresh. "That was the worst."

"No, please do be serious."

"I must. It was serious. There was a heavy fall in silk. In the street. And I shall be blamed for that."

Denis continued to laugh.

Nicolette drew away as though hurt.

"Denis," she expostulated, "please. Please answer my question. What is the worst, the utmost, that can happen to you for what you have done to-night?

"If you won't tell me, I won't go to Avignon," she added firmly.

"Well, darling, when I asked you if you'd wait eight years for me, I wasn't altogether joking," he said.

"Eight *years*! You mean eight years *in prison*? They'd do that to you, Denis?"

"I doubt it. They might, but . . . Depends on how the Colonel takes it."

"Denis!"

"You'd wait for me?" he asked.

"I shall wait for you for the rest of my life . . . But eight years! In prison! Why, it . . ."

"Oh, nice open-air life," interrupted Denis. "Not actually in prison, you know. Out in the desert. Making roads, and forts, and other little things like that. All good exercise."

"Eight *years*!" whispered Nicolette. "Denis!"

"But it won't be eight years. The Colonel isn't a bad old sort, and I've done him no real harm. His reputation has been quite safe in my hands. Lots of people will think all the better of him," and he began to laugh. "Eight years! Good Heavens, no. More like sixty days cells after a bit of solitary.

"Besides, I'm not caught yet," he added.

"Denis! Let's stop the carriage at once. I'll go on to the station, and you drive back to the Barracks as quickly as you can go," begged the girl.

"No. I am going to see you safely into that train, and the train safely out of the station. It would be a nice thing if the picket wouldn't let you go through!"

"Why should they interfere with me?" demurred Nicolette.

"They shouldn't. But you don't know these Legion Sergeants. They're not all Frenchmen, you know. You might very well find a bullying Prussian brute of the filthiest sort. And if it just entered his head to make you lose the train, he'd do it. Pure *schadenfreud*. Pretend your papers were out of order, or something of the sort. . . . Might say he suspected you to be the seven-foot Russian who deserted last week, trying to make his get-away after lying low in the bazaar somewhere. . . .

"No, I'm coming with you to the station," he concluded decisively.

"Oh, Denis! I shall be so anxious. So worried."

"I shall be all right. All you've got to do is to get safely home—and wait for me. I won't keep you waiting long, Nicolette."

"How I shall pray for you, Denis. Every day I shall burn candles to St. Antoine, St. Christophe, St. Michel, and to the Blessed Virgin. . . . Oh, how I shall pray for you."

"Then what harm can come to me?" smiled Denis. "Well. Here's the station. . . ."

If the Sergeant in command of the picket felt any surprise at the sight of his Colonel escorting a girl to the station with the obvious intention of seeing her off by train, he concealed it admirably, and called the Guard to order, to attention, and the presenting of arms, as though this were an unfailing nightly routine of Sidi-bel-Abbès Railway Station. . . .

As he stood by the door of the train, Denis Ducros found that, of the infinity of things he had to say, there was nothing of which he could speak coherently.

He could only beg her to take care of herself, to trust in him implicitly, and to wait for him—a reasonable time.

"I shall not expect you for eight years, Denis," said Nicolette softly, as she held his face between her hands.

"And at the end of eight years?" he asked.

"Then I shall begin to wait," she smiled.

As the train started to move and he kissed her again, "*I shall wait for ever*," Nicolette said.

"I shall come soon," Denis answered.

CHAPTER XIII

BACK TO THE PATH AGAIN

THE thoughts of Sergeant Igor Schlentczic were long, long thoughts, as he witnessed the parting ceremonies between his austere strait-laced Colonel and *cette très jolie jeune fille.*

Moving only his eyes he scanned the faces of the Guard

as they stood immovably to attention. Like himself, they had obviously seen nothing.

As he passed, the Colonel punctiliously, if absent-mindedly, returned their salute.

He walked on air.

Not Heaven itself could take away the solid fact, the glorious truth, that he had found Nicolette, fallen in love with Nicolette, and had actually saved Nicolette by his own wits and will-power.

There was no play-acting about that. Not but what the play-acting had been marvellous, wonderful, glorious. It would have been a hundred times worth punishment; and whatever that might be, he would not grudge or regret it. But the reality, the truth, the fact—of Nicolette —was a hundred times worth any punishment that the General Court Martial of Oran could inflict upon him— short of death.

It must not be that.

He must not die now. Now that he had found Nicolette.

But these were morbid and foolish thoughts. If the Colonel did send him to the Oran Court Martial, the utmost they would give him would be eight years with the Penal Battalions. And what was that to weigh against this new-found, wonderful happiness? Why, he'd enjoy the eight years, knowing that Nicolette would be there at the end of it.

But that again was morbid and foolish thinking. The Colonel would deal with him, himself. Probably give him all he'd got, and that was only sixty days cells.

Punishment? A mere joke.

And ever more buoyantly he trod on air.

What had he better do now? . . .

Get back to barracks as fast as he could—in the somewhat thin hope of replacing the Colonel's uniform, and satisfactorily explaining his absence if he had been missed.

No. Perish the thought! The play must go on. What sort of an actor was it who left the stage in the middle of playing his part?

He, Denis Ducros, who had waited all his life for the chance to act a big part on a great stage, to be unworthy of the opportunity when it came! To be weak, to be cowardly, to be too little for his part, to be unequal to his *rôle*!

Let the play go on—until the curtain falls.

While Denis Ducros could play the part of Colonel Louis Rochefort, he would play it for all he was worth.

As he left the station, Denis Ducros saw something that he had seen before, in different circumstances.

A pale boy in Legion uniform, obviously a wretched recruit, was standing staring with hopeless, tortured, longing eyes at the railway, symbol of escape and freedom. Obviously one of those—and there are many of them, as Denis knew—who find the beginning almost too hard for human endurance. Perhaps he was not physically equal to the strain of the day's work that begins at dawn with gymnastics, running-drill, and marching, on an empty stomach.

Perhaps he had fallen foul of some brute of a barrack-room bully, or of a corporal, or instructor.

Perhaps, and here Denis' heart was moved to acutest pity, he simply could not bear separation from the girl he had left behind him.

The boy started and stared, as though unable to believe his eyes. Was this the dread Colonel himself, bearing down upon him; the martinet of whose discipline he had heard such tales? He would know instantly that a recruit, *soldat deuxième classe*, would not have a late pass, and what was more, the Colonel would know quite well what he was doing down there.

With a brave attempt at the smart and soldierly swagger of the *vieux moustache*, the youngster saluted; and, to his dismay, the Colonel halted as he came abreast of him.

"Ah, my boy!" said he, in pleasant fatherly manner. "On late pass, I see! And taking a stroll out of town to have a look at the station . . . I know . . . I know . . . I used to do it myself when I was a young—er—ahem!—officer. But it isn't wise, *mon enfant*. It isn't wise. It only makes things harder, and God knows they're hard enough at first.

"But they get easier very quickly . . . very quickly.
. . . You'll hear some of the old rascals say it's the first
five years that are the worst. But don't you take any
notice of them. Why in three months' time you'll be
enjoying it. Absolutely enjoying it, and you wouldn't
want to go back home if you could.

"Stick it out. Do your best to be a good soldier—and
you'll be all right. Believe me.

"I shall keep an eye on you. Understand?"

"*Oui, mon Colonel!*" faltered the boy.

"And I expect to see you become a credit to the Regiment. You will, won't you?"

"I'll try, *Monsieur le Colonel.*"

"And you'll succeed. Take the rough with the smooth.

"If you can find any smooth," he added, with a grim
smile. "But you didn't come here to look for smooth
things, did you?

"Now then—back to Barracks. And remember I'm
your friend."

And the boy departed, also walking on air.

A sergeant passed him, and the boy saluted smartly.

"Hey!" called the Colonel, and the astounded sergeant,
scarce believing the evidence of his senses, positively
galloped across the road.

"Know that *bleu*?"[1]

The sergeant stood statuesque and still, the back of
his fingers at the peak of his *képi*.

"*Oui, mon Colonel.*"

"Then keep an eye on him. He's a good lad. Understand?"

"*Oui, mon Colonel.*"

The sergeant quite understood, or thought he did;
and to himself he said, "Good Gracious!" or words to
that effect.

"*Bon!* . . . *Rompez!*[2]" snapped the Colonel.

The sergeant fell away into the night, his mind interest-
ingly occupied with thoughts of princes in disguise, missing
heirs, illegitimate sons, and other colourful speculations.

"That two-*sous bleu*! The Colonel interested in him,

[1]recruit.   [2]Dismiss.   Break off.
208

eh? Well . . . What the Old Man said—that went. He'd have to blast the soul out of Corporal Kellermann, who, he seemed to remember, had a down on the creature."

"That would probably march, all right," reflected the Colonel. Sergeant Brausch was an ambitious climber and would put any commandment of the Colonel's before the other Ten. And it was quite probable that Sergeant Brausch, like a great many other people who had met Denis Ducros that night, would never know whether his interview had been with the genuine Colonel Louis Rochefort or not.

Anyway, he had done his best for the youngster, and at the very least he had given him a little pleasure, comfort, and brief happiness. Better still, hope. He'd feel a new man, and sleep like a child that night. Do him no harm, and perhaps do him a lot of good. And at best, it would make the wily Brausch a friend to the lad. Not a true friend of course, but a friend in need and a friend in deed.

He strode on, head in air, a giant refreshed.

Nicolette! . . . *Nicolette!* . . . *Nicolette!* . . . sang his heart.

As he approached the gate in the City rampart, he saw, passing beneath a lamp, a man of unmistakable figure and bearing, a man whom he greatly admired and liked, Captain le Sage, whom *le légionnaire* Denis Ducros, *ordonnance* to Colonel Rochefort, knew to be a very important member of the Legion's Military Intelligence Department.

An idea entered his uplifted mind, an idea that pleased his rash and soaring spirit. He'd try himself out against the wits of the cleverest man in the Nineteenth African Army Corps. If Captain le Sage saw through him, he'd brazen it out and puzzle him. He'd have a duel of wits and wills and personalities. He'd order him back to Barracks, and tell him to consider himself under close arrest.

It would be great fun; and if he succeeded in deceiving le Sage, he'd have a pleasant chat with him, and—*bon Dieu*, what an idea—he'd make use of the brilliant officer.

He'd put him on to one or two useful things that would interest him; and on to one or two people too.

Now that would be a useful bit of sport; and, pulling himself together, summoning every ounce of his undeniably great powers as an actor, he became Colonel Rochefort more authentically than at any time that evening.

"Ah! Le Sage!" he said in the Colonel's severe and quiet voice, as Captain le Sage blew out the match with which he had lighted his cigarette.

Captain le Sage's left hand, containing the cigarette, dropped smartly to his side, while his right hand rose swiftly in salute.

"Good evening, Sir," he said. . . . What was the Old Man doing down here at this time of night?

"Going to the Station?" pursued the Colonel.

"Yes, Sir. I am rather expecting that an interesting person may arrive to-night, very incognito."

"And you're going to introduce him to himself, eh?"

"And myself to him," smiled Captain le Sage.

Now was there anything behind that poker-faced smile? wondered Denis.

No, he believed not. Even the clever le Sage saw nothing unusual. But of course it was pretty dark; and, like mere ordinary people, le Sage saw what he expected to see. What he saw inside the Colonel's uniform must be the Colonel—naturally . . .

There was the voice, though. It must be a pretty good imitation; but if Denis Ducros, gifted impersonator, couldn't imitate a voice he heard all day long, and half the night, it would be a pity!

Le Sage must be wondering what Colonel Louis Rochefort was doing at the station at this time of night.

"I've just been seeing an interesting person off," he said. "And talking of interesting people, I want you to keep an eye on the *vaguemestre*, Stalheimer. I think you'd find a brief study of that gentleman's methods quite rewarding. And in more ways than one. I happen to know that he is robbing the men. Also that he is getting much more money than he could easily account for . . . from a foreign source."

Captain le Sage gave a quick direct look into the Colonel's eyes. This was very interesting. He didn't know the Old Man went in for that sort of thing. He had never supposed that he had an idea outside his own particular sphere of duty—wherein he was undeniably and uncommonly competent, behind that wooden façade of his.

On second thoughts, was his face and manner quite as wooden as he had always thought? He was certainly human enough to-night, and very much alive. . . . Eyes sparkling . . . Expression almost warm . . . Unusually friendly . . . Something had gingered him up . . . Well, he had just said he had been seeing somebody off. Perhaps they had opened one more bottle.

"Money comes from Berlin," continued the Colonel, "and not from kind father, loving mother, or devoted wife, for Stalheimer has no family. Not even a Rich Uncle Kurt. . . . He was a slaughter-house hand before he was a German soldier.

"Yes, he's a real *mauvais sujet*, that one; and I think that one or two of his letters, addressed to Berlin, might prove very interesting."

Certainly the Colonel was interesting to-night, thought le Sage, whatever Stalheimer was. Probably the Old Boy had been getting anonymous letters from some German *légionnaire* whose little remittances were not arriving regularly.

"German agent, do you think, Sir?" he said.

"Yes. Sure of it. And I'll tell you another thing, le Sage. He works with a damned scoundrel, as big a *salaud* as himself. That mass of corruption they call Bacchus. You know him of course? A bloated hairy fellow, a typical *faux bonhomme*."

"I know him," le Sage answered. "A detestable brute; but I don't know anything against him."

"Well, put him under your microscope. In conjunction with the worthy *vaguemestre*. And I think you may see signs of active insect-life which will quite intrigue you."

"Well, well, well!" thought le Sage. "Out of the mouths

of Colonels and Commandants they'll be convicted!
Someone is certainly keeping the Old Boy posted. Mare's-
nests and . . ."

"And I'll give you an address, le Sage," the Colonel's
voice interrupted the current of the surprised officer's
thoughts. "Make a note of it. And put a good man on
to it, with instructions to contrive to be present at one or
two of the little meetings that are held there.

"You might go yourself," he continued, with a dry
smile, "disguised as—er—your batman, or something
of the sort. I believe you'd really enjoy yourself."

Curiouser, and curiouser, thought Captain le Sage.
Whoever would have thought it? One never knew;
and when one did, one was generally wrong. Colonel
Louis Rochefort was shedding quite a new light upon
himself. Just imagine his knowing so much about his
men, and particularly that sort of much!

Anonymous letters! That's what it was. And the
Old Devil was coming the oracle and mystery-monger
over poor stupid le Sage of the Intelligence!

"*Rue Raspail, dix bis; Rue de Daya.* Top front room.
And they meet there on Sundays after evening *soupe.*"

"Thank you, Sir," said le Sage, making a note of the
address in a small book which he drew from the breast
pocket of his tunic.

"I expect you're wondering how I happen to have that
piece of information," said the Colonel.

"I am, Sir," admitted le Sage. "I am filled with
curiosity."

"*Ah! . . . Indeed?*" said the Colonel, and brushed his
moustache.

"Good night," he added abruptly, and marched off,
leaving an extremely clever man, extremely puzzled.

There was more in Colonel Louis Rochefort than met
the eye, and a good deal more than met the ear, as a
rule.

And as Denis Ducros went on his way rejoicing, he
rightly surmised that he'd given his admired Captain le
Sage something to think about; and there was no shadow
of doubt in his mind that Captain le Sage would think

about it to some purpose. He'd get that rogue the *vague-mestre* all right, and that lousy swine Bacchus, and the gang of rotten depraved parasites who did their dirty work and ran their filthy errands.

Yes. Le Sage must be wondering how Colonel Louis Rochefort knew quite as much as he seemed to know.

But in point of fact, there were precious few people in Sidi-bel-Abbès who knew as much as Denis Ducros, with a foot in neither camp, and one wide-open ear in the Colonel's club, and the other in the Barrack canteen.

It was of course, speaking generally, quite against one's principles to tell tales of one's comrades to an officer, but these men of whom he had spoken were not comrades. They were despicable criminals who were a disgrace to the Regiment.

One of them was a murderer who had also been the cause of two or three suicides; and one was that lowest form of low thief who used official powers and position to rob his subordinates. And, what was perhaps worse, although Denis Ducros wasn't personally greatly concerned in such matters, they and their hireling gang were, by all accounts and many indications, traitors to the country whose pay they took and to whom they had sworn the oath of *"Honneur et Fidelité"*.

No. Denis had no qualms of conscience about this little piece of work. It was a thoroughly good job, well done.

On he strode, trailing clouds of glory.

Still the all-powerful Colonel, who interfered in the lives of men, who put down the evil-doing mighty from their seats, and raised up the humble and meek.

The potentate whom men feared and whom women were . . .

Hallo! What was this? The first of a smart procession of carriages drew up beside him, as he turned to cross the small square of the *Place Bougeaud*.

A girl sprang from it, and flung herself upon him.

"I knew it! I knew it!" she cried. "I knew it was our own dear friend, *Monsieur le Colonel*.

"Here he is, girls!" she screamed; and, as the other carriages came to a halt in the rear of the first one, the

213

girls jumped out and came running to join Odette, and gather round the Colonel.

It could not be said that their hearts were too full for speech. Words did not fail them, nor kisses; and the heart of the Colonel was warmed within him, warmed by sympathy, affection and kindness; warmed by anger and indignation at the thought of Madame—and that such things should be.

And might not he have done more for these girls than send them for a drive?

To what was it due, but to pure selfishness on his part, that Nicolette was now speeding through the night, saved, released, set free—and these her companions, were still the slaves of the unspeakable Madame.

He felt that he had not risen to the full height of his opportunity, and that he had failed them. If he could save one, he could have saved them all.

Was it too late?

Raising his hands and waving them above his head, the Colonel, in mock despair of being heard, cried,

"*Mes enfants! Mes chères filles!* Listen! Listen! I want to make a speech."

"Speech! Speech!" cried the merry and excited girls.

"Up there, *Monsieur le Colonel!*" urged Odette, and pointed to where, behind him, stood upon a low plinth the statue of a French general, arrayed, for some reason, in the garb of a Roman senator; about his bald head a laurel wreath; across his stomach a close-fitting garment of bronze; pendent from his middle a kilt of dangling bars of metal; clasping in his hand the roll of manuscript without which no Roman of any class was ready to be photographed, painted, or done in enduring stone.

"Excellent idea!" said the Colonel, and stepped on to the plinth, sharing for the first time in his life the pedestal of fame with a general of repute.

With laughter and cries of encouragement, the girls gathered about him. He began to speak, and in a moment they had fallen silent.

"*Mes enfants,*" he said, "you've had an hour or two's freedom, and you seem to have enjoyed yourselves. Is there any real reason why you should return to Madame's house at all?"

The girls laughed dutifully at the Colonel's idea of a joke.

" . . . Because if you don't want to go back—now is your chance.

"Nicolette has already gone . . ."

"What?" breathed Odette, while the rest of the group stood staring, speechless, stricken silent.

"I saw Nicolette off, myself, from the station, half an hour ago. She will be out of Africa to-morrow, and in France a day or two later."

"Mon Dieu!" whispered Odette. "And Madame let her go?"

"And gave her her fare," replied the Colonel.

"At *Monsieur le Colonel's* orders, *sans doute*?" said Odette shrewdly.

"I did suggest it . . . And what is more, I'll suggest the same thing for all of you—or for any one of you, who wishes to leave Madame's house," declared the Colonel.

He stopped speaking, and glanced quickly from girl to girl. In the brilliant moonlight he could see clearly to read the expression upon each of the up-turned faces.

It was an expression common to them all.

Though the face were vacant, greedy, cunning, stupid, shrewd, bovine or vicious, each expressed refusal and rejection—rejection more or less contemptuous.

Before anyone spoke, he knew what the answer would be.

They would not go.

They did not want to go.

And in his heart, there mingled with regret and sorrow for them, a feeling of gladness and pride.

Nicolette was different. Nicolette was not as these.

Nicolette . . . Nicolette . . . Nicolette . . . sang his heart.

These were people quite different from Nicolette. Nevertheless he must do his best.

A girl laughed scornfully, a sound that conveyed as plainly as speech, her bitter thanks for empty nothing.

"Odette?" he asked.

The girl stared at him wide-eyed, her mouth set in hard lines.

"Wouldn't you like to go home?"

"I have no home, *Monsieur le Colonel.*"

"Oh, surely you have relations or friends, who . . ."

"My friends are in Sidi-bel-Abbès, *Monsieur le Colonel,*" said the girl shortly.

"Wouldn't you like to leave Africa?"

"In *Monsieur le Colonel's* company?" asked the girl pertly.

"I am not leaving Africa at the moment. . . . Do you really wish to remain—with Madame?"

"I wish to remain with Madame.

"And to accompany her to Hell," she added. "It will give me a great satisfaction.

"Home!" she spat with a bitterness and venom that he found pitiful indeed.

"Fifine?" he asked. "Wouldn't you like to go home?"

"Blague!" laughed the girl. *"Monsieur le Colonel se moque de nous autres."*

"No, no, Fifine. I . . ."

"And pray who will take me to my happy little home in German Poland, where we get nearly as good a time as the cattle? Not quite such nice byres, or so many mangel-wurzels, you understand, but . . ."

"But one knows when one's getting white bread," grinned Annette.

"So," agreed Fifine with finality. "Believe it or not, *Monsieur le Colonel,* I prefer a fine house in Sidi-bel-Abbès to a stinking pig-sty in Solcszysch. Madame's a good many things, but she's not a German policeman.

"Home!" she added softly, and laughed, with a dreadful amusement, at the vision the word recalled to her mind.

"Justine?" asked the Colonel of a girl who stood with beautiful wide-open eyes and an also beautiful wide-open mouth, gazing at him in placid, bovine incomprehension. "What about you? Wouldn't you like to go away from Sidi-bel-Abbès?"

"I? *Monsieur le Colonel?* Go away? Go away from Sidi-bel-Abbès? Where to?"

"Well, isn't there any place to which you'd like to go —to get away from here, to get away from Madame?"

"*Mais oui, Monsieur.* I should like to go to Paris," she said, and added ere he could reply,

"If Monsieur could find me a nice house like Madame's."

"A house? Like Madame's?" asked the Colonel, disappointed. "Wouldn't you like a change? A fresh start in life?"

"No, thank you, *Monsieur le Colonel*, I do very well."

"You don't want to leave Madame?"

"Madame's all right, *Monsieur le Colonel*. She's a thief, a liar, a fit wife for the Devil, and a half-caste bitch, *mais que voulez-vous*?

"What would you?" shrugged the girl, "these Madames are not angels. And should *Monsieur le Colonel* be at any time looking for an angel, it is not among them that he'll find one."

Some of the girls laughed, without great amusement.

"But if *Monsieur le Colonel* is inviting *me* to go to Paris with him, there is a train to Oran at . . ."

"I am not going to Paris at the moment, *ma belle*," interrupted the Colonel. "But look! Wouldn't you like to go by yourself, and find a job of work which . . ."

"*Work?* What is that?" enquired Mademoiselle Justine.

Unhelpable, thought the Colonel, unemployable . . . vicious . . . born in the bone and bred in the flesh . . . from birth . . . poor doomed soul.

Complete silence held the group in the little *place*.

"Isn't there one of you who'd like to . . . escape?" he asked again. "I'll see that you get a ticket for France, Algiers, Tangier, your own country, anywhere you want to go."

No answer.

"Come on, girls," laughed Odette. "Before *Monsieur le Colonel* corrupts us. If we listen any longer, he'll make us want to cheat our dear kind Madame, who loves us so," and leaping lightly up on to the plinth, she once again flung her arms round the Colonel's neck and kissed him.

"*Dieu vous bénisse!*" she whispered in his ear, and, turning to the now laughing and applauding group, cried,

217

"Come on, girls. Start the procession up again. Right through Sidi and out the other side, and half-way to Saida."

Back to their respective carriages went the girls, still more like schoolboys let out of school for an unexpected holiday.

As Odette got into the last *fiacre*, she turned to the Colonel, to whose arm she still clung.

"Nicolette," she whispered. "Did you really mean that she has . . . *gone*? You've helped her to get away? Oh, I am glad . . . glad . . . glad. She was never one of us. But, oh, how I shall miss her."

"Yes," replied the Colonel. "She is in the Oran train. Going home. Safe. Now *she* . . ."

"You are a darling," she said. "You are a girl's dream of St. Louis! . . . Nicolette was different.

"You want to be, oh, so kind; but you don't understand us others. We are . . . damned . . . we are finished . . . we are doomed . . . destined . . . done for. . . . Goodbye!"

And a minute later the procession resumed its cheerful and noisy way.

"Yes," mused Denis Ducros, as he stood looking after the last retreating vehicle. "Nicolette is different."

CHAPTER XIV

A LITTLE MORE GLORY

AND once again, secure in this glorious certainty, he resumed his amazing journey with a light and happy heart.

A short cut through a dark, narrow and sinister alley brought him into a still-busy and crowded bazaar.

Here and there a *légionnaire*, suddenly realising that he must be drunker than he felt, thought that he came face to face with his Colonel, saluted the grim vision, and made resolutions for immediate reform.

These salutes the Colonel returned with an absent-minded raising of the fore-finger vaguely in the direction of the peak of his *képi*.

Suddenly he caught sight of a man whom he liked, admired and pitied from the depths of his vast experience. Poor Hagues! He remembered that man as a model *adjudant*, the perfect *sous-officier*, who would certainly have been sent to the St. Maixent College, to be trained for a commission, had he not suddenly taken to drink.

And, alas, he had done this as thoroughly as he did everything else; he had drunk his way down the ladder far more quickly than he had fought his way up it.

Drunk on parade—reduced to Sergeant-Major; drunk on duty—reduced to Sergeant; drunk on guard—reduced to Corporal; drunk on escort-duty and reduced to the ranks.

And now in the ranks, drinking to escape, drinking to drown the dreadful sense of failure, disgrace and ignominy. He, the smart *adjudant*, now the butt and victim of every blackguard whom he had ever punished.

"Halt there, Hagues!" said the Colonel. "I want to speak to you."

Hagues stood swaying, doing his utmost to keep stiffly at attention and at the salute.

"Stand easy. Come in here," and taking him by the arm, the Colonel actually led him into a small semi-Arab café of which the door stood invitingly open.

The fat proprietor scuttled across the cavern-like smoky room when he saw the gold braid.

Bowing low, automaton-like, he indicated the largest and cleanest divan.

"In one moment, noble Sir, the dancing girls . . ."

"Silence," growled the Colonel. "Coffee. The best. Strong. Nothing added."

That would be the best thing for Hagues in his present condition, and he personally preferred his coffee without the addition of vanilla essence, cheap cognac, Dutch oil-of-orange, a spot of hashish, or anything else.

"Six cups each, and Allah help you if . . ."

The fat hybrid galloped off, but quickly returned with

a tray of his small clay cups of most excellent coffee—none better until he started improving it with assorted flavours and stimulants.

"Drink some coffee, Hagues," said the Colonel. "Pull yourself together and listen to me."

The bewildered, incredulous, and intoxicated *légionnaire* obeyed. By the time he had drunk three or four cups of the strong hot coffee, he decided that this was not a drunken dream; he realised that he was sitting in Abdullah's, face to face with Colonel Louis Rochefort—which was absurd.

No, it wasn't true. It was either absurdly impossible, or impossibly absurd. Which? He'd see the answer in a moment, through the haze of wine.

He was drunk.

He wasn't drunk.

It was the Colonel, and he was talking to him—as to a friend.

"You can do it," he was saying. "And nobody but you can do it. You've got to save yourself. I could put you straight back to *adjudant*, but what would be the good of that? You'd be in trouble again in a week. No earthly good my doing anything for you until you've done something for yourself. You stop drinking, and you'll get your Corporal's stripe back very quickly. Keep off it, and your Corporal's worsted stripe will change to your Sergeant's gold stripe, while you watch it. And soon nothing can prevent your becoming Sergeant-Major, and then *adjudant* again, except your own weakness and folly.

"You know I'm right, don't you? You know you can climb back. And though you may not be aware of it, I shall have my eye on you. But I can't and I won't do anything for you, until you do something for yourself.

"Stop it, man, here and now—and be a man, not a hog. Damn it all, you don't want to live on the level of the animal Bacchus and his gang of sottish scum, do you?"

"*Monsieur le Colonel*," faltered the man, "I . . . There was a letter. . . . It knocked me down into the dust."

"Get up again then," snarled the Colonel. "The dust isn't the place for a man."

"She was my . . . life. . . . She wrote that . . . And I had her put on a level with the Holy . . ."

"Don't whine," growled the Colonel. "You're not the first man who . . ."

And suppose this poor devil loved and trusted her, as he loved and trusted Nicolette?

"Look!" he said, his voice, human and sympathising. "She proved worthless, eh?"

"Worthless, *Monsieur le Colonel*."

"Well, *mon enfant*; let's suffer and fight and die for something worthy, eh? Something worth while. Why all this misery and degradation, leading to downfall, ruin and death, for something *worthless*?

"Give everything you have—your honour, reputation, life itself if necessary, for the woman who loves you; but don't be such a fool and weakling as to throw . . ."

"*Monsieur le Colonel*, I loved her better than life itself. I loved her so that I would not marry her until I was an officer, and once again, a gentleman. And she . . ."

"And she wasn't worth it all, Hagues. But because you built up that fine pedestal so quickly—for her, why knock it down again because she is not equal to standing on it?

"Stand on it yourself, man," continued the Colonel.

"It's gone, *mon Colonel*. I am done for. Finished."

"Then I am done too—with you. Finished—with you. I am sorry, for I had had some hopes of you. I had really thought you were, in some ways, something like a man."

The Colonel leaned back, folded his arms, and stared into Hagues' miserable eyes.

"Listen, poor weakling; poor sniveller," he said. "I had actually thought it conceivably possible that, when you had been to St. Maixent Military College and got your commission, I might have seen you Captain some day; Major; and, if you were lucky, *Chef de Bataillon*. . . . But I was a fool of course. I was quite mistaken in you.

"Because one of five hundred million women is a what-shall-we-say, you at once become—what you are—a poor drunk, a disgrace, a sot and a rotten soldier. . . . *Pah!*"

The unfortunate *légionnaire* flushed, shuffled, and moved his hands and feet nervously.

"*Monsieur le Colonel*," he began, "I am . . ."

"Yes, of course you are," interrupted the Colonel in a tone of encouragement. "You are ashamed of yourself. And you are going to start afresh. Going to turn over a new leaf. Now. Not another drop of *tchum-tchum*, or any other bazaar filth. And no more *pinard* than the regulation allowance. And—mark my words—you'll go up like a rocket, once it is realised you are back on the water-wagon, and you are on the job again.

"Don't expect anything from me—except watchfulness. I shall have my eye on you, Hagues.

"Well?" he asked sharply, and extended his hand.

Hagues hesitated to accept so great an honour, and again his face flushed.

"*Monsieur le Colonel* is too kind," he faltered, his eyes unwontedly bright. "I will do my best I promise.

"God help me," he cried, and, rising, swiftly saluted, and fled, incredulous, overwhelmed, and unable either to trust his voice or control his feelings.

The Colonel!

He took an interest in the fate of such a grain of dust as Guillaume Hagues, dust blown along the road to Hell on the wind of adversity.

The Colonel himself!

What a man!

Guillaume Hagues would be deserving of his kindness. He would not fail him.

What an accursed fool he had been. As the Colonel said, he was a weakling, a coward and a cur. Imagine wrecking a successful career and ruining one's life because a woman was—a woman. As though such suicide would do him any good, or her any harm. *Assez!*

And so thought and hoped Denis Ducros as he rose to depart.

"How much?" he growled at the salaaming Abdullah.

"But nothing, nothing, nothing, *Sidi Général*," replied Abdullah, trying hard to abase himself lower and lower, while rising higher and higher in the Colonel's estimation —he hoped.

" 'How much'? I said," growled the Colonel, on his deepest note.

"Oh noble Sidi! Give your servant the honour!"

"Give your servant the bill," interrupted the noble Sidi, "and let him take it to my servant at my house," and walked out of the smoky little cavern, reflecting on the peculiarities of the ritual of credit.

He seemed to have gone a very long way, that evening, on the strength of the gold on his sleeves—though there was none in his pocket.

Poor Hagues! Would he have the guts to hold on? He might. And again, he might not, for he had undoubtedly taken a terrible knock, and he, Denis Ducros, could understand the force of it.

What sort of interest in life would he feel if, when he reached Avignon, he found no Nicolette, and learned that she had gone off with somebody else? Poor Hagues! Poor devil! Poor, poor devil!

Well, he had done his best for him; and now he must do his best for himself. And They'd look after him all right, once They saw that he had pulled himself together, and really meant to make good. Captain le Sage had the highest opinion of him, and had told the Colonel so, at the Officers' *popotte*,[1] one evening, in camp.

The Colonel had agreed, for at that time, Hagues was not only a model *adjudant*, but the latest model.

He remembered that le Sage had advanced a theory—which was more likely a piece of private knowledge—that *Adjudant* Guillaume Hagues had been not only an officer in the Belgian Army, but a Staff Officer, and Aide-de-camp to the King.

What a downfall! And what a tragedy! Weak streak somewhere, of course. Drink probably—and that terrible form of disease which impels a normally sober and moderate man, occasionally, though perhaps very rarely, to collapse into a bout of steady and determined drinking. Just swinish.

Probably in Hagues' case it only happened under great stress and strain. Or violent emotion . . .

[1]temporary Mess.

Hullo! What was this?

A crowd of soldiers and civilians had suddenly burst forth from a *bistro*, shouting and knocking each other down, as they struggled through the doorway.

"Run! Run!"

"Look out! He's got a knife!"

"Murder! Murder!"

"He's mad! He's mad!"

"He has killed Pedro!"

"He has cut his throat!"

"Nearly slashed his head off!"

These and other cries intrigued the Colonel, as the occupants of the place stumbled out into the alley. Positively signs of life!

And signs of death too.

It would probably be the excellent Zidenski, fighting-drunk again. He'd kill somebody one of these days.

"Well?" he barked, at a tall bearded *légionnaire*, who pulled himself up short in his head-long career, saluted, and blinked in amazement at this apparition.

"Zidenski! *Monsieur le Colonel*," he gasped. "Gone mad. *Cafard*."

"Well?" growled the Colonel.

"Got a great knife, *Monsieur le Colonel*. Murdering everybody."

"Well?"

"Mad ... Blood ... Murder ... Knife ..." gulped the *légionnaire*.

"And why have you not taken him back to Barracks?"

"Because he's mad. Because he has a knife, *Monsieur le Colonel*."

"Any other reason?"

"No, *Monsieur le Colonel*," faltered the big *légionnaire*.

"Yes, *Monsieur le Légionnaire*," mocked the Colonel. "There is another reason. Because you are a coward.

"Like the rest of these scum," he added, as other soldiers either stopped, saluted and stood at attention, or, with greater presence of mind, achieved an absence of body, by promptly wheeling about and taking to their heels, on catching sight of the Colonel.

"Fall in! You, and you, and you!" he ordered, indicating some half-a-dozen *légionnaires*, "and await orders."

"You, Allones, in command," he added, addressing a grizzled *soldat première classe*, whom he knew to be the senior man present; and turning on his heel, crossed the road and entered the *bistro*.

Here was a scene of terror and confusion.

Behind the bar, across which they had vaulted, were three *légionnaires*, armed with empty bottles. Behind them again, cowered the fat little Pedro, the Spanish proprietor of the wine-shop. In corners of the room shrank soldiers and civilians, men and women, behind such fragile barricades as a couple of benches, chairs, iron-topped tables.

In the middle of the floor lay dead, dying, or shamming, a citizen, the peak of whose mountainous stomach rose far higher than any other tract of the surrounding area of his anatomy. Even his big, up-turned feet looked short and small.

About him, danced a little *légionnaire*, who—in spite of the facts that his eyes blazed madly brilliant in a dead white face, that foam flecked his lips, and that he brandished aloft a blood-stained knife—irresistibly reminded the Colonel of an india-rubber ball.

He seemed to bounce as well as to bound; to rebound as well as to leap; for his flying feet scarcely seemed to touch the floor. Undeniably, as the Colonel entered, he bounced, he rebounded, from the resilient summit of the loftily protuberant centre of the prone citizen.

On all the soldiers, with the exception of the drunken madman, discipline laid its compelling hand of steel. To a man they stood to attention, at the salute, even while death threatened them, and the homicidal maniac leapt around, about, and upon a fellow creature whose fate they might at any moment share.

So sudden was the silence that fell upon the room, that even the *cafard*-stricken lunatic noticed it, and, completing the tight-rope balancing progress which he had been making along the prostrate man's body from his feet to his face, he leapt about as though to meet a new enemy, and beheld an old one—the Colonel!

The effect was instant and electrical.

He screamed, a horrible inarticulate sound, without words or meaning; raised the knife to stabbing position; and, like a panther stalking its prey and about to spring, he crept tense and crouching, towards the man he feared and hated more than any other.

Denis Ducros instinctively assumed the attitude which Colonel Louis Rochefort would have adopted in such circumstances.

With his gloved left hand in which he held his riding-switch, resting lightly on his hip, he stood at ease, the bare right hand hanging loose, but very ready. With steady level gaze he met and held the madman's glare.

Closer and closer crept Zidenski, murder in his hand and eye.

No other actor moved on that sordid stage, of which Denis Ducros saw himself the centre and the star.

One more step and the hand went back to strike.

"*Halt!*"

Crisp, clear, sudden, the familiar command fell upon the ears of the man who had obeyed it a million times.

He obeyed it.

"*About turn!*"

Prompt obedience.

"*Quick march!*"

"*Left turn!*"

"*Left turn!*"

Each order instantly and automatically carried out.

The madman reached the door.

"*Halt!*"

"*Stand at ease!*"

The man obeyed.

"'*Shun!*" shouted the Colonel suddenly and loudly; and, dropping the knife, the man placed his hands, open and flat, in correct position.

"*Quick march!*"

The madman marched out through the door, into the alley.

"Guard!" called the Colonel, and Allones brought his squad to attention.

"You, *Légionnaire* Allones, arrest this man. Take him back to Barracks, and hand him over to the Sergeant of the Guard.

"Cells," he added grimly. "I'll deal with him to-morrow."

And, a minute later, the drink-sodden, *cafard*-stricken Bulgarian found himself in a familiar situation.

What that one wanted was another tour of active service, reflected Denis. No drink, no *cafard*. Meanwhile, no liberty, no murder. A cell was the best and safest place for him.

What a night! What a night!

Love and Death and . . . doings.

Quite a good job that he chose the Great Holiday night for his great escapade.

But he didn't really choose it.

It was chosen for him—by Fate.

No. Let him say rather by *le bon Dieu*, who intended him to meet and to love and to save his Nicolette. . . .

Ah! Here came a nasty piece of work, and he'd give him a nasty jolt; he'd try to pay off one or two old scores. For in the days before he, Denis Ducros, became the Colonel's batman, Lieutenant Guani had, for some reason, taken a personal dislike to him, and had made a personal matter of it.

The greasy little Italian cur. All flash and bombast. Completely bogus.

For, truly or falsely, his half-company considered that he was no real fire-eater. Not of rifle-fire anyway.

Old Pinard had put the idea into appropriate words, as usual, with the casual remark that Lieutenant Guani was really more of a tactician than an ordinary fighting soldier, and had perfected the art of leading from behind, which was much superior to following in front—whatever Pinard meant by that.

However, Pinard admitted that the man was a good leader, and declared that nobody ever led a retreat better or further.

227

What cramped Guani's style, according to the same authority, was that the Legion never retreated, and so Guani's career had been hampered and slowed down. He had never had a chance to show what he could really do in command of a body of troops. Retreating by yourself might be spectacular, but it really led nowhere—save to the rear—and the Higher Command was not as yet sufficiently advanced in military theory to understand and appreciate the value of initiative shown in the great art of strategic retirement, without orders.

Those heavy-sterned Generals certainly mentioned an original and enterprising officer who used the tactic—but it was not in despatches.

Well, most bullies are cowards, if not all; and Guani was a hectoring bully to subordinates and a fawning sycophant to superiors. . . .

Lieutenant Guani, a plumpish, blue-cheeked man, with protuberant eyes and over-ripe lips beneath a tiny curled moustache, gave an obvious start of surprise, and smartly saluted his Colonel, a man whom he hated as much as he dared, and admired more than he wished to do.

A sudden thought struck Denis Ducros, and made his blood boil.

He saw red.

This loathsome, swaggering, upstart brute was probably on his way to visit *chez* Madame.

Man proposes—to call Lieutenant Guani a man. For once Denis Ducros would dispose—appointing himself God's agent in the matter. And if it came to pass, obviously it was ordained that he should be just that.

He returned the Lieutenant's salute with the merest upward movement of a finger.

"Ah! *Ce bon Lieutenant Guano!*" he murmured.

"Halt you, and stand at the salute, while I tell you one or two things I have had on my mind for some time.

"You have been one of the things, Lieutenant Guano."

"Guani, *Monsieur le Colonel*," corrected the Lieutenant, and his face flushed angrily.

"I *said* Guano," agreed the Colonel.

"Guani, *Monsieur le Colonel*," ventured the Lieutenant, who had dined well and supped better.

"My good creature, I'm not deaf. Neither am I blind, nor yet, in spite of my years and station, quite imbecile. I *heard* you say Guano. I *see* you are Guano. And I am not so ignorant as to be unaware as to what to do with Guano."

A pulse beat in the Lieutenant's cheek, but he had sufficient self-control to stand like a statue.

The Colonel appeared to be following a train of thought. He sighed.

"Yes. Very useful . . . But not yet. Some day you'll be buried, though. Very fertilising."

"Where are you going?" he suddenly snapped.

"Er—I was . . . I was going to a rendezvous, *Monsieur le Colonel*," replied the junior officer, burning with resentment.

What right had the Old Devil to make puns on his name, and then to ask where he was going, when he was off duty?

"Oh! Excellent! Night march and exercises! Your men have already marched off, eh? I hope you didn't turn the poor fellows out until their holiday expired—at midnight."

The Old Man was being funny, surely. His idea of humour.

"Not a military rendezvous, to-night, *Monsieur le Colonel*," and the Lieutenant permitted himself a little nervous giggle.

"Rather a case of Wine, Woman and Song, *Monsieur le Colonel*," he smirked. "Holiday occasion and . . ."

"Well, I see you've had your wine," interrupted the Colonel unsympathetically. "More than enough of it. I cannot imagine that any woman could possibly desire your society. And Heaven preserve us from hearing your song.

"So there will be no more Wine, and neither Woman nor Song for you to-night, Lieutenant.

"You have my permission to go," continued the Colonel quietly.

"Back to Barracks," he added with a parade-ground rasp.

The Lieutenant's arm fell to his side. He saluted again and turned about.

"When I have told you the one or two things I have had on my mind, for some time," pursued the Colonel.

"In the first place, I wish to bring to your notice the fact that you are, in my opinion, as well as that of all your superiors, by far the most . . ."

Lieutenant Guani brightened up, stood more stiffly, and assumed the air proper to one who, with conscious modesty, receives a decoration.

The Old Man had been pulling his leg.

". . . the most inefficient, slack, lazy, incompetent and objectionable officer in the Battalion; and, almost certainly, in the whole Foreign Legion. You are a drunken, dissipated, dishonest, disreputable and detestable character, Lieutenant Guano; a bully, a braggart, and a bad officer. I don't think you'll hold your present rank much longer—certainly not long after I have sent in my next report on you.

"Those are the little matters I had on my mind concerning you.

"Now march yourself straight back to your quarters, and put yourself under close arrest. . . . You'll hear why in the morning; and you can spend the night in guessing which of the many probable reasons is the real one.

"Dismiss!"

And as the crestfallen Lieutenant, stricken, frightened and thoroughly apprehensive, turned about and took his dejected way, the Colonel smiled in the well-known Rochefort orderly-room manner.

"A taste of your own medicine, you dog," he growled, and as Colonel Rochefort was wont to do, made the motion of one who dusts his fingers.

It had been in bad taste to misuse this fellow's name like that, but one had to meet people of this sort on their own ground. He needed a touch of the whip that he was so very fond of wielding—vilely insulting remarks on subordinates' personal peculiarities, as though it were a man's own fault that he was short and thick-set, tall and lean; had a big nose, a wall eye, bat ears, or a mouth like that of a hippopotamus.

Why, the pernicious little swine used to exercise his wonderful wit on the subject of the face of a man who had been scarred and slashed when tortured by Bedouin tribesmen, had been picked up for dead, and had been decorated for the tremendous courage and resolution he had shown on that occasion!

Yes; his mutilated face had struck Guani as very funny, but it would strike the Company as something much funnier if Guani himself ever got himself a decoration for valour. . . .

Well, he'd let that animal get well ahead, and then he must really think about making his own way back to Barracks.

Positively he was beginning to feel tired.

And no wonder!

What a night!

He'd loathe to end it.

It would be with a positive pang that he would put off the uniform of glory.

Henceforth he would feel as a Colonel reduced to the ranks. But he would have had his hour, an hour which heaven itself could not take away; his crowded hour of glorious life, itself the first of many years of glorious life with Nicolette.

So no regrets. . . .

It would have been a splendid and wonderful thing if he could have finished his great night on an appropriate and satisfying note, so to speak; then have just taken off his uniform, folded it up, gone to bed in peace, a Colonel fulfilled—and awakened in the morning a batman restored.

After all, uneasy walks the figure that wears the uniform of rank, and happy low lies down the humble and obscure man, be he only a batman—who has found his Nicolette.

So back along the weary road—no, no, the happy golden road—to Barracks and the green apron, *and* to Nicolette.

The golden road to Samarcand—to Avignon and to Nicolette.

Perhaps one more little drink on the way?

Thus, gaily bedight, this gallant knight in moonshine and in shadow, journeyed along singing his song— *Nicolette! ... Nicolette! ... Nicolette! ...*

CHAPTER XV

"THE LAST ACT CROWNS THE PLAY"

AND as he came to a large restaurant whence issued again the appealing and disturbing strains of *Donna è Mobile*, he halted in his magnificent stride.

Ah! The *Cabaret Espagnol*, a crowd of good lads still going strong; and the wine had been flowing freely.

It should again flow freely, at his command; for they must have spent their pay by now—and a bottle of it should flow down his own tightly-encircled neck.

Appropriately enough, at this moment, the music changed, and broke into the *Funeral March of a Marionette*. Appropriate, timely, and most amusing— rather sinisterly amusing. . . .

The Colonel entered in style.

Silence spread in an ever-growing circle from the door, until there was no sound in the big room, save the notes of the mocking music.

Half a hundred soldiers stood, or did their best to stand, correctly at attention.

"Stand easy! Stand easy, *mes enfants*!" he cried. "And now sit easy."

The astonished soldiers obeyed with soldierly promptitude, one or two seating themselves, somewhat heavily, upon the floor.

"A bottle for everybody," he ordered, turning to the proprietor of the restaurant.

This was the Colonel himself? The Old Devil in person? Name of a Name of a Scalded Cat! What the Hell?

232

It might be the Great Fête Day of Madame la République, but it wasn't the Day of Judgment too, was it?

No. Nor did the Old Devil look as though he had come to do any judging.

"A bottle for everybody," repeated the Colonel blithely, "of your best.

"And a still better one for me," he added with a merry laugh.

A be-medalled *légionnaire* in whom wine had weakened the bonds of discipline, habit, fear and inhibitions, called loudly for three cheers for the Colonel, and a *tohuwabohu* of joyous cries burst forth from the joyous rout. Hurrahs, mingled with *bravas*, *hochs*, *vives*, and other strange national shouts of joy and approval. Undrowned in the roaring surging sea of noise, the Colonel clearly heard a lone but dominant,

"*Rah—Rah—Rah! Attaboy!*" and glanced to where a long lean saturnine *légionnaire* stood supporting a wall with one hand, a bottle with the other, and cried aloud with open mouth and tight shut eyes.

And, hullo! Who was that sitting beside him, but the grand old rascal Michel Aubraine.

Yes, and there were Ivan Dobroff and Hans Müller with him still. They must all have got out of barracks after he left.

Now, clever Master Michel, let's see if Denis Ducros can bring off as good a one as your *Monsieur le Maire* escapade! And you yourself a witness, eh, my boy?

As the cheers died down, a lady who had seen better days stepped on to the low dais at the back of the hall.

And, as a little black-eyed Spaniard, pale and wan, struck a chord on the tinny piano, she burst into strident song.

Ere, assisted by the entire company, she had finished screeching the uncommendable ditty "*Pan, pan, le gobinois,*" the Colonel had also finished his bottle. He ordered another.

As the lady concluded her song, the Colonel applauded loudly, beating with the empty bottle on the zinc bar by which he stood.

"*Bis!*" he cried, and the singer, proud and pleased, obliged most willingly. Even deeper and louder than before, was the chorus that the enchanted warriors supplied.

"More wine, you rascal!" ordered the Colonel. "Keep those rogues of yours busy with those bottles. Are the soldiers of France to go thirsty on the Fête Day of France?"

And, nothing loth, the proprietor drove the Arab waiters yet harder.

Having finished his second bottle, the Colonel took it by the neck, raised it on high, and bade the pianist play "*Père Dupanloup en chemin de fer.*"

There was a roar of approving laughter; the Spaniard, who evidently knew every air that the Legion knew, smiled and smote the piano with all his strength. The Colonel, stepping forward, used the upraised bottle as a baton, and personally conducted the choir and music.

The song concluded, the choir, orchestra and conductor applauded themselves loudly.

"And what shall we have next?" asked the Colonel, genially, as the applause at length died down.

"Name your favourite song, somebody."

Many were called, and all were chosen; some being led by the *cantatrice*, some being passed by her in a prudent but not prudish silence.

Breaking the peace of exhaustion which followed the singing of the last song, the doors were thrown open and there entered two senior non-commissioned officers, bearded and bemedalled men of a severity and dignity all their own, and worthy of their rank and years of service.

All eyes turned toward this apparition, the *légionnaires* torn between discipline, promptings to rise to salute, and the knowledge that the Colonel himself had given them orders to remain seated.

The *sous-officiers* stared, unwilling or unable to accept the reality of what they saw. Each knew that he was perfectly sober, but felt that nevertheless he was beholding a strange and somewhat nightmarish vision.

"*Les huiles!*" suddenly exclaimed the Colonel, turning about to see what could be the counter-attraction at which his audience was staring, "*Nom d'un pipe! Les huiles!*" to the completely incredulous amazement of the astounded *légionnaires*.

That the great and grim Colonel Louis Rochefort should come into this *casse-croute*; that he should stand unlimited wine to the whole company assembled; that he should join in the chorus of a very low song, and then select and take an actual part in the singing of a still lower one, was enough to make the dead arise and run away.

But that he should know and use such a term as "*huiles*"—applied to non-commissioned officers—was enough to knock the fleeing dead back into their graves again.

That he, the cold hard Colonel Louis Rochefort, the aloof unapproachable aristocrat, product of St. Cyr, who had never spent a day in the ranks of the Legion, nor any other regiment—that he should know and use such a piece of barrack-room *argot* as that, was the last straw to break the back of the camel of credulity.

And indeed, as far as the two grave and reverend senior Sergeant-Majors were concerned, it was the case of the last straw which breaks the camel's heart.

But the heart of Denis Ducros was uplifted within him and he was strong, bold and outrageous with the heady fumes of good wine and brave love.

"Outside, *salauds!*" he bawled, with the well-known imperious dismissing gesture of his hand.

"Outside! Go on. Get out of here you abominable blackguards. This place is reserved for honest *légionnaires*, and for them to be able to drink and enjoy themselves in peace.

"Get out as quickly as your aged limbs can move—and a bit quicker. . . . And stay out," he shouted.

There was a roar of delighted, if slightly nervous, laughter, as, looking nearly as hurt and broken as they felt, the two *sous-officiers*, models of discipline, duty and deportment, saluted and obeyed; while the Colonel, gleefully rubbing his hands, laughed not only merrily, but most derisively.

Then, taking the hands of the fat *chanteuse*, with a cry of *"Vive la compagnie!"* he led her to a table and called for more wine—wine for the lady, wine for himself, wine for everybody.

He knew he was foundering and that the end was near; but he would go down in a blaze of glory and a sea of wine. He was bewitched, again uplifted, *tête montée*, in love.

Wine is another man and he would remain another man to the last moment.

Gone were all prudent thoughts of getting quietly into barracks, removing this enchanted uniform of glory, brushing it humbly, dutifully, and folding it away.

"Wine for *les légionnaires*!" he cried to the proprietor, who also felt he was a little bewitched, or at any rate, bemused and bewildered.

And *Messieurs les légionnaires*? They saw, they heard, and they realised—how drunk they must be. It was a Soldier's Dream of Bliss. Only a dream. But the wine was real—or seemed to be . . .

Silly . . . ! There must be a catch in it.

However, wine is wine; orders are orders; and when, once in a life-time, your Colonel sits down with you in a Bar and bids you drink, well, by all the Gods of War and the laws of the Legion—you drink.

They drank.

Those who could still drink a lot; those who felt that, as a matter of strict fact, they had drunk a lot but were still functioning; those who felt they could not drink another drop, all undeterred, drank deeply of the Colonel's wine.

The din grew louder and the fun more furious—but scarcely as furious as the two Sergeant-Majors, when, on recovering their senses, they realised that they had actually been driven away, like bazaar curs, from the wine-shop that they had considered it their duty to enter.

They, men of power and importance, ridiculed, in-

sulted, and humiliated in front of the very men whom it was their main duty in life to discipline.

And by the Colonel himself!

Colonel Louis Rochefort, the finest stickler for discipline that ever backed-up a zealous non-commissioned officer in his arduous and difficult work of breaking and making military toughs.

"It *was* the Colonel, wasn't it?" asked Sergeant-Major Sleicher, at the end of a long and bitter silence.

"You saw him," growled Sergeant-Major Goertz.

"You heard him, too," he added.

" '*Huiles'!*" growled Sergeant-Major Sleicher beneath his breath.

"Has he gone mad, do you think?" asked Goertz.

"*Cafard*, I should say," muttered Sleicher.

"Colonels don't get *cafard*," objected Goertz.

"Well, whether he's gone mad or not, I swear there are a few of those scum who'll think *I've* gone mad before I've done with them."

"Did you mark down any of the *scélerats?*"

"I did. Didn't you?"

"What do you think? There was that scoundrel Aubraine, and his two *copains*, and Zerro and his gang."

"Yes. And I saw that big baboon, Seminoff, and his jackals. I'll give Seminoff something to laugh about, as he's so fond of laughing—and plenty of time to do it in too."

"In the dark," growled the other, "with some dry bread and salt water.

"*Laugh!*" he added unpleasantly, grinding his teeth.

But if, at this stage of the affair, the rage of these noble minds burned so fiercely as to be almost uncontrollable, what was it when they met their friend the *vaguemestre* and received from him a piece of news that rendered them temporarily speechless?

Literally speechless with rage.

For when Sergeant-Major Sleicher, the more articulate of the two saw the *vaguemestre*, he beckoned him across the road, with a view to pouring out the vials of his wrath and woe.

237

He must tell someone or burst, and, what was more, he must tell people of the proper rank and standing— and understanding; people whose sympathy would be extremely practical. Every non-commissioned officer in the depôt was concerned in this, and must make it his business to be very actively concerned too.

Oh yes, *Messieurs les légionnaires* should have plenty to laugh at. Some of them should laugh for days—and nights.

"Hullo!" said the *vaguemestre* as he joined them. "Going back to Barracks? I've got to find Captain le Sage before I can turn in. Colonel's very ill and can't sign a . . ."

"*What?*" interrupted both *sous-officiers* simultaneously. The *vaguemestre* jumped, so fierce and menacing was the anguished cry.

"*What* did you say?" asked Sergeant-Major Sleicher.

"The Colonel's very ill, I said, and . . ."

"*Ill? . . . Where?*"

"In his sacred bed, of course!" replied the *vaguemestre* testily. "Where do you suppose? Under the kitchen sink?"

"But he isn't! He . . ."

"All right! All right! Médécin-Major Barrade is a liar then," interrupted the *vaguemestre*.

"What the *Hell* are you talking about?" burst in Sergeant-Major Goertz, a good man whose mind was not quite so strong and active as his fine body.

"I don't know. Don't ask *me*," snarled the *vaguemestre*. "Sleicher knows all about it. He knows everything. *I* was only under the impression that possibly the Colonel is ill, because Médécin-Major Barrade has given the strictest orders that he is not to be disturbed! . . . I personally don't know anything because it wasn't *I*, of course, who went to his quarters half an hour ago with an '*Urgent*,' and had my head nearly bitten off by the blasted doctor. . . . One doesn't suppose that *he* knows anything about illness, of course. Merely thinks he does. . . .

"Or about the Colonel. Merely thinks he does. . . .

"Anyway, he thinks the Colonel's so damned healthy

238

that he has issued the strictest orders that he is not to be disturbed by anyone on any account whatsoever. Not by *anyone*. . . . Not even by me."

It will be perceived that the *vaguemestre* was, unlike Sergeant-Major Goertz, a fluent speaker; something of an orator, *en effet*.

"So the Colonel's ill? Ill in bed, is he?" said Sergeant-Major Sleicher, having patiently heard the *vaguemestre* out.

"No! No! No!" roared the latter. "He's dancing on the tiles, stark naked. He's mad. He's . . ."

"Listen!" said the Prussian, with sinister quiet. "*Monsieur le Colonel Louis Rochefort* is not ill in bed. Nor is he dancing on the tiles, stark naked."

"No! No, of course not! Never ill in his life. Never been on the tiles in his life. Never was such a person in his life," spluttered the *vaguemestre*.

"Where the Hell is he then?" he asked. "And what is he doing, since you know all about him?"

"He's in a *bistro*, the *Café d'Afrique*. Boozing with a herd of swine. When any *sous-officier* enters, he insults and abuses him, and bids the swine to laugh at him.

"The swine laugh," he added.

The *vaguemestre* stared open-mouthed at the solemn and stolid Sergeant-Major Sleicher.

"Go in and see for yourself. You'll enjoy it," advised Sergeant-Major Goertz.

"Let me see now, what have I drunk to-night?" pondered the *vaguemestre*, in the tone of one who makes careful retrospective calculation. "A little wine for the stomach's sake—with water. So it cannot be that I am so drunk that, having come straight from the Colonel's sick-bed, I am imagining that two intoxicated gorillas are telling me that my dying Colonel is drinking from a trough in a pig-sty and insulting all who pass. . . .

"No. I am as sober as Satan on a Saturday night."

The tone of his voice suddenly changed.

"Be ashamed of yourselves!" he admonished them sharply. "And get back to Barracks at once and sleep your liquor off. You'll be losing your stripes like poor

Hagues, if you go on like this. . . . The Colonel boozing with the men in a low pot-house!

"You're looking for trouble, that's what. And you'll find it too. Better not tell a yarn like that to anyone else.

"He'd break you like a couple of rotten sticks," he concluded viciously.

Sergeant-Major Sleicher dug deeply and laboriously with his huge fist in the pocket of his tunic, and, before apoplexy ensued, or his empurpled face turned black, produced a ten-franc note—big money in the Legion.

"See that?" he asked.

The *vaguemestre* replied that he did, and added that he had seen one like it before, though not waved in front of his eyes by the Sergeant-Major.

"Very well then. I'll wager *that*," and he gave the note which lay upon one large palm, a resounding smack with the other, "I'll wager *that* to a copper *sou*, that Colonel Rochefort is at this moment in the *Café d'Afrique*, boozing *and* singing with a rabble of *légionnaires*. Yes, and conducting the music—with a bottle. . . . Tight as a tick. Now then?"

"Done," responded the *vaguemestre* promptly producing a copper coin.

"Come on then," urged the two Sergeant-Majors as one man, and a few minutes later, the door of the *Café d'Afrique* was again flung open, and through it, swelling with importance, strode the confident figure of the *vaguemestre*.

Behind him, obviously diffident and anxious, lurked, inconspicuous, two unusually unobtrusive Sergeant-Majors. They forbore to follow their rash leader into the lion-like Colonel's temporary den. Sufficient unto the moment to witness from a safe distance, and through the doorway, what might now befall.

And it was while the Colonel was himself on the dais and actually in the middle of favouring the company with a song—of which, one regrets to admit, the *chanteuse*, the pianist, and every man present knew not only the tune, but the words—that the sudden rude interruption occurred.

The Colonel indicated the fact that he noticed the man's intrusion, by an angry glare and a Rochefortian frown, but continued his song, the end of which he had almost reached.

The *vaguemestre* stared in utter bewilderment. He could see that this was the Colonel, and he knew perfectly well that it was not.

Instinct told him that this man was not Colonel Louis Rochefort.

Common sense supported instinct.

Would Médécin-Major Barrade nearly bite his head off and nearly kick him out of the place because the Colonel was far too ill to be disturbed—if the Colonel was not there at all, but was out on a bend, raising Cain in the grog-shops.

He was certain, absolutely certain, this was some new trick of these anointed devils of *légionnaires*.

But, God of Battles! *Wasn't* that Colonel Rochefort?

Colonel Rochefort, sober, he knew only too well, but Colonel Rochefort, drunk, was a sight no *vaguemestre* had seen. Was this the Colonel, drunk?

No.

And as, really rather bravely, he approached the dais, shoving his way roughly and angrily through the laughing and applauding crowd of licentious soldiery, he suddenly noticed one drunken rascal, that *mauvais sujet, légionnaire* Michel Aubraine, throw his hands up toward Heaven, then in an ecstasy of joy clasp his stomach with both arms, double up with laughter until his head almost reached his feet, and then, rising, murmur drunkenly, as he wiped his streaming eyes.

"*Magnificent! Marvellous!* I give him best! Most *perfect* piece of acting! ... *C'est incroyable!*"

And then the *vaguemestre* knew.

He had known that he knew.

He was right. ...

Now they should see something.

The Colonel acknowledged the applause genially, and then deigned to deal with the intruder.

"Well I'm damned!" he said, "Another *huile*!"

There was a loud laugh, and all eyes turned to the hitherto unremarked *vaguemestre*.

The angry blood of that derided man came to the boiling-point, and his rage was such that he could scarcely speak.

They'd laugh at *him*, would they?

Stepping on to the dais, he thrust the forefinger of his outstretched hand almost in the Colonel's face.

"Y-y-y-you're a s-swindler," he stuttered.

"*Ah!* . . . *Indeed?*" drawled the Colonel, suddenly sober as a judge; and as a judge, austere, cold, hard and stern.

The *vaguemestre* recoiled.

The Colonel drew the scented handkerchief from his left cuff and held it beneath his nose.

"Get further away," he growled. "Get off this platform. Get out of this Bar. In fact, get back to Barracks, and report to Captain le Sage. He'll put you under arrest. . . . Oran Court Martial for you my man. A little matter of *stealing from the letters of les légionnaires*."

There was a low and ominous growl from *les légionnaires*.

The *vaguemestre* quailed before the blaze of the Colonel's eye, and the import of these terrible words.

Involuntarily stepping backwards, he left the dais with unintentional suddenness, and was only saved from falling on the floor by the agile and skilful movement of a very large Turk, whose knee shot up just in time, and just in the right place.

Not only was the *vaguemestre* saved from falling backward, he was propelled upward and forward.

"Filthy *huile*!" observed the Colonel dispassionately, and that settled the matter in the *vaguemestre's* mind.

Never in this world would Colonel Rochefort have called a very senior non-commissioned officer a *huile*, much less a filthy *huile*.

No. He was being fooled. And the men were in it. What had *légionnaire* Aubraine just said?

Springing on to the dais again, he turned to the men,

"Here, you scum!" he shouted. "Frog-march this pollution of an anointed acrobat back to Barracks.

"You . . . and you . . . and you . . . and you," he pointed. "Take him. Throw him into a cell, and tear that uniform off him. Strip him naked."

"'*Huile*', eh?" he added, turning to Denis, "what about *une bonne ration de l'huile de cotret*,[1] eh? A dose of stirrup-oil. I'll oil you, you impudent hound . . . What about a pint of *huile de ricin*[2]? . . . I'll give you oil enough to keep you greasy for the rest of your life—which may not be as long as you expect."

The *vaguemestre*, foaming at the mouth with rage, was forced to pause for breath.

"This dog's gone mad!" observed the Colonel.

"Dangerous. Throw it out."

And sweeping the wildly excited and somewhat inebriated assembly with the eye of the true commander of men, he pointed imperiously to the door.

Headed by Michel Aubraine, the *légionnaires* obeyed their Colonel. It was not every day, not even every Fête Day indeed, that they were invited, nay commanded, by superior authority to throw a *sous-officier* out on his ear.

This one fell almost at the feet of his friends who had not advanced to his support. . . .

"Well? What did I tell you?" gloated Sergeant-Major Sleicher.

"I said you'd enjoy it," said Goertz.

The *vaguemestre* picked himself up.

"Listen, you bone-headed camels. You poor, half-witted, half-blind bat-eyed beetles. You make me sick . . ." he raged.

"Go it, then," encouraged Sleicher.

The *vaguemestre* spat.

He then invoked Heaven's assistance in the retention of his sanity.

"*Bon Dieu de Dieu de Sort!*" he cried, making as though to cast his *képi* on the ground. "That's *not* the Colonel. It's a damned dog's-tail of a *légionnaire* dressed up in his uniform! *Légionnaire* Aubraine knows him

[1] a good thrashing. [2] castor oil.

243

too! . . . You apes . . . you asses . . . Listen! Guard that door, and when he comes out—*get him*! I'm going to run back to Barracks, and I'll send you every man I meet on the way, and the picket, *and* a party of . . ."

"*And* the real Colonel!" jeered Sleicher.

"Have the *Assembly* sounded, while you're about it," suggested Goertz.

The *vaguemestre* went through the motions of tearing his hair, and turned to run, at the *pas gymnastique*.

"Wait till to-morrow," he shouted. "You'll tear the chevrons off your own cuffs, you bloody fools."

Almost it seemed to the now laughing Prussians, that the poor *vaguemestre* wept.

"The good animal is imbecile," observed Goertz, in the didactic Prussian manner.

"He'll be thinking *he's* Colonel, next," sneered Sleicher.

The two men regarded each other enquiringly and somewhat doubtfully.

"Well, what do we do now?" asked Goertz. "Leave 'em to it?"

"Yes. Clear out while we can, and let the *vaguemestre* get on with it. He may have caught a cartload of Colonels by daylight.

"Not but what I am going to have another squint through the crack of that door," he added.

"They seem quiet enough now. Settled down to some serious drinking, I suppose," replied Goertz, and longingly smacked adequate lips.

Quietly approaching the door of the *Café d'Afrique*, Sergeant-Major Sleicher paused, listened, and pushed it open a couple of inches.

There was the Colonel—of course it was the Colonel—on the dais, and, in a quiet voice, earnestly addressing the now silent *légionnaires*.

For Denis Ducros had had enough.

He was tired, and he realised that, beyond telling, he wanted his Day of Days to finish quietly, decently, and in order—a weary Colonel, taking off his uniform and going to bed.

It would spoil everything—or go far toward spoiling

it, for nothing could destroy the glory and the beauty of his love for Nicolette—yes, it would nearly spoil everything if, as that swine of a *vaguemestre* had said, he was seized, knocked about, frog-marched to Barracks, stripped naked and thrown into a cell.

Lucifer! Lucifer! . . .

Ichabod! . . .

As the last chorus died down, he had raised his hand for silence, and was the severe, yet still kindly Colonel once again, the man with whom no son of woman took liberties.

"Now, *mes enfants!*" he said. "That will be enough, I think. We've had a good time together this Fête Day, and now we'll call it a day—as the Day is over.

"When I give the word, you will file quietly out of the place, and march back to Barracks in a smart and soldierly manner. I wish every one of you *bonne chance.* Now then:—

"Légionnaires! . . ." But before he could say more, a soldier who did not appear to be drunk, but undoubtedly had drink taken, cried in a loud voice,

"Three cheers for the Colonel! By God, the very finest man that ever wore the Legion's uniform! God preserve him, and the Devil admire him!"

And the eyes of Michel Aubraine met those of Denis Ducros with the faintest flicker of an eye-lid.

"Thank you, my man," acknowledged the Colonel, and again Michel Aubraine was convulsed with ecstatic laughter as the enthusiastic cheers rang out.

Again the Colonel raised an inhibitory hand.

"Légionnaires! . . ." he cried. *"Garde à vous!* . . . *Fixe!* . . ."

And with practised skill his merry men raised their heads above the encircling rosy fumes of wine, and stood practically to attention.

"Rompez! . . ."

And the *légionnaires* turned about and went quietly and respectfully from the presence of their Colonel.

Sergeant-Major Sleicher hurriedly left his observation post and rejoined Sergeant-Major Goertz.

"Come on! Quick!" he said. "The Old Devil's dismissing them."

"*Of course* it's the Colonel," he added. "No doubt at all. The *vaguemestre's* been whooping it up."

"And pouring it down," agreed Goertz.

"Nice to be *vaguemestre*," observed Sleicher, as they marched away. "No stint of the best of everything."

"But silly to flash the cash you pinch," said Goertz.

"Well, he won't flash my ten francs anyhow," decided Sleicher. "Look out, here comes the Colonel. Let's turn down here."

In the wake of the returning men whom he had been entertaining—and for whose entertainment Colonel Rochefort would very soon be invited to pay—Denis Ducros marched hopefully.

Le bon Dieu had been so truly kind and helpful this night that it was perfectly possible, almost probable, indeed, that He might grant him safe return from his wonderful escapade, his brief excursion into an upper world, clad in the Uniform of Glory, to the wearer of which all men had accorded recognition, respect and obedience.

All men . . . All women . . . And the One Woman. *Nicolette! . . . Nicolette! . . . Nicolette! . . .*

Yes, he thought, and the One Woman valued the uniform at its true worth—coloured rags—and valued *him* for what he was worth, and saw in him a fellow human-being, warm with human kindness.

Love! . . .

The men marched on. . . . He loved them too. . . . Good fellows. . . . How they responded to a little human kindness. . . . They were as quiet as lambs. . . .

Down the lane between the Spahis' Barracks and those of the Legion, through the Barrack gate, they filed at last; and there was not a man with whose deportment the Sergeant of the Guard could find cause for complaint.

And after them—the Colonel.

The Colonel flicked a perfunctory salute, and passed on in the darkness towards his house.

Behind him one came running, and his heart sank within him.

"Pardon, M'sieu' le Colonel!" panted a most respectful voice. "But the *vaguemestre* is most anxious to find you. Most urgent message, I believe. . . ."

"Ah! . . . Indeed?" said the Colonel, as he paused in his stride. "I have already heard that he has either got *cafard*, or has had too much to drink. . . . When you see him, tell him to report to Captain le Sage, who will doubtless put him under arrest—for conduct unbecoming a *sous-officier*.

"I'll deal with him in the morning," added the Colonel grimly, and strode on.

CHAPTER XVI

THE UNIFORM IS TAKEN OFF

SAFE in his dressing-room, the door locked, the Colonel reluctantly removed his uniform and folded it away.

Denis Ducros, also reluctantly, resumed *his* uniform.

Before covering it with the green baize badge of servitude, he turned up the light, viewed his image in the mirror, and, in low but eloquent voice, addressed an imaginary company of—*huiles*.

"Little men!" he whispered. "Little earth-bound men, do you know what I am?"

With one accord, and one opinion, they seemed to tell him what he was.

From the heights of his wine-flown eminence, his *tête montée* glory, his vast pride of Love, he laughed his bitter contempt of those poor oppressors.

"Imbéciles! Goats! Asses! Mules! Camels! It is as I thought. Ignorant. Blind. *I* will tell you what I am— for I have just remembered.

"I am the great Caliph of Baghdad, and henceforth you have my permission to call me The Great Caliph, *Haroun al Raschid*."

Yet that was not at all what they called him.

Happy as he had never been before in all his mal-adjusted life, Denis looked into the Colonel's room, showed himself to that convalescent, then retired, un-dressed, crept into bed, and composed himself to dream of Nicolette . . .

Only six more months, and his time in the Legion would be up!

Nicolette! . . . *Nicolette!* . . . *Nicolette!* . . . and Denis Ducros . . . the little Soldier of Fortune and the little Daughter of Joy, brought together, for ever, by his wear-ing, for an evening, the Uniform of Glory. . . .